MW01127708

A SPIRITED TAIL

MYSTIC NOTCH BOOK 2

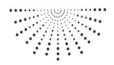

LEIGHANN DOBBS

This is a work of fiction.

None of it is real. All names, places, and events are products of the author's imagination. Any resemblance to real names, places, or events are purely coincidental, and should not be construed as being real.

A Spirited Tail

Copyright © 2014

Leighann Dobbs

http://www.leighanndobbs.com

All Rights Reserved.

No part of this work may be used or reproduced in any manner, except as allowable under "fair use," without the express written permission of the author.

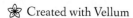 Created with Vellum

CHAPTER ONE

One of my favorite things about living in the White Mountains of New Hampshire is the fresh, clean smell after a summer rain shower. Up until this morning, I didn't think there was anything that could ruin that smell. But now I knew better. There *was* one thing ... the stench of a dead body.

I covered my nose with my hand and tried to tear my eyes away from the body, which was difficult given the unusual graffiti on its forehead. There were actually two bodies lying in the grass, but thankfully, only one of them was dead. The other was real estate agent Ophelia Withington, whose eyes had rolled up into their sockets shortly before she fainted after her brain came to grips with the fact that there was a dead body in the backyard of the old, abandoned mansion she was about to list for sale.

"Ophelia!" I squatted down, feeling a slight sting in my left leg—a reminder of the near-fatal accident over a year ago that was one of the catalysts for my move back to my home town of Mystic Notch. The accident had left me with a slight limp, a bunch of scars and a few odd side effects I didn't like to dwell on.

Pushing away the wet blades of grass that tickled my nose, I roughly shook Ophelia's shoulder.

She moaned, then rolled her head and squinted one blue eye up at me. "What happened?"

"You fainted."

She scrunched her perfectly made-up face, then her eyes went wide. She covered her nose and swiveled her head toward the body. "Is he ...?"

"Yep."

She scrambled up and away from the body. Her face took on a greenish tinge as she turned away, then bent over to serenade me with loud retching noises.

I pinched my nose closed and tried to focus on controlling my own gag reflex. A whining sound tugged my attention away from Ophelia and I looked across the body at the Golden Retriever who sat patiently beside it.

My heart tugged when my gaze met the wounded, brown eyes of the dog, which obviously belonged to the dead guy. The Golden's mournful whining had caused us to investigate the side area of the house in the first place. If it hadn't been for him, Ophelia and I would have simply gone about our business inside the dilapidated mansion, never knowing someone was lying dead outside.

Glancing at the bent-over real estate agent, I felt a twinge of regret at offering to help her appraise the book collection inside the house.

I wasn't actually sure why I *had* offered to help. The collection had been locked away in the house for fifty years and was reputed to include many rare volumes. I guess my love of books had been the reason rather than any kind of friendship I had with Ophelia. Because I wouldn't actually categorize us as 'friends'.

In fact, I hadn't even liked the overzealous real estate agent much at all when I'd first moved back to Mystic Notch to live in the large antique Victorian home I'd inherited from my grandmother. Ophelia seemed hell-bent on persuading me to sell it—through her real estate agency, of course—and she was annoyingly aggressive about it.

Much to her dismay, I had no intention of selling Gram's house, and up until this past spring our relationship could best be described as adversarial. She'd been mean, shrewd, and money-hungry back then, but I had to admit she'd changed a lot since being the prime suspect in the death of our town librarian—whose body I'd also discovered.

I wouldn't say we were best buddies now, but she

had done a few things to redeem herself in my eyes and I found her to be more tolerable than before.

And now here we were, discovering a dead body together.

Another whine pulled my attention back to the situation at hand. I stood and walked closer to the dog, holding my hand out for him to sniff. "Hey, buddy. Are you friendly?"

The dog glanced down at the body and then up at me, as if realizing his old master had departed and was sizing me up as a replacement. I guess I didn't pass muster because he didn't move a muscle.

"Okay, suit yourself."

I brushed off my jeans and waded through the overgrown grass toward Ophelia. The extra exertion of trying to navigate through the grass made my limp more pronounced. Ophelia was no longer retching. She stood before me, her usually perfectly coiffed blonde hair sticking up from the top of her head like the crest of a bird. I bit back a laugh. I didn't think she was going to be too happy the next time she looked in the mirror.

"You okay?"

She nodded. "Who *is* that?"

"I was hoping you knew."

She shook her head, then gestured toward the body. "And what's wrong with his forehead?"

Good question.

It was bad enough to stumble across a dead body first thing in the morning, but this one had a strange mark on his forehead. It looked like a triangle with a dot in the middle and it almost seemed to be glowing in the early morning sunlight.

Why would someone do that?

"Do you think it's some kind of cult?" Ophelia's eyes darted wildly toward the woods.

"I don't know. Do we have any cults around here?"

Ophelia shrugged, and I turned her away from the body and toward the front of the house, glancing backwards at the dog who didn't seem to be in any hurry to leave his post.

"Let's go out front and call Gus," I said, referring to my sister, Augusta, the town Sheriff.

I led the way to the front of the house, eager to escape the stench emanating from the body and the buzz of flies that had already discovered it. It had stopped raining and the sun had made an appearance, but my legs were soaked from brushing against the tall, wet grass.

The front yard was mostly dirt and weeds, a sharp contrast to the field that had taken over the side and back of the house. I perched on the granite step that led to the porch and went through the motions of inspecting my legs for ticks, congratulating myself for having the good sense to wear long jeans and tuck them into my socks before venturing into the grass.

Even though I'd been a city dweller down in Massachusetts for most of my adult life, I'd grown up here in the White Mountains, and my eyes were still trained to pick out those small brown pests, so it didn't take long for me to give myself the once-over.

"What are you doing?" Ophelia eyed my gyrations as I twisted around to get a look at the back of my legs.

"Looking for ticks. The grass is probably loaded with them."

Ophelia made a strangled squeak and I glanced over to see a horrified look on her face as she darted her eyes around her beige linen suit and stabbed her fingers into her hair. I grimaced, remembering how she'd been lying on the ground. No one wanted ticks in their hair.

"Do I have any on me?" Her lip quivered, her face turned pale and I was afraid she'd pass out again.

"I'll check for you while I call Gus." I dug the cell phone out of my pocket and checked for a signal. Reception could be spotty up here in the mountains, but I was in luck. I punched in Gus's number and started my inspection.

"Don't mess up my hair," Ophelia commanded as I listened to the phone ringing. I didn't want to tell her it was already pretty messed up.

"Wilhelmina? This had better be an emergency." Gus's voice bellowed over the phone. I cringed at the use of the long version of my first name. She always used that when she was mad. Normally, she just called me 'Willa' like everyone else had for the past forty-eight years.

"Well, it's not exactly an emergency anymore ..." I plucked a tick off the hem of Ophelia's skirt.

"What's wrong?"

"There's a dead guy up at the Van Dorn house."

"You found another one?" I could practically *hear* Gus rolling her eyes. Earlier in the summer, I'd stumbled across the body of the town librarian murdered in the library, and Gus hadn't been pleased. I wasn't sure why she got so upset with *me*; it wasn't like I found these bodies on purpose.

"Afraid so."

"Who is it?"

"I'm not sure. It's hard to tell because he's been ... umm ... defaced."

"Defaced?"

"Yeah, he has a symbol on his forehead. Not sure how to explain it—you kind of have to see it for yourself."

"Oh, for crying out loud, we'll be right there." Gus's voice turned stern, like our mother's when we were kids. "Don't leave and don't touch anything."

She snapped the phone shut without even saying good-bye.

I had to laugh at her warning. I knew enough not to touch anything, but Gus was probably thinking I'd be snooping around, trying to get involved in the case. I

7

could hardly blame her, though. I *did* have a habit of getting involved in solving crimes. I supposed it had to do with my previous career as a crime reporter. Sometimes I just couldn't help but get involved ... and sometimes I didn't have much choice.

"You're all set." I gestured at Ophelia's outfit.

"You didn't find any on me?"

"Nope," I lied. I'd found four, but since they were just crawling around and not feasting, I'd simply flicked them off. I figured she was better off not knowing that.

"I suppose we need to wait outside." Ophelia glanced at the weather-beaten door and worn wooden floor of the front porch.

I nodded, knowing that Gus wouldn't take kindly to us venturing inside until she'd been able to check things out herself.

Ophelia shrugged, brushed off a spot on the top step and sat down. Feeling worried about the dog, I strolled over to the side of the house and peeked out back. My heart squeezed at the sight of him, still sitting in the same spot, guarding his master.

"I hope there won't be a problem with the dog when the police come," I said as I eyed the porch. Years of neglect had taken their toll and the once-grand area now boasted rotting boards, loose railings and missing columns.

I brushed at a section of the top step carefully, so as

not to jab my hand with the splintering wood, and plopped down beside Ophelia, wincing at the pain in my left leg.

"Me, too," Ophelia said. "I'm sure they have ways of handling it."

"Maybe." I wasn't so sure they did and I was already feeling responsible for the dog.

"I hope this won't impede the selling of the house." Ophelia brushed some dirt off her skirt. It was just like her to be thinking about her bottom line instead of about the dead guy in the back.

"So, what's the deal with this house, anyway?" I asked. I could see it was probably a hundred years old, but I knew it had been abandoned for decades. I had vague memories of rumors of it being haunted when I was a kid, but couldn't remember exactly why.

"Oh, it was the victim of a family squabble, I guess. The owner died a long time ago and didn't have any heirs. Left the house to his two brothers, who couldn't agree on selling terms. So, it sat all this time. I guess the last brother finally died and the house passed to the nephew. He contacted me to see if I could sell the house and its contents. Honestly, it's in pretty bad shape from the looks of things out here. I don't know if it's worth trying to find a buyer." Ophelia waved her hand at it dismissively.

I glanced back at the house with its crooked, paint-peeling shutters and weather-beaten wood door. A few bricks were missing here and there, but otherwise, the brick facing was in good condition. Many of the windows had been boarded up and the old, wavy glass on the ones that hadn't been were caked with dirt. You could barely see inside ... except for one window at the end of the porch where a frantic movement caught my eye.

My stomach tightened.

I hope that isn't what I think it is.

"What is it?" Ophelia looked at me curiously.

I jerked my head to face forward. "Oh, nothing."

But I couldn't help myself. A few seconds later, I was looking at the window again out of the corner of my eye. I saw the same misty, swirly motion I had before. I squinted, alarm spreading in my chest as I realized what was in there.

It was as I had feared—there was a ghost in the house and it wanted to talk to me.

CHAPTER TWO

*G*hosts were the other side effect of my accident, and the reason why I didn't have much choice about investigating certain murders. Ever since the accident, I'd been able to talk to the dead. And, as if it wasn't disturbing enough that I could have conversations with them, it usually turned out that they wanted something from me ... like investigating their murder.

Judging by the way the ghost in the window was gesturing for me to go inside, I figured he was no different than the others.

"Is something over there?" Ophelia craned her neck in the direction of the window.

"No. I was just trying to see what was inside." I certainly wasn't going to tell Ophelia that I talked to ghosts. The only person who knew was my best friend, Pepper St. Onge, and I wanted to keep it that way so I

turned around and ignored the ghost's wild gesturing
while I waited for Gus and her crew to arrive. Somehow,
I'd have to get inside and talk to him, but not with
Ophelia around to hear us.

"I wonder what's inside, too." Ophelia turned around
to look at the door. "The house is supposed to be loaded
with furniture and all the household items and, of course,
the books."

And ghosts.

"No one has been in there yet?" I asked.

Ophelia shook her head. "Nope. I'm meeting with
the client today. He wants me to catalog the items. He
said he'd probably sell them off first, then list the house.
But I tell you, it's going to need some work if he expects
to get anything decent for it."

I nodded, then drowned out her chatter as I tried to
figure out how to get in without her. The house was
located off the beaten path, away from town and no
nearby neighbors. I noticed how still and silent it was out
here. Even the usual cacophony of bird sounds were
absent, as if the birds were maintaining a moment of
silence out of respect for the dead. Only the forlorn cry
of a mourning dove could be heard above the distant
sound of the approaching sirens.

"Here they come." Ophelia stood and brushed off the
back of her skirt. "I hope she'll let us get in today. I need
to take a good look before meeting with the client."

"Me, too." I glanced at the window to see my new friend still gesturing.

I pulled my jeans out of my socks and brushed away black flies as the sirens got louder. The sun peeked at me from the tops of the pine trees. I realized I was going to be late opening my bookstore and felt glad I worked for myself with no boss to admonish me when I came in late.

The now-deafening sirens turned into the circular driveway, which I assumed had once been crushed gravel. Most of the gravel had disappeared and now it was mostly dirt, weeds, and a few stones.

Mercifully, Gus cut the siren as her police-issue brown and tan Crown Victoria pulled to a stop. She hopped out of the driver's side and her young deputy, Jimmy Ford, got out of the passenger side. Two of the crime scene techs got out of the other car, loaded down with various pieces of equipment.

"The ambulance is a few minutes out," Gus said. "Had to take Miles Warner to the hospital with a gallstone attack."

I nodded. The small town of Mystic Notch only had one ambulance. I was pretty sure it wasn't going to help the guy in the backyard, anyway.

Gus raised her left brow. "So, where's the body?"

"Over here." I tilted my head toward the side of the house and Gus marched off in front of me, her long blonde ponytail swinging behind her. I watched for a second before

13

falling in behind her. I still got a kick of seeing my little sister in her police uniform. Eight years separated us and she was just a teenager when I'd moved down South. Now, twenty-five years later, we were just becoming acquainted as adults and I guess I still thought of her as that teenage girl, sometimes, even though she was forty years old.

Gus turned the corner, her hawk-like eyes taking in the scene in front of her. Her new deputy, Jimmy Ford, scrambled along behind her with his notebook out, ready to jump at Gus's every command.

I felt a twinge of sympathy for the poor kid. Fresh out of the police academy and barely old enough to shave, he didn't seem to have much confidence and could usually be found following close behind Gus like a puppy eager to prove himself.

The dog was still there. He let out a low growl as we neared the body.

Jimmy stopped short. "Is that dog vicious?"

"What?" I scrunched my face up at him. "No. He's perfectly nice. Just guarding the body. I imagine he must belong to the deceased."

"He does," a gritty voice rasped from behind me. The voice sounded like its owner had drunk a bottle of whiskey and munched on rocks for breakfast and I turned to face the county medical examiner, Gertie Sloan, trudging through grass that was almost as tall as she was. Gertie must have been ninety if she was a day, but somehow managed to keep the job as chief M.E. Probably because no one else wanted it.

"You know him?" I asked.

"Yep. That's Ranger. Belongs to our victim, Bruce Norton." Gertie bent over to get a look at the body, then turned to me sharply. "What in tarnation did you do to him?"

"Me? I didn't do that ... he was already like that." I gestured to his forehead. "I don't think I've ever heard of him. Is he from Mystic Notch?"

Gertie ignored me and returned to inspecting the body.

"You probably wouldn't remember him," Gus said without looking up at me. She continued walking around the area, her eyes glued to the ground searching for clues. "He kept pretty much to himself."

Gus finished her circling of the area and started issuing commands. "Tape off the area. Establish a search grid around the body."

Jimmy scrambled to get to the yellow police tape. The crime scene techs started opening their boxes and pulled out various implements of the trade. One of them started taking pictures. Another started placing yellow numbered evidence markers.

Ranger watched the activity with weary eyes.

"So, what happened to him?" Ophelia had joined us and was peering over my shoulder.

"Someone killed him," Gertie stated the obvious.

"What about his forehead?" Jimmy looked at the body and then blanched. His face turned pale, making the red dots of pimples stand out even more than usual. He jerked his eyes away and got busy with the crime-scene tape.

"The markings are very odd." Gertie rubbed her chin. "They do seem somewhat familiar, but I can't quite place them. It seems someone is trying to send a message."

"A message?" Ophelia asked. "To whom?"

Gertie shrugged and walked around the body to inspect it from another angle.

"Did you guys trample the crime scene?" Gus asked accusingly, pointing at the area of tamped down grass where Ophelia had fainted.

"No," I said defensively. "Well, Ophelia fainted there, but other than that we stayed as far away as we could."

Gus twisted her mouth up and gave me the evil eye. "You didn't touch anything?"

"Nope." I shook my head and lifted my hand up beside my face holding the first three fingers up and bending my thumb and pinkie in toward my palm. "Scout's honor."

Gus narrowed her eyes at me. "Did you see anyone here ... maybe pass someone on the road?"

I thought back to my ride up the winding mountain road. I hadn't seen anyone. Ophelia was already here when I arrived. I glanced over at her and she shook her head.

"I don't remember seeing anyone," I said.

"Me, either," Ophelia added.

"There's no car here," Jimmy pointed out eagerly. "So how did the victim get here? He probably came with the killer."

"Or walked." Augusta pointed to the west. "Bruce lived over there not too far and there're a lot of trails in the woods. He could have been taking Ranger for a walk and maybe stumbled on the killer doing something he shouldn't have been doing."

"I wonder why a killer would be *here* ..." Ophelia glanced around uneasily.

"Me, too," Gus said. "But even more than that, I wonder why *you* are here."

"I'm listing the house," Ophelia said. "Willa met me here to help appraise the book collection that is supposed to be in there."

"You haven't been in?" Gus asked.

"No."

Gus glanced over at the large house. "I thought this place was abandoned."

Ophelia explained how the sale of the house had been held up by the brothers of the previous owner and how the nephew had now hired her to sell it. "You don't think that has anything to do with the murder, do you?"

Gus pressed her lips together. "It's hard to say. I don't know why Bruce would be out here. He was quite a recluse and I'd heard some say they thought he might be getting dementia. He *was* getting on in years."

"Not everyone who is getting on in years gets dementia," Gertie bellowed from her position at the side of the body.

A smile flitted over Gus's lips. "True."

"Why would anyone want to kill an old man?" I asked.

"That's the question." Gus fixed me with a pointed stare. "And I hope you don't feel the need to take it upon yourself to find the answer."

I plastered a look of innocence on my face and slid my eyes over to the house. I had no intention of getting involved in a murder investigation ... but my new ghostly friend might have other ideas.

"Can someone help me roll him over?" Gertie yelled, catching Gus' attention.

Gus walked over next to Gertie, but as soon as she bent down, Ranger started to growl.

"Oh, come on now, Ranger." Gertie stuck her hand out and the dog whined and licked her wrist just above the purple latex glove she wore. "Better get him out of here. He might not like strangers messing around with Bruce."

"I'll call Mel at the dog pound and have him come," Jimmy offered.

"Pound?" My heart twisted at images of the grieving dog sitting in a cage, cold and unloved flooding my mind. He'd just lost his master—hadn't he been through enough? "No way. I'll take him until we can see if any family members want him."

"I don't care where he goes, just get him out of my crime scene," Gus said.

"Is there any rope around here?" I surveyed the area near the house, but came up empty.

"There's some in the car," Jimmy glanced at Gus. Gus gave a curt nod and Jimmy jogged off toward the Crown Vic.

Gertie grabbed on to Ranger's collar and led him toward me. I squatted down and reached out, letting Ranger sniff me, which he did hesitantly.

"Good dog." I nodded up at Gertie, who let go of his collar. Ranger seemed to understand what was going on and let me tie the rope Jimmy had brought to the ring on his collar.

Ophelia cleared her throat and we all turned to look at her. "I don't suppose we could go in the house now ...?"

LEIGHANN DOBBS

Gus' eyes slid from Ophelia to the house. "We need to check it out first. Do you have a key?"

Ophelia held up a weather-beaten brass house key. "My client mailed me this ... he said it should open the house but I haven't tried it."

"Okay. Open the door and let Jimmy check it out. Stay outside until we say you can go in."

"Yes, Ma'am." Jimmy practically saluted Gus and ran off to the front with Ophelia close behind. Gus stared after them, her lips quirking up in a smile. I knew she got a kick out of the way the young deputy idolized her, but I also knew she wasn't on a power trip about it—she truly wanted to take him under her wing and teach him the ropes.

Gus turned her attention back to helping Gertie roll the body over and I turned away, focusing my attention on rubbing Ranger's coarse fur.

"Looks like he got whacked pretty good." Gertie's emotionless voice carried across the grass. "Been dead a while. He was hit with something pretty big. A shovel, maybe. I'll need to get him to the lab to tell more."

Instinctively, I looked around for a big shovel, or some other implement that could have done the deed. My search came up empty.

"The ambulance should be here shortly," Gus said.

"Okay." Gertie stood amidst various popping noises.

"I can't do much more here, so I'll meet the body back at the lab."

"Thanks." Gus smiled up at Gertie who nodded curtly as she stripped off her purple gloves.

Gertie picked up the bag she'd set on the grass beside her. It reminded me of an old doctor's bag from the 1800s. I found myself thinking it wouldn't surprise me to find it was that old ... or even that Gertie herself was.

More popping noises came from her knees as she squatted beside Ranger.

"You be a good boy, now." She looked from the dog to me. "You're in good hands."

Ranger's big brown eyes followed Gertie as she stood and walked to her car.

"Okay, boy. Let's go out front." I tugged the rope. Ranger looked up at me uncertainly, then stood and followed me, taking one heart-breaking glance back at Bruce.

Ophelia turned from her post at the open doorway where she was peering into the house, trying to get a glimpse of what was inside.

"It's just like he said. Everything is in here," she whispered, then frowned at Ranger. "Are you taking him?"

"Yep. Well, at least until I can find him a good home. Maybe one of Bruce's relatives wants him."

"Well, don't bring him near my car. Tatters is in there and I don't think she likes dogs."

I jerked my head around to stare at her brand new Lincoln with the cream-colored leather interior. I was relieved to see that she had the windows cracked and the air conditioning on so the cat wouldn't overheat, but a little surprised that she'd brought her cat to work with her. As I stared at the car, a little black and white head poked up on the passenger side. I noticed one of its ears was still a little tattered. The engine of the car purred so quietly, I hadn't even noticed it was running.

I'd been surprised earlier that summer when Ophelia had adopted the little homeless kitten with the tattered ear, because I couldn't picture the selfish real estate agent caring for anything but herself. She'd proved me wrong, and it looked like she'd grown very attached to the kitten.

"You bring your cat to work with you?"

"Yes, of course. Tatters comes to the office with me every day. Just like you bring Pandora with you to the bookstore. You don't think I'd leave her home alone, do you?"

I glanced down at Ranger and wondered if he liked cats. Then I wondered if Pandora, the cat I'd inherited along with the bookstore and house, liked dogs. I took Pandora to the bookstore with me every day and, since that was where I was headed after I finished up here, I guessed I was going to find out soon enough.

The ambulance arrived, interrupting my vision of bookshelves clattering to the ground spilling books all over my store as Ranger frantically tried to escape the hissing and clawing cat.

When the EMTs appeared from the back with the body on a stretcher, Ranger stood at attention and let out a series of barks. I put a reassuring hand on his head as they loaded his former master into the back. He looked up at me with pleading eyes that squeezed my heart.

"Don't worry. I'll make sure you get a good home."

They shut the door on the ambulance and Ranger lay down, pushed out his breath in a big sigh and curled in a ball, looking for all the world as if the life had been drained from him.

Gus came around the corner, snapping off her gloves just as Jimmy appeared in the doorway.

"Did you find anything in there?" she asked.

"Nope. It doesn't look like anyone has been in here in years." Jimmy pointed to the floor. "The dust hasn't been disturbed in any of the rooms."

Gus nodded to Ophelia and me. "Okay. I guess you two can go in, but if you find anything suspicious, let me know."

"Great!" Ophelia practically pushed Jimmy out of the way in her haste to get inside. I hesitated, looking down at Ranger. He appeared to be sleeping, but I wondered if he'd be okay out here while I was inside. I didn't want him to wander off, so I looked for a safe place to tie the other end of the rope where he couldn't get tangled or stuck. I squatted and slipped my fingers under his collar, just to make sure it was loose enough that he could slip it off if he did somehow get tangled in the rope.

Jimmy eased his way down the steps, giving Ranger a wide berth.

"He won't bite," I said as I made a loose knot in the rope.

Jimmy cast a few glances in the dog's direction. Ranger opened one eye and looked at Jimmy, then sighed and closed it again.

I rubbed Ranger's ears and he rewarded me with a meager twitch of his tail. "See, he likes being petted."

Jimmy tentatively held out his hand and Ranger opened both eyes while he sniffed at it. Stretching even closer, Jimmy touched the dog's head, petting him cautiously with his fingertips. Ranger gave him an unenthusiastic tail wag and then tucked his head back under his tail and went to sleep.

"I guess he's probably kind of depressed," Jimmy said.

"You comin'?" Gus called from the car. Jimmy whipped around and scurried off toward her.

Gus opened the driver's door, then looked over the top of it at me, a mischievous gleam in her eye. "Now remember, Willa, no investigating or I'll have to tell Striker on you."

I felt my face flush at the mention of the handsome sheriff from nearby Dixford Pass. I'd met him during the investigation for the last dead body I'd found and we'd been on a few dates. A few very good dates. Just the thought of him made my heart flutter like a teenager, which felt downright embarrassing at the age of forty-eight.

I remembered that Striker had lots of homicide experience and Gus had none and found myself hoping she'd call him in to consult on the case. Which made my face even warmer and tied my tongue in a knot.

Gus' laugh interrupted my thoughts and I tried to give her a mean look.

"Seriously, Willa, a killer is on the loose and I don't want you getting hurt, so no investigating."

"I know. I'll stay out of it."

"Good. See ya." Gus slipped into the driver's seat and started up the car.

I turned toward the open door as she drove away, glancing at the windows to see if my ghostly friend was there waiting for me. He wasn't.

"Willa, are you coming? Better bring a flashlight. It's kind of dark in here." Ophelia's voice drifted out from somewhere in the house.

The few windows that hadn't been boarded up let

minimal light into the house. I hadn't thought to bring a flashlight, though, so I guessed my eyes would just have to get used to the dark.

Hesitating on the threshold, I took a quick look back at the warm, sunny outdoors before heading into the dark gloom of the house.

CHAPTER THREE

*T*he blanket of humidity left by the rain shower made my red curls frizz into an unruly mess. I pushed the hair out of my eyes as I looked around the large foyer. To my right, a wide staircase curved upwards, the ornately carved railing thick with dust.

An opening on my left led to what appeared to be a living room. The sheet-covered furniture gave the dimly lit room an eerie appearance. Shafts of sunlight filtered in between the cracks of the boards used to cover up the windows. It was the perfect setting for a ghost ... except there was no sign of the one who had seemed so anxious to talk to me before.

"Come in here and check out this china—it's Limoges!" Ophelia's excited squeal rang out from the end of the hall and I followed it to a butler's pantry. Ophelia had her head buried in a cabinet, the paneled, mahogany doors wide open.

"It's a full set." Ophelia's eyes gleamed with excitement. "And look at this cut crystal."

I opened another cabinet to reveal a hoard of sterling silver candlesticks, salt shakers and serving trays. "Looks like the nephew is going to make a bundle just on the contents of the house alone."

"Yep. And the house isn't actually in that bad of shape on the inside." Ophelia squinted into the dark kitchen where I could barely make out a large commercial range and dark wood cabinets complete with Victorian drop knobs. "Did you find the library?"

"Not yet."

"I think it's over there." Ophelia pointed to a hallway on the left. "I'm going to poke around in here and uncover some of the furniture while you check out the books. I lost a lot of time with everything going on this morning so I only have about a half hour now before I have to meet another client."

"Me, too. I have to open the shop. I'll just take a quick look now and come back later to do a more in-depth evaluation."

Ophelia nodded, then returned to rummaging in the cabinets and I headed off in the direction she'd indicated. On my way, I kept my eyes peeled for the ghost, but he didn't seem to be around. Probably just as well, since I couldn't actually talk to him in front of Ophelia without her thinking I was crazy.

The house was bigger than it had looked from the outside. I passed a dining room complete with an ornate chandelier, a bathroom, and a strange room lined in dark velvet drapes that had only a large oval table and chairs in the middle.

The ceilings were twelve feet high and the hallway paneled with mahogany. A large portrait of a man in eighteenth century garb hung on one wall. My neck prickled as I looked at it and I was reminded of those old movies where the eyes of the portraits move to follow the innocent victim. I walked past, then stopped short and turned quickly. The eyes didn't move, and I laughed at myself for being so silly.

The further I got into the hallway, the darker it became, but I could see one room at the end that had light spilling from it. I headed toward it and found myself standing in the doorway of one of the most stunning private libraries I'd ever seen.

Bookshelves covered three of the walls from floor to the twenty-foot high ceiling. The fourth wall was dominated by a fieldstone fireplace, the opening almost large enough for me to stand in. A moose head mounted in the center kept watch over the room.

The tall, hand-rounded top windows were framed by long, sweeping curtains. A sheet-draped sofa sat opposite the fireplace with a chair on either side. A rolltop desk sat open at one end of the room. A pen and paper lay on top, almost as if the former inhabitant had just gotten up from writing. But the best part of the room was the scent of leather and vanilla musk—the smell of old books.

I stepped inside as if in a dream. Looking down at the rug, I could see it was once a beautifully colored oriental, but centuries of dust had dulled the color. I didn't care so much about that, though. It was the books that held my interest.

I started at the bookshelf closest to me, just looking at first. The dust lay thick on the shelves and tops of the books, but otherwise, most of the volumes seemed to be in good condition. Most were leather-bound, which would add to the value.

Walking down the row of bookcases, I could see the previous owner had varied tastes. My heart thudded with excitement as I walked past volumes of poems, history books and some of the popular novels from the 1950s and '60s. A polished mahogany ladder ran on a track around the room allowing access to the books on the higher shelves, but I didn't need to venture up there yet—I had plenty to occupy me within reach.

At the end of the row, I noticed a large section devoted to books on the occult, including some rare books from the 1700s, and a later edition of Leonardo Vairo's *Major Treatise of Demonology: Three Books of*

Charms, Spells & Sorceries. I knew the original had been printed in the 1500s, but this book surely couldn't be that old. If it was, it was worth thousands.

Glancing around the room, I realized the books in here could be worth tens of thousands ... maybe even more. I had yet to crack one of them open and was itching to find out if any were first editions.

I moved away from the occult section. Call me superstitious, but I felt creeped out looking at books on the occult in a haunted, abandoned house, outside of which, a murder had just happened. I stopped in front of an early edition of Poe's *The Raven*, its spine bound in tan leather with stamped gold lettering. I reached out, pulling the spine toward me gently with my index finger to reveal the gold-leaf tops of the pages inside. A cloud of dust floated out, causing me to sneeze and dislodge more dust, causing more sneezing.

After the sneezing stopped, I pulled the book out and opened it carefully. A slightly spicy mildew aroma wafted out and I closed my eyes, savoring the smell. Inside, the yellowed paper was of high quality, almost silky to the touch. I thumbed through the book, engrossed in looking at the fine print and wonderful illustrations.

"Hands off the books!"

I spun around, the rapid movement causing a sharp pain in my leg. Fumbling the book, I dove forward, catching it just in time. My heart thudded against my ribcage and I sucked in a deep breath, cradling the book to my chest.

"Who are you?" I demanded of the swirling mist before me, which I figured was the ghost I'd seen in the window earlier.

At first, I'd just assumed it would be the ghost of the recently deceased, but now that he was in front of me, I could see it wasn't. The face and hair looked different, though it was hard to tell through all the swirling mist. This gentleman was dressed in formal-wear and was somewhat old-fashioned looking, with a large mustache and a regal air about him.

"I'm Charles Van Dorn." The ghost bristled at me. "Who might you be and what are you doing with my books?"

"I'm Willa Chance. I own the bookstore downtown." I resisted the urge to extend my hand out for a handshake.

"Last Chance Books?" Van Dorn cocked an eyebrow at me, referring to the bookstore I'd inherited from my grandmother.

I nodded, glancing uneasily toward the door. Could Ophelia hear us? Hopefully, she was too busy with the china and silver to come looking for me down here.

"You must be Anna's granddaughter, then. She was a nice woman." Van Dorn leaned in toward me as if sharing a secret. "She parted the curtain to the other side a while ago."

I nodded, waiting patiently for him to get to what he wanted.

Van Dorn glanced out the window, where the crime scene techs were still taking pictures and searching for evidence. "What is going on here? It's like Grand Central Station. I really just want to be left alone in my own home ... like I have been for all these years."

"There was a murder out there." I jerked my chin toward the window.

"Oh dear ... again?"

My radar perked up. "What do you mean, *again?*"

Van Dorn looked contrite. "There was a bit of a scandal back in my day ... I guess that just added to my brother's dislike of me, but I imagine it's also what's allowed me to keep living here alone. Which I like very much ... so if you don't mind, I'll have to ask you to leave."

"Well, I hate to tell you, even if I leave you won't be alone for long. Your house is being sold."

"Sold?" Van Dorn's eyebrows shot up and his mustache twitched. "I thought Joshua would never sell it due to the controversy."

"By controversy do you mean the murder?" I made a mental note to look up the history of Van Dorn and the murder.

"That, and also my brother thought I was a fraud."

"Why would he think that?" I looked at him quizzically, my curiosity piqued. For the first time, I wondered how Van Dorn had come about the money that allowed him to afford this big house and expensive book collection. "What did you do?"

"Why, I was a spiritual medium. Don't tell me you haven't heard of the great Charles Van Dorn?"

"Sorry, no."

"Harrumph! I was quite well-known. Of course, there were those who resisted believing as they always do, and my brother Joshua was one of them." He peered at me closely. "*You* believe in mediums, though, don't you, Willa?"

I tilted my head to the side. I could hardly doubt that people could talk to the dead, since I was doing it myself right now.

"Well ... I don't deny people can communicate with ghosts."

Van Dorn's booming laugh surprised me. "I should say not! Oh, I was the real deal just like you ... but then things went wrong and ... well, I ended up on the other side, as you see me now. I've been content to stay here, and was hoping things could just continue as they have. I figured Joshua would rather see this house rot than sell it, because he hated everything I represented."

"Well, you're probably right about that. I heard something to that effect, actually. But I'm sorry to tell you, your brother has passed on and your nephew is putting the house up for sale."

"Oh, dear. That means people will be moving in." Van Dorn wrung his hands. "And my stuff will be sold?"

"I guess so."

"I guess I really need to move on then, so it's a good thing you are here."

"Why haven't you moved on before this?" Ghosts always had a reason why they were still lingering around. I didn't have a lot of experience with them at this point, but near as I could tell, they all wanted to 'move on' to whatever was next, but some of them couldn't do it on their own.

That's where I came in.

After my accident, I'd apparently become some sort of mediator that could help them do what needed to be done. I didn't really know how that had happened. Maybe my near death had caused me to make some sort of deal with the guy upstairs ... or downstairs.

Van Dorn sighed and plopped down on the couch, causing a round wet area on the sheet. "Unresolved issues."

"Let me guess. You want me to help you."

He brightened. "How did you know?"

"Let's just say, it's happened before."

Van Dorn twirled the end of his mustache between

his index finger and thumb. "Back when I was alive, I had many clients come here for readings and séances."

I remembered the curtained room with the round table I'd passed and nodded. "Go on."

"We had smashing parties. Celebrities flocked here. I was the toast of the town." He smiled, apparently remembering all his séances and parties.

"And ..." I drew out the word.

His face turned sad. "Unfortunately, there were a few untimely deaths."

"And that's why you took your own life?"

Van Dorn speared me with a glare. "No, you see, and that's why I can't move on."

"I'm sorry, but I don't understand."

"I didn't take my own life ... I was murdered."

CHAPTER FOUR

The first thing I discovered after I'd inherited the bookstore from Gram is that it came with a crew of regulars. The four of them had been congregating at the store first thing in the morning for decades, and they figured my grandmother's passing was no reason to stop the tradition.

So, when I pulled in an hour late, I was met by four senior citizens standing impatiently with coffees in hand.

"Willa! You got a dog?" Cordelia Deering's inquisitive, bright blue eyes flitted from Ranger to me.

"Well, sort of." I looked down at the Golden Retriever whose tail was tucked down low, his head hanging and his ears flopping. He looked depressed. "There was some trouble up at the Van Dorn mansion."

"Oh, is that why you are late?" Bing Thorndike raised a bushy white eyebrow at me.

"Yes. Let's go inside and I'll tell you all about it."

They parted to let me open the door and I pulled the unenthusiastic Ranger into the shop. Once inside, Josiah Barrows, the retired postmaster, handed me a Styrofoam cup filled with coffee. I accepted it gratefully.

"So, what's all the mystery? What's going on?" Hattie Deering, Cordelia's twin sister, asked. Her blue eyes had the same sparkle as her sister's and I noticed they were wearing almost identical outfits—something they did quite frequently as they had for the entire eighty-five years of their lives.

Four sets of eyes stared at me expectantly. I wasn't sure how to tell them about the murder. I hoped it wouldn't spook them since they were, after all, senior citizens and might be disturbed to learn a murderer was on the loose. I decided the best way was to just blurt it out.

"Someone was murdered up there."

"Oh, how exciting!" Hattie's eyes were as big as saucers.

"And you found the body?" Bing asked.

"That seems to happen with you a lot," Cordelia said. "Why, it was not even six months ago you stumbled over Lavinia Babbage dead in the library."

"Who was it this time?" Josiah asked.

They were taking it a lot better than I had expected.

"Gus said it was someone named Bruce ..." My voice trailed off. I'd forgotten his last name.

Bing snapped his fingers. "Bruce Norton! He had a Golden Retriever just like that one."

"Yes, that's it," I said.

"Oh, dear, not Bruce," Cordelia said. "Why, I haven't seen him around in ages."

The four of them found seats on the purple micro-suede sofa and chairs I had bought for customers to read books on while I untied the rope from Ranger's collar and let him loose. He seemed disinterested in the shop and simply plopped down in a patch of sun, curling up in a tight ball. I felt a tinge of uneasiness. My cat, Pandora, was not going to be happy when she saw a dog lying in her sunny spot. I glanced around the shop nervously for the persnickety feline who I'd dropped off when I'd come in at the crack of dawn to catalogue some inventory before meeting Ophelia. She was nowhere to be seen.

"What happened?" Josiah asked. "Are you sure it was murder?"

"Oh, it was murder all right. There was something really weird, too."

"Do tell," Cordelia and Hattie said at the same time, then clinked their Styrofoam cups together.

I opened the tab on my coffee lid and took a sip. "There was a strange mark on his forehead. It looked like a triangle with a dot inside it."

Hattie gasped. "I'd forgotten all about that."

"What?"

Cordelia leaned forward in her chair, her face as serious as a heart attack. "The Van Dorn Curse."

Hattie nodded solemnly beside her. "Back when Charles Van Dorn was alive there was a strange death connected with him."

"Some say he was a devil worshiper," Cordelia added.

"He had séances and all kinds of things going on up there." Hattie said. "Some said he was a fake, but I don't think so. Do you, Bing?"

"Yeah, didn't you know him pretty good?" Josiah turned to Bing.

Bing had been a magician all his life—and a good one, too. He'd toured the world with his magic act and even taught me a few tricks when I was a little girl. It made sense he'd probably have known Van Dorn, as they would have been about the same age.

Bing took a deck of cards out of his pocket and started shuffling them. "I did know him. He was pretty good at what he did. And he was a first class magician, too. But whether he was a real medium or not, I have no idea. Either way, it was a terrible thing that happened to that girl."

My brows shot upwards. "What girl?"

"Well, back then, a lot of young Hollywood types liked to hang around with Van Dorn. He had a lot of parties. There was one girl in particular—Lily Johanson." Bing's eyes took on a faraway look as he worked the cards. "She was a real beauty."

"And what happened to her?" I watched him work the cards, mesmerized on the movements of his hands.

"She died under mysterious circumstances. Some say there was a love triangle involved. Others say it had to do with the occult." Bing paused.

"Tell her the weird part," Josiah prompted and I leaned forward, eager to hear 'the weird part'.

"When her body was discovered, she had a strange mark on her forehead ... just like the one you described Bruce as having."

"What?" I straightened back up. "No way, that's just too strange."

"It's the Van Dorn curse, I tell you." Cordelia nodded.

"Tell me about the curse," I said over the top of my Styrofoam cup.

Bing shrugged. "Some say Van Dorn conjured up an evil spirit that killed Lily. The thing was, that symbol— the triangle with a dot in it—is very similar to the symbol Van Dorn used as his logo. His was a triangle with an eye in the middle."

"So naturally, everyone thought Van Dorn killed her," Hattie said.

"And he killed himself out of guilt," Cordelia added.

That's what you *think.*

"Was there ever a trial or anything?"

Josiah shook his head. "Nope. No need, really. His suicide note spelled it all out."

Suicide note?

That was strange. Van Dorn didn't mention any note to me. Which made me wonder—did he kill Lily and then himself? Did his ghost kill Bruce? Why would he lie to me? And, if all that was true, what exactly did he think I could do to help him?

Years of being a crime journalist had instilled a natural curiosity in me and I felt it kick in. I started to make a mental checklist of how to go about investigating the circumstances surrounding Lily Johanson and Charles Van Dorn's deaths. Gus had warned me not to get involved in Bruce's murder, but she never said anything about investigating the fifty-year-old cases.

"I'm curious, Willa. Why were you up there in the first place?" Bing asked.

"Van Dorn had a huge library filled with books. They are all still in the house."

Bing stopped shuffling the cards. "I didn't realize there was anything still in the house after all these years."

"It looks like everything is still there. I guess the sale of the estate was held up by Van Dorn's brother or something and it seems like people were afraid to go near it, so, thankfully no one looted it. I remember when I was a kid there were rumors about it being haunted," I said. "Anyway, it's being sold now and the seller wants the contents sold off. I was there to appraise the books."

"I remember reading that Joshua died. He and Charles didn't see eye-to-eye," Josiah said.

"Then why'd he leave the house to him?" Hattie asked.

Josiah shrugged. "Joshua was his only family. I guess he had no one else."

"So did you get a chance to look at the books?" Bing asked.

I nodded. "He had a wonderful library. Huge. But I didn't get to look in-depth because most of the time I had allotted was spent waiting for Gus to investigate the house."

"Was anything amiss in there? Any clues from the killer?" Cordelia dipped her tea bag in and out of the Styrofoam cup.

"No. It looked like no one had been in there in decades."

"So what's going to happen to all the stuff? Will you have a sale?" Hattie asked.

"Ophelia Withington said the nephew who inherited it all is planning on selling the contents and then putting the house up for sale. She wanted me to appraise the books to get an idea of their value."

Bing started shuffling the cards again. "Well, I hope

you will let me take a crack at buying any unusual books."

I remembered that Bing had taken to collecting books. A vague memory of selling him a special and rare antique book floated to the surface of my brain, but I couldn't recall exactly what the book was, though I did seem to get the feeling that it was very important. I tried to focus on the memory, but it was too fuzzy. My mother had always said that my steel-trap of a memory would start to fade once I hit forty-five. I didn't believe her when I was younger, but now that I was a few birthdays past the forty-five mark, I realized she'd been right.

We all fell silent, watching Bing shuffle the cards. The repetitive movements he used were mesmerizing—I felt relaxed, almost like I was in a trance.

"I'd be particularly interested in any journals or notes you find from Van Dorn," Bing said while continuing to shuffle. "He had some special magic tricks that he might have written the secrets to."

"I'll let you know if I find any," I said.

Bing stopped shuffling and put the cards back in his pocket, then stood up. "Well, I best be going."

"Me, too," Josiah said. "But I wonder. Who would have wanted to kill Bruce Norton? He was practically a recluse. I can't imagine anyone having a beef with him."

"It looked like he might have just been in the wrong

place at the wrong time," I said. "Maybe he stumbled across someone who didn't want to be stumbled across."

"Yeah, but *what* was he doing at the Van Dorn mansion?" Hattie picked up the Styrofoam cups and walked to the trash.

"I heard that he had dementia. Maybe he just wandered off," Cordelia offered.

"Okay, well, if that's the case, then who else was at the mansion and what were they doing that was so secret that they'd kill him just for being there?" Hattie raised her brows at her sister.

"Good question," Cordelia answered. "And why would they put that creepy symbol on his forehead?"

"Another good question, sister." Hattie took Cordelia's arm. "I think this begs further investigation."

"Meow!" Pandora came racing around the corner in a ball of gray fur. She skidded to a halt when she noticed Ranger lying on the floor. Her back arched and she let out an unwelcoming hiss. She glared at me, her greenish-gold eyes shooting daggers across the room.

Ranger merely opened one eyelid, shoved his nose further under his tail and went back to sleep.

"Well, looks like you might have a bit of a problem on your hands." Bing chuckled as he watched Pandora sniff Ranger as if he were an alien species.

"Indeed," Cordelia said. "We'll leave you to it, then. Be sure to let us know if you find anything else out about the murder. We'll hit up the Mystic Notch grapevine and see if we can come up with anything."

And with that, the four of them left, shutting the door behind them and leaving me to deal with one furious feline.

CHAPTER FIVE

*P*andora stared at the noxious-smelling ball of golden fur, unable to believe her eyes.

Who had let a dog in here?

She looked up at Willa incredulously. Didn't she know how dirty these things were? Surely, her human had more sense than to bring one here. But the next words out of Willa's mouth proved she didn't.

"Now, you be nice, Pandora. Ranger's just lost his master."

Pandora's heart hitched. She knew what it was like to lose her human. She remembered the pain she'd felt when Anna had died.

Did dogs feel the same way about their masters?

Pandora wasn't sure, but she put aside her natural dislike for the species and vowed to try to be nice ... at least until the creature proved she should act otherwise.

She went around to the back end and sniffed the tail cautiously, ready to unleash her razor-like claws and scratch the beast's eyes out should it try to bite her.

The dog did not move a muscle.

She worked her way to the front, taking in the various smells on its coat. She could tell the dog had been near death. She smelled fear and loneliness and her heart started to soften.

Maybe dogs did have feelings. She had to admit she didn't know much about them. She'd always avoided having anything to do with them as she considered them to be inferior creatures.

She sat down near it's head.

"Hello there," she said, attempting to establish communication.

The dog didn't even acknowledge her presence. It was just as she suspected—dogs were rude, self-involved creatures.

She stood and turned her back on the dog. She was working on picking out the sunniest spot on the wide sill of the front window when she heard a pitiful whine escape the beast.

"What was that? Did you say something?"

"Leave me alone," Ranger said. His face was partially tucked under his tail and he looked up at Pandora with one tormented eye.

"Fine by me," Pandora replied haughtily. *"You're the one encroaching on my territory."*

"I lost my best friend today." The pathetic whining tone of his voice tugged at Pandora's heart and she sat back down next to him.

"I lost my best friend once," she said. *"It was a sad day. But then I inherited Willa and I miss my old friend less and less now."*

Ranger flicked his eye up to look at Willa behind the counter and then back down to look at Pandora. *"No one can ever come close to my master."*

Pandora shrugged. *"Well, cats don't have masters. We are the masters. So I really can't help you there."*

"Just leave me alone, then. There's nothing for me to do now but sleep. I can still hear him arguing. I'm a bad dog."

"Arguing?"

"With the man at the special house."

Pandora moved closer, her curiosity getting the better of her. *"What special house?"*

"The house my master takes me to when we go for a walk. I can sense he thinks it is special. So I think it is special, too."

Pandora considered that for a moment. What would make a house special? She had no idea, but suddenly was overwhelmed with wanting to find out.

"Where is this special house?"

Ranger's forehead creased into furry lines as he thought. "It's through the woods, down the path with the birch trees and past the place where the deer come at night."

Pandora narrowed her eyes at him. Apparently, dogs weren't very good with directions. Better start a different line of questioning.

"So, why are you a bad dog?" she asked.

Ranger blew out a strangled sigh. "I couldn't save my master. I was out sniffing in the woods and by the time I heard him cry out, it was too late."

Waves of guilt radiated from the dog and Pandora backed up a few inches so as not to be engulfed in them.

"Are you saying your master was murdered?"

"Yes."

This was getting interesting, Pandora thought. Not that she didn't feel bad about Ranger losing his master to violence; she did. But murder usually meant the presence of evil, and her task on this earth was to protect humans from evil. Something told her this particular murder might be one she should pay attention to.

"You feel guilty because you couldn't save your master?" she asked.

"Yes, what good is a dog if he cannot fight for his master?"

True, Pandora thought but didn't voice her opinion. "But you saw the other man. The one who killed him."

"No. I would have chased him down!" Ranger lifted his head, feeling insulted. Did the persistent cat think he wouldn't have attacked the man and taken revenge for his master if he'd had the chance? "By the time I came back to the clearing, the bad man was driving away and master wouldn't wake up."

"So, you didn't see him? You don't know what he looks like?"

Ranger let his head fall again, depression overwhelming him. "No, I did not see him ... but I'll never forget his scent."

THE SHOP HAD BEEN quiet since my regulars left, which gave me a chance to enter some books I'd acquired into the database and put price stickers on them. Glancing over the counter, I was relieved to see that Pandora and Ranger seemed to have called a truce and were staring at each other warily.

"Good girl, Pandora." I tried to encourage the cat, whose kinked tail flicked on the floor nervously. I'd had visions of having to play referee all day to prevent her from injuring the depressed dog, but since it looked like they were getting along, I figured I'd take the opportunity to stock the books on the shelves.

As I scooped up a pile of books and headed toward

the shelves, my mind wandered to the Van Dorn library. I hoped it didn't seem callous considering a man was murdered outside the house, but I was practically salivating to be able to spend more time in that library.

I was also curious to find out more about Charles Van Dorn and Lily Johanson's deaths. Was it really murder like his ghost had said, or was he lying? What did their deaths have to do with Bruce Norton's murder? It was hard to picture them being related with a fifty year gap in between, but the triangle symbol on Bruce and Lily was too much of a coincidence. The deaths *had* to be related.

I knew I probably shouldn't get involved, but I couldn't tame the instincts I'd honed while spending over twenty years as a crime journalist. They were ingrained in me, and now I just couldn't help but investigate any mysteries that crossed my path—much to the dismay of my sister and Eddie Striker.

"I hope I can get back to the Van Dorn house soon," I said aloud. I'd gotten into the habit of talking to Pandora when the store was empty. Call me crazy, but most of the time it actually seemed like she was listening and understood me.

"Did you say Van Dorn?"

The voice scared the bejesus out of me and I dropped the book I'd been trying to shove into a slot on the bookshelf. I spun around to see the swirling mist of another of the 'regulars' that inhabited my shop. Unlike the four senior citizens, this one was of a more ethereal persuasion. A ghost. Robert Frost's ghost to be exact.

Yep, the poet. He'd lived in New Hampshire during a good part of his career and apparently liked it so much he'd decided to spend a good part of his afterlife here, too. I wasn't sure why he'd picked my bookstore to spend it in, but I had a large selection of books featuring his poems, and I think he felt flattered.

"Yes, I did say Van Dorn." I answered his question while retrieving the book from the floor and placing it on the shelf.

"As in Charles Van Dorn?" He swirled in front of me, blocking my access to the shelf.

"Yeesss." I drew out the word and stepped to the left, shoving the book into a space before he could move in front of me again. I didn't like passing my hand through ghosts—they felt cold and clammy. Not to mention that it just seemed like a rude thing to do.

"Oh, I knew Charles." Robert Frost smiled. "He used to channel me. Back then, I was newly dead you know. Oh, we had a grand old time. Though I did so wish I could have attended his parties in the flesh."

"You knew him?" My investigative radar honed in on this little tidbit. "What happened to him?"

"He's dead," Frost said, as if I didn't know. "Been

hanging around his house ever since—or so I've heard. I guess he can't move on."

"Oh, that is so sad when that happens." A voice behind me spoke up. My other ghostly regular—Franklin Pierce, the fourteenth President of the United States—who was also from New Hampshire. I wasn't sure why he'd picked my store either, but ghosts never seem to have a good reason for doing some of the things they do.

"I'll bet he wants you to help him." Robert Frost ran his finger along the edge of the bookshelf, leaving a trail of condensation.

"Yeah, how'd you know?"

He looked at Pierce and they both shrugged. "We're ghosts; sometimes we just know things."

I pressed my lips together, a thought occurring to me. "How come you guys never want me to help *you*? Don't you want to move on?"

"Who, us?" Pierce looked at me and I could see a gleam in his eye even though he was mostly transparent. "No way, it's too much fun here."

Robert Frost laughed. "It sure is. How about the other day when Mrs. Woolridge was looking in the naughty romance section and you swiped the book onto the floor."

Franklin Pierce laughed and slapped his knee. "I thought she was going to jump out of her saggy pantyhose."

My lips curled up in a smile at the image of pious old pinch-faced Mrs. Woolridge looking at sexy romances and then being surprised by a book slamming to the floor. The boys did this to my customers a lot. Apparently, they thought it was great fun. I usually had to spend a few minutes each night walking the aisles to pick up any stray books that had fallen to the floor.

"So, if you guys know stuff, then what do you know about Bruce Norton's murder?"

"Murder? There's been a new murder in town?" Frost consulted Pierce, who shook his head.

"We don't know a thing about it," Pierce said.

"Nope. We don't know everything, you know," Frost said.

"We're not psychics—just ghosts," Pierce added.

"But I do know one thing." Frost leaned toward me. "Van Dorn has some very nice volumes of my poems in his library. Be sure to acquire those for the store."

"Oh, and if there are any biographies on my life, get those, too," Pierce added. "Books about me are so hard to find."

The bells over the front door tinkled and the two ghosts evaporated, leaving a wet spot on the rug. I leaned backward to look down the aisle toward the door and saw my best friend, Pepper St. Onge, scooting inside with a tray loaded with goodies from the teashop she owned two doors down balanced in her right hand. She stopped

short as soon as she spotted Ranger, who was still lying in
the same spot.

"Well, hello there." She slid the tray onto the counter
and squatted to pet the dog, who ignored her.

"Hi," I yelled from my spot as I slid the last book into
place before joining her.

"I brought you some refreshments." She turned
concerned, green eyes on me. "I heard about what
happened at Van Dorn's and wanted to make sure you
were okay."

"Oh, I'm fine." I eyed the silver tray, noticing it had
my favorite molasses spice cookies along with a dainty
china teapot. Wisps of steam curled out of the spout of
the teapot. There were two chintz teacups, a tiny pitcher
of milk, sugar cubes and a row of thinly sliced lemon all
perched on top of antique lace doilies on the tray.

"You adopted a dog?" Pepper pointed to Ranger, who
hadn't moved a muscle. Some watchdog he was.

"No. That's Ranger, Bruce Norton's dog. He was
hanging around the ... err ... body. The police were going
to take him to the dog pound, so I took him instead."

Ranger let out a pained whine at the mention of his
former master's name, pinching my heart and causing
Pepper's face to crumble with concern. She broke off a
tiny piece of cookie, squatted and presented it to the dog.

"Treat?"

Ranger slit one eye open, sniffed, and then closed his eye without taking the food.

"He must be in a bad way, poor thing," Pepper said.

"Did you know Bruce?" I asked her.

"When I was younger." Pepper took the tray to the couch and motioned for me to join her as she talked. "I heard he'd become quite a recluse in his old age. Rumor had it he was suffering from dementia. I didn't know he had a dog. Are you going to keep him?"

"No. I don't think so. I figure I'll see if any of Bruce's relatives want him, and then find him a good home if not.

Pepper scrunched up her face. "I'm not sure Bruce has any relatives. He never married. I'm not sure about brothers or sisters."

She got busy pouring the tea and handed me a cup. I looked into the cup, then narrowed my eyes at her. "You didn't put anything in here, did you?

Pepper leaned back, a smile on her face. "Of course not."

Pepper had fancied herself to have a way with herbs since she was a teenager. She claimed she could use the herbs in her teas to help people feel better and push them along the 'right path'. I'd always been skeptical, especially since her teas usually had the opposite effect of what she intended. Though I had to admit, they did seem to work sometimes ... like earlier this summer when her teas had seemed to change Ophelia Withington from mean and bitter to nice and generous.

"So, go on, tell me what happened. I heard Bruce was found at Van Dorn's. What were you doing there?

I broke a cookie in half and nibbled on it while I told her about finding the body. Normally, I'd scarf down the whole cookie, but I'd noticed my jeans getting a little tight in the waist and figured I'd better start watching what I ate. Her eyes got wide when I told her about the mark on Bruce's forehead. I finished the story by telling her about Charles Van Dorn's ghost and the death of the starlet, Lily Johanson, fifty years ago with the same mark on her forehead.

"So, you think Charles lied to you about being murdered?" she asked.

"I have no idea. He left a note and confessed to killing Lily. But why would he lie to me?"

Pepper shrugged. "Who knows with ghosts? Maybe he's up to something. But those murders have to be related. Does Gus know about the old murder?"

"If she doesn't, I'm sure she'll find out soon enough."

"Well, this sure is turning out to be a mystery. Do you think Charles' ghost killed Bruce?"

"It would make sense, but why would he do that? And how?" I wasn't sure if ghosts were capable of bashing someone on the back of the head and leaving marks on their forehead.

"Maybe he just wants to be left alone and figured a new murder would scare people off for another fifty years."

"He *did* say he wanted to be left alone, but also that he wanted me to find his murderer so he could move on."

"Well, it sounds like you've got a real mystery on your hands." Pepper's eyes sparkled at me over the rim of her teacup. "You *are* going to investigate it, aren't you?"

"I really shouldn't. Gus warned me not to, but I have to admit, I am curious."

"Pfft. Gus always warns you not to and you never listen. Are you sure you're not hesitant because you know Striker will get mad at you?" Pepper teased.

I felt my face flame. I certainly didn't decide whether to investigate or not based on if I thought my sort-of boyfriend would get mad. Did I? I mean, heck, we'd only had a few dates, and I wasn't going to let anyone tell me what to do.

"No. It has nothing to do with him," I said, a little too forcefully. "And besides, I never said I *wasn't* going to look into it. I'm just not sure how to go about it. I wonder if Van Dorn knows more than he's letting on."

"He was in the house and probably saw the whole thing. When do you go back?"

"I'm going to call Ophelia and see if we can go back tonight. I think she said the nephew was coming in today." I glanced over at Ranger and Pandora. They were sleeping peacefully, Ranger on the floor and Pandora in the window. Could they be trusted alone together? Probably not. "Will you watch Ranger if I go back up there tonight? I can swing by your place and fill you in when I pick him up."

Pepper's face brightened. "Sure. I love dogs."

"I hope I get a chance to talk to Van Dorn, because if he didn't kill himself over guilt for killing Lily, then maybe he didn't kill Lily."

"And if he didn't kill Lily, he probably didn't kill Bruce."

"Which means the killer could still be out there somewhere."

"And he's still killing."

CHAPTER SIX

I closed shop at four p.m., leaving Pandora sunning herself in the window. After dropping Ranger off at Pepper's teashop, I drove up to Van Dorn's to meet Ophelia and the nephew. Pulling into the driveway, I noticed the police were gone, but the yellow crime scene tape remained. I wondered if the fact that a murder had been committed there would spook the new owner.

I made my way onto the sagging porch, glancing anxiously at the windows. I didn't see any signs of a ghost and I felt anxiety building in my chest. I had hoped Charles' ghost would be around—I had some questions for him.

One of the double doors gaped open and I tapped on it, reluctant to enter uninvited.

"Hello?" I yelled into the house.

"Come on in!" Ophelia's reply echoed down the front hall.

Inside, the house looked different. Sheets had been pulled off a few of the pieces of furniture and boards pried from some of the windows to let more light in. I realized the inside of the house was in a lot better condition than the outside. I could see the house had been a showplace in its day. Carved moldings framed the doors and windows and intricate, scrolled details enhanced the ceiling fixtures and wall panels. The furniture, while outdated, looked to be of the highest quality.

"We're in here." Ophelia's voice drifted toward me and I followed it to the kitchen. Boards had been removed from the windows and the room was bathed in the waning late afternoon light, allowing me to get a better look than I'd been able to earlier that morning.

Large, dark wood cabinets ran the length of two walls. A soapstone sink set under a tall window interrupted the wooden counters and two ovens, one on top of the other, sat opposite it. A long, stainless steel prep table ran down the middle of the room. Ophelia had her head in one of the bottom cabinets, her back-end sticking up in the air in a most uncomplimentary way. A tall, thin man with longish, wavy brown hair was pulling things out of an open drawer and loading them into a cloth shopping bag.

It looked for all the world as if they were looting the place.

I paused in the doorway. "Hi."

Ophelia backed out of the cabinet and the man turned to face me.

"Willa Chance, this is Steven Van Dorn, the new owner of the house." Ophelia waved her hand between Steven and me. "Willa is an expert on books. I've asked her to appraise your uncle's collection."

Steven extended a large, callused hand toward me. I judged him to be near sixty years old and his face had an edge to it that said he'd had a hard life. His handshake was rough and the way he eyed me made me uneasy.

"You can call me Steve," he said.

I glanced at the bag he held. "Packing up already?"

"Let's just say I'm in need of immediate cash and this stuff is gonna sell like hotcakes on eBay." He leaned closer to me and lowered his voice. "Especially now with the Van Dorn curse coming back into the public eye."

I slid my eyes over to Ophelia, who shrugged.

"You don't mind that someone was murdered in the backyard?"

"Mind?" He laughed. "Heck no, that's gonna make this stuff more valuable! There's already an interest in old occult legends and this new development is going to make the personal items of Charles Van Dorn highly collectable."

I took a step backward, a bit put-off with his attitude. He seemed completely insensitive to the fact that a man was dead, focusing only on how much more that death would allow him to profit.

I turned away. "I guess I'll go start on the books."

"So, what about those books? Are any of them any good?" Steve asked.

Just thinking of the beautiful books in the library warmed my demeanor. "I didn't get a chance to look too closely earlier, but it does seem your uncle had some valuable volumes. Just the sheer number of books is incredible. You might consider a specialty auction. I believe you'll get the most money that way and it will be easy for you to consign the whole lot."

I felt a little sad about seeing the library empty of books, but at least an auction would ensure they went to good homes.

He narrowed his eyes. "Well, I don't wanna get ripped off. I have important uses for this money."

"Oh?" I had a sneaking suspicion what he thought was important and what I thought was important were two different things.

He narrowed his eyes at me. "Well, I can't really say what they are, but it's not all just going to me."

"Don't worry, I'll write up a full appraisal and list the most valuable books. You can double check those on eBay or with another appraiser if you want." It was none of my business what he did with the money. It was my responsibility to do a good job appraising the books, and I took my responsibilities very seriously.

That seemed to satisfy him.

"Okay, you get to it, then. I gotta grab a few bags from here and then get back to the motel and start listing. This time tomorrow, I might be upgrading my room." He flashed a grin, which I noticed was missing several teeth, and turned back to the drawer.

I headed down the hall, past the butler's pantry and the curtained room that I figured had been Van Dorn's séance room. I was glad Ophelia and Steve would be busy in the other part of the house. I wanted to be alone in the library in case Van Dorn felt like making an appearance.

I pulled out my notebook and shut the door, wondering where to start. It made sense to pick a corner and work from one end of the room to the other, so I made my way to the opposite end, then crouched down to start with the books on the bottom shelf.

Scanning the books, I pulled out the ones that would have the most value and combed the insides to get an estimate of condition as well as look at the edition, whether it was signed, and the publisher, all of which I recorded in my notebook. For me, it was relaxing work. I loved working with the books and was soon immersed in my own little world, barely aware of my surroundings.

I'd made my way halfway around to the edge of the fireplace when I felt something cold and wet at my elbow.

"Who is that odious man in my kitchen?" Charles Van Dorn's ghost whispered into my ear.

"I hate to tell you, but that man is your nephew."

Charles made a face, his form dissolving, then swirling back together. "Little Stevie? Why, he's practically giddy over selling off my kitchenware!"

"Apparently, the popularity of the Van Dorn curse makes your kitchenware very profitable. How come you didn't mention the curse to me before?"

Van Dorn made a dismissive gesture with his hand. "That whole curse thing was sensationalism, manufactured by the press to sell newspapers. There is no curse."

"But what about the markings on Lily Johanson's forehead that match your logo? Did you kill her?"

"Certainly not!" Van Dorn's face turned hard. "That's what everyone thought, I know, but I didn't do it."

I slid another book out of its place to inspect the jacket, then snuck a sideways look at Van Dorn. "Did you know the man killed in your yard this morning had the same mark on his forehead?"

His eyes widened. "You don't say? That is odd. You don't suppose the same person that killed Lily did this other person in, too?"

"I don't know. Didn't you see the murder? It was right outside the house here."

"I'm afraid I was off in the nethers and didn't witness it. His spirit must not have been restless as I didn't even know something had occurred until I saw you out there." Van Dorn glanced out the window. "Tell me, who was it that was murdered?"

"Bruce Norton."

Van Dorn gasped. "No!"

"Oh, you knew him?"

"Yes, he used to come to my ... umm ... parties back in the day," he stuttered. "I guess you could say we were friends."

"Why do you think he would be in your yard, now, though?"

Van Dorn's brow wrinkled, causing wisps of mist to swirl up toward the ceiling. "That's a good question. I really cannot say."

"And you didn't have anything to do with his murder?"

"Of course not! How could I kill someone? I'm merely vapor and energy with no physical form to inflict harm."

I chewed my bottom lip. What he said was true. I knew I could pass my hand right through him if I wanted. Then I remembered how the ghosts of Robert Frost and Franklin Pierce were able to pull books off the bookshelf in my store. If they were able to do that, then maybe Charles Van Dorn's ghost was able to smash in Bruce Norton's head.

I regarded Van Dorn with renewed suspicion. "Are you sure you were really murdered? From what I hear, you killed yourself out of guilt after killing Lily Johanson. There was even a suicide note."

"Staged!" he boomed. "I told you someone murdered me. I'm sure it was the same person who killed Lily. I believe they were trying to frame me—someone who was jealous and wanted me out of the way. That's why they put my logo on her forehead."

"Jealous?"

"Of my popularity and skills, I assume."

"Oh, not like a jealous lover?"

Van Dorn looked insulted. "I should say not. What kind of a guy do you think I am?"

I shrugged. *Was he protesting a little too vehemently?*

"So you weren't involved with Lily romantically?"

"Of course not. My work was my whole life. And even if I was, which I wasn't, then why would I kill her?"

I studied him while he swirled and misted anxiously. He did seem sincere and I couldn't figure out what he would gain by lying to me. The scenario he outlined was entirely plausible. I made a mental note to dig up whatever I could about his death and see if they'd even entertained the thought of it being murder.

As if reading my mind, Van Dorn spread his arms, smiled and said, "What would I have to gain by lying to you? I'm seeking your help so that I can pass on to the next realm, which I would have done already had I not been held back by the unresolved issue of finding my killer, and the fact that I was quite comfortable hanging around in my own home, *undisturbed.*"

He did have a point. I decided to accept his story for the time being.

Crash!

Van Dorn grimaced and looked in the direction of the crash. "What *is* he doing in there? It's so disrespectful. I have a good mind to head in there and do something otherworldly to spook him. That will teach him to come skulking around here at all hours of the day and night, touching my things."

"Well, technically they are *his* things now," I pointed out.

"Oh, dear, I suppose they'll be going through everything." Van Dorn wrung his hands, watching me closely as I went back to my task of inspecting the books. I hated to be rude, but I had to speed things up or I'd never be finished.

"Are you going to look at every single book?" he asked.

I shrugged. "Well, I'm just inspecting the valuable ones, but eventually they'll all be removed. The whole house will be emptied. I think Steve might send the books to auction."

"Well, then, I pray my instructions have been followed so my secret will be safe," he whispered in a barely audible voice.

Did he just say something about a secret? My interest was piqued.

I stared up at him. "Secret?"

Van Dorn was distracted by another crash. "What? Did I say secret? I must have been confused. Really I *must* go see what they are doing in there."

"Wait—"

But he had already disappeared.

I turned back to my work with a sigh. I'd been hoping to get answers from the ghost, but all I'd gotten were more questions.

I pulled out several more books, then coming to the very edge of the fireplace, I was just about to start on the next shelf up when one book that was sticking out past the others caught my eye. Upon attempting to push it back in, I noticed it seemed rather light for the thickness of the spine.

My heartbeat picked up speed as I pulled it out and flipped open the cover. It was hollow inside—a fake book. Nestled in the hollow were several pages of handwritten notes, all bound in a red ribbon.

I held my breath as I took them out of the book.

Could these have something to do with the secret Van Dorn was just talking about?

I pulled one of the pages out of the ribbon and was just about to read it when the library door flew open.

"Chance, I thought I'd find you in here!"

I whirled around to see all six foot two of Eddie Striker, his broad shoulders taking up most of the doorframe. Striker and I had gotten off to a rocky start when I'd been his number one suspect in the murder of town librarian Lavinia Babbage. He liked to call me by my last name, which he said was appropriate because I took a lot of chances, especially when it came to investigating murders. He acted like that bothered him, but I think he secretly liked it.

My face flushed, my heart fluttered and I shoved the papers in the back of my notebook, unsure as to why I was hiding them, but certain it was the right thing to do. Knowing Striker, he'd think it was some kind of evidence and make me turn them in and I didn't want to do that, at least not until I'd gotten a chance to read them.

"Hi, Striker." I tried to act cool, even though his dimpled smile turned me to jelly.

He walked toward me and I closed the book, shoved it into the bookcase and stood.

"Impressive library. You must be in your glory here."

I smiled. "I am. I wish I could transfer the whole thing to my house."

He leaned his palms against the bookshelf on either side of my head, trapping me. Not that I wanted to get away. I breathed in his fresh, clean smell and closed my eyes. Then my thoughts turned suspicious.

"What are you doing here?"

"Gus wanted me to consult on this new murder case. I was looking over the crime scene."

My eyes flew open. "Really? Did you find any clues?"

Striker's gray eyes narrowed. "Why so interested? I hope you're not launching another investigation ... last time, you almost got killed and I would hate to see that happen."

"Who, me?"

Striker removed his right hand from the bookcase and ran it down my arm to my hand. Earlier in the summer, I'd burned that hand in an explosion, which was a result of my investigating another murder. I guess I could see why he didn't want me to get involved in this one. He turned my hand over gently in his palm.

"I see this has healed up nicely, so let's not do anything to hurt it again." He leaned back and his gaze raked my body. "Or any other part of you."

Suddenly, I found it hard to speak. "Okay."

He pushed away from the bookcase and took a step back, much to my disappointment.

"Good. Then carry on. I saw your car outside and wanted to stop in to say hi. Are you going to be finishing up soon?" He looked at me hopefully. "Because if you are, I could stop by your house after I'm done."

I nodded my head up and down like an overzealous puppy, then admonished myself for acting like a teenager in heat. I actually was feeling pretty hot, but that probably had more to do with a hormonal hot flash than Striker.

"I should be done in about an hour," I managed to say. "But I have to get Pandora and then stop at Pepper's to pick up Ranger."

"Ranger?"

I filled him in about the dog and he said he'd swing by in two hours, which should give me just enough time. I waited until I saw him moving around in the backyard and then I took the letters out of my notebook.

I vaguely remembered Bing saying something about a journal or some notes on magician's tricks and I wondered if that was what was in the letters. It didn't take long before it became clear the letters didn't have anything to do with any magic tricks.

They were love letters.

CHAPTER SEVEN

By the time I arrived home two hours later, Striker was already waiting in the driveway. I parked the car and Pandora shot out across my lap and over to the farmer's porch to be let in. Ranger was not nearly as enthusiastic and I had to open the back of my Jeep and coerce him out.

By the time I got into the kitchen, my nerves were frazzled, my stomach was grumbling and my leg was aching.

"So this is Ranger?" Striker knelt down in front of the dog that stood listlessly at my side.

"He's kind of depressed," I said.

"Meow!" Pandora glared at me expectantly from her place next to her food dish.

"Of course he's depressed. Poor guy lost his best

friend." Striker rubbed the fur on Ranger's head as I started to fill Pandora's bowl.

Ranger whimpered and twitched his tail.

I finished with Pandora's dish and got a large, ceramic bowl out of the cabinet for Ranger, thankful that Pepper had had the foresight to supply me with a small bag of dog food.

I poured out the food and set it down, along with a bowl of fresh water. "Here you go. You must be hungry."

Ranger flicked his eyes from me to the bowl. He approached cautiously, sniffing around the edges, then he sighed, lumbered to the corner of the room and plopped down, resting his head on his paws.

"Hey, you have to eat." I grabbed a few pieces of food and squatted beside him, wincing at the pain in my leg. I put the food under his nose. He sniffed at it, then curled up in a ball and ignored me.

"Maybe he doesn't like it," Striker said.

"I think he's still upset about the murder." I pushed up from the floor and limped over to the fridge in search of supper for Striker and me.

"Is your leg bothering you?"

My heart hitched at the way he said it. Like he was genuinely concerned. I shoved my head further into the near-empty fridge. "I don't have much in here ... some cottage cheese, mustard, jalapeños, cream cheese and Ritz crackers."

"You keep crackers in your fridge?"

I shrugged and pulled everything out onto my counter. "Do you think you can turn this into dinner?"

Striker's lips quirked up in a smile as he looked at the ingredients skeptically. In the few months we'd known each other, I'd learned he was an excellent cook, which worked out well because I couldn't cook to save my life. My meals usually consisted of take-out, frozen pizza and English muffins with whatever was in the fridge on top. Tonight I didn't even have the English muffins.

"Looks like we'll be having appetizers for supper." Striker took out some plates and I watched him spread cream cheese on several crackers, then apply a dot of mustard, then top it off with a jalapeño slice. He made a trayful, then we sat at the kitchen table.

The crackers were surprisingly good. The spice of the mustard and heat of the jalapeños were soothed by the smooth cream cheese, and the cracker added a satisfying crunch. We munched in silence for a few minutes, my mind drifting to the love letters I'd found at Van Dorn's.

They were safely tucked away in my notebook and I was dying to tell someone about them ... but not Striker. I knew the letters didn't have anything to do with Bruce Norton's murder, but I figured it was better for me to keep their discovery to myself until I was sure what they meant. They could help me figure out who killed

Charles Van Dorn if he actually was murdered like he claimed. Although his ghost *seemed* sincere, I was starting to have my doubts, especially since he'd clearly lied to me about having a love affair—the letters proved that. The only problem was, the letters didn't reveal *who* he was having the affair with.

Striker broke the silence. "Pandora's being awfully cordial to her new guest."

I glanced over at the sleek, gray cat who was circling Ranger, sniffing every inch. She shot me a reproachful look as if to let me know she took a dim view of having a dog as a houseguest. I felt a swell of pride that she was acting so respectful and made a mental note to give her some extra catnip.

"I guess she must sense that he's in distress," I said. "I have to admit, I was leery of bringing him here because I didn't know how she'd react, but it looks like they're getting along."

"Well, at least she's tolerating him for now," Striker said. "Are you going to keep him?"

I munched on the last cracker thoughtfully. "I don't think so. I'm hoping Bruce had some relatives who might want him."

"Gus said Bruce had no next of kin."

"Oh, that's kind of sad." I glanced at Ranger, wondering what would happen to him now. He moved his eyes in my direction and my heart pinched. "I guess it's up to me to find Ranger a good home, then."

Striker raised his left brow and I realized that *he* didn't have a pet. *Everyone* should have a pet. I glanced from Striker to Ranger, mentally sizing them up as a potential match, but decided it was too soon to mention it to Striker.

"I heard Bruce was a recluse," I said. "I guess that explains why I didn't know him. But Hattie and Cordelia said they thought he might have been getting dementia and just wandered onto the property."

Striker pressed his lips together. "Maybe. Of course, whether he wandered there or went there on purpose doesn't really matter so much. What we need to find out is why the other person—his killer—was there."

I saw the perfect opening and took it. Plastering on my most innocent voice, I asked, "Got any clues as to who that might be?"

Striker shrugged. "I really shouldn't discuss it, but I can tell you no witnesses have come forward and there're very few clues. Gertie estimated the time of death at two a.m. and Ruth Walters said she saw a yellow car drive by, but swears it was closer to six. She claims people were racing up and down the road all night and suggested we put up a speed trap."

I snorted. "Well, that's not the first time Ruth has

suggested that. One car goes by and she complains that they've been drag racing up the road all night."

"That's what Gus said, so I'm taking her testimony with a grain of salt."

"Probably a good idea." I pulled an empty chair out from the table and gritted my teeth as I swung my leg up onto it. I angled my chair to be more comfortable, and something glowing in the living room caught my eye. The round sphere on my coffee table had caught the setting sun from the window and was reflecting lovely gold and pink light into the room. The sphere—I guessed it was some sort of paperweight—had been a gift from my grandmother's friend and neighbor, Elspeth Whipple, and I made a mental note to check on the old woman. Gram had asked me to do that in her will and I hadn't looked in for a few days.

"That's hurting you," Striker leaned forward and pushed my pant leg up to my knee. "I told you, you should keep massaging it."

"Uh-huh." I closed my eyes as he pressed his thumbs deep into the tissue, providing what I could only describe as 'painful relief'. "Do you think Bruce's murder could be related to the murders during Charles Van Dorn's time?"

"Murders? I thought one person was murdered and Charles confessed and killed himself."

"Right." I couldn't tell him that Charles himself

claimed differently. "Don't you find it odd the two victims both had that symbol on their forehead?"

"They did?"

"Yeah. You didn't know?" I felt a momentary surge of superiority, thinking I'd out-investigated the police.

Striker narrowed his eyes at me. "No. What do you know about it?"

"The morning bookstore gang told me about the symbol. Apparently, it all had something to do with Charles Van Dorn's career as a medium. Lily had the same symbol on her head as Bruce did. They thought it was some sort of curse."

Striker laughed. "You don't believe in all that mumbo-jumbo, do you?"

Yes.

"No." I wasn't ready to reveal my secret pastime of talking to ghosts to Striker yet.

"Anyway, it's unlikely the two crimes would be done by the same person as the original killer would have to be at least seventy years old by now. I don't know if they would have the strength to swing hard enough to wield the blow that killed Bruce Norton. But the markings are an odd coincidence. Our new killer must have known about the original case."

"Right. So, what did kill him? I mean, what was the murder weapon?"

Striker looked at me sideways as he worked his way

up my leg, past the knee to my thigh, his face getting closer and closer to mine. "Sorry, Chance, that's privileged information. I can't give you all the clues. Besides, I don't want you to have too many of them or you might go off investigating on your own. And I can't have you doing that."

And with that, he leaned in and pressed his lips against mine. The relaxing after-effects of the massage and the feeling of his soft, warm lips must have gone right to my head because I forgot all about clues, murders and the Van Dorn curse.

PANDORA GLANCED *up at Willa and Striker, her whiskers twitching in disdain. Didn't they know lips were for helping to pull the fur off mice? She turned her attention back to Ranger, ignoring the strange noises the two humans were making.*

"You really should eat, you know. You won't be able to keep your strength up."

"Why would I need strength? I lost my master and now I have no one and no purpose."

Pandora let out a sigh. She was finding Ranger's doldrums to be quite tiresome. "Well, you could get a new master."

"Who would want me? I couldn't save my old master. Certainly no one will want a dog like that."

Ahhh, so that's the problem, *Pandora thought. Ranger just needed a little boost of confidence. And she'd have to be the one to give it to him, otherwise he might never find another home and she sure as heck didn't want him spending the rest of his days in hers. Not that he was that bad ... he was tolerable. But she was set in her ways and used to having Willa to herself.*

"Maybe you couldn't keep your master from being murdered, but you still might be able to help him."

Ranger picked his head up off the floor and eyed her skeptically. "What do you mean?"

"You could help find his killer and make sure he's brought to justice."

"How would I do that?"

Pandora rolled her eyes. She'd forgotten dogs were used to being led around on leashes by humans. She realized they must have a hard time thinking for themselves, which meant she'd have to do all the brain work and let Ranger think it was his idea.

She picked up her paw, licking the pink, callused pads underneath. "I guess you would do what humans do ... visit the scene of the crime and look for clues."

The golden fur in between Ranger's eyes ruffled together and Pandora could see he was giving it great thought.

"What kind of clues?"

Pandora let out an exasperated sigh. Would she have to do everything?

"I'll help you look. Do you think you can show me where the special house is?" While Pandora wanted to help the dog get out of his funk, the truth was she also wanted to check out this 'special house'. She was filled with curiosity about it. And also about the murder. Something told her she'd best keep close tabs on the situation and Ranger seemed to have the most information.

"I might be able to," Ranger said cautiously. He wondered if he could trust the cat ... he'd heard they could be furtive and sneaky. But the idea of avenging his master's death appealed to him and he wasn't sure how to go about it on his own.

"Good." Pandora nodded toward the bowl Willa had filled with dog food. "Then you should try to eat something ... you may need the energy."

PANDORA KNEW Ranger wouldn't be able to fit through the cat door, so later that night after the humans had gone upstairs, she took him through her secret escape route in the basement. He barely fit through the loose board that led into the root cellar—where Willa never went—and almost didn't make it out the narrow tunnel Pandora had spent all of last summer digging.

At first, he wasn't sure of which direction to go, but once Pandora got him to focus, he homed in on the special place and they trotted off up the mountain.

"I really miss my master, but Willa seems nice," Ranger said as they ran through the woods, using the stars as navigation points. "Maybe things aren't as bad as they seemed yesterday."

Pandora slid her eyes over toward him, her whiskers twitching. She was glad the dog was coming out of his funk, but not glad enough to want to share her home with him. Or her human. Sure, he might come in handy for blaming things on, but she doubted Willa would believe he was the one that threw up a hairball on her new bedspread or left the headless mouse on the porch.

"Willa is nice, but you need a new master, not mistress," Pandora said.

"I don't deserve either." He stopped and sniffed the air. "The special place is up ahead."

They spilled out of the woods and Pandora paused at the edge of the yard. A large brick house loomed in the distance and a variety of smells hovered in the air.

"Wait here," she said.

Pandora sniffed the air. Slinking low on her belly, she skirted the edge of the yard, moving in circles closer and closer to the house. The cloying smell of death lingered, but it wasn't strong. She smelled anger, fear, greed and betrayal. But none of that was here now. Satisfied that no other souls, human or otherwise, were in the yard or the house, she signaled for Ranger to join her.

"This is where it happened." Ranger stopped in a spot behind the house where the tall grass had been trampled down. Pandora could smell many humans, their scents and emotions intermingled, making it impossible to single out that of the killer or Ranger's former master. If she had been able to, she might have at least gotten a clue as to if Bruce knew his killer or the emotions surrounding the murder.

She glanced at the large house which loomed over them, silhouetted by the full moon. Her whiskers tingled. The hairs on her back stood up with static electricity.

Something important was in that house.

Not something to do with the murder, though. This was something bigger than that—this had to do with her purpose of helping the humans keep the scales of good and evil balanced on the side of good.

Should she go in? A quick glance at the house told her there would be many ways she could slip inside, but she had no idea what to look for. Better to wait and seek advice from the others of her kind.

She turned to Ranger. "Why is this house special?"

"I'm not sure." Ranger's eyes clouded over. "Master used to take me for walks here all the time. I could feel he thought it was special. He told me he used to come here when people lived here. Good times."

"But he never said why it was special?"

"No, but I could feel it. The house and the special thing he had at home."

Special thing at home? Pandora narrowed her eyes at the dog. How many 'special things' did his master have? She wondered if the special thing at home was related to whatever it was she sensed in the house. She would have to see if Ranger could take her there and show her.

"You lived nearby?" she asked.

"Yes." Ranger looked off to the west, his eyes moist.

"Can you take me there and show me the special thing?"

Ranger whined, nodded his head and started off to the west. Pandora remembered the reason they'd come— she still needed to help him solve the murder or he might never find a new master. "Not yet. First tell me what you remember from that night your master was killed."

"I followed the rabbit smells. Master lets me off the leash here when we come. There are rabbits that live here. I heard the voices, but I was chasing the rabbits." Ranger's ears lowered and he looked at the ground, his head hanging. "When I came back, Master was laying on the ground. I licked his face, but he did not move. I smelled death."

Pandora nodded sympathetically. "And you never saw the other man?"

Ranger shook his head, his eyes still cast downward.

"Did you stay with your master the whole time?"

Ranger frowned. "No. I followed the man's scent in two directions, but I did not find him. Then I came back and stayed with Master."

"Two directions?" Pandora wondered why the man would have gone in two directions. Wouldn't he have killed Bruce and run away? She assumed he had a car so one of the directions would have been the driveway, but what was the other? "Show me which directions."

Ranger nodded toward the front of the house. "That way."

"The driveway. He probably drove away in a car."

Ranger nodded. He'd already figured that out on his own. Then he jerked his head toward the woods on the other side of the road. "And that way."

Pandora squinted at the woods. Why would the man go over there? She could think of only one reason.

"Can you still follow his scent?" she asked.

Ranger sniffed at the ground. He walked around the trampled area in a circle his nose twitching as he tried to pick up the scent. "Maybe. It's not strong, but I will try."

"Good, let's see where he went in the woods. I think it might help us find out who it was."

Ranger's ears perked up and he sniffed even harder,

leading Pandora up the road and into the woods to an area near the shallow river. They didn't have to go far before a metallic odor flooded Pandora's senses. Blood.

They both stopped, Pandora homing in on the origin of the blood smell and Ranger sniffing in circles to pick up the trail.

"This is where his scent trail ends, isn't it?" she asked Ranger.

"I think so."

Pandora knew why. The murder weapon was here somewhere. She could sense that people had been here searching and assumed it was the police. They'd looked for the murder weapon but had not found it and she knew why. It was buried, right beneath where she was standing, cleverly covered up with leaves and forest debris so no one would notice the ground had been dug up. She herself wouldn't have noticed if she hadn't smelled it with her finely tuned senses. It was no wonder the police had not discovered it.

"Help me dig here." She pointed to a spot on the ground and Ranger used his powerful claws to dig. He didn't have to go far before he hit something—a heavy piece of white-painted wood that looked like it came from one of Van Dorn's porch columns.

"Hold it." The blood smell was stronger and Pandora could see the dirt caked on one end of it along with something that looked like it had been sticky—blood.

Ranger sniffed and started to whine. "Master!"

"You did well," Pandora said to him.

"I did?"

"You found the murder weapon. This will help the police find the killer of your master."

Ranger's ears perked up and he held his head high. "Good dog?"

"Yep." Pandora answered. "Now that we have that taken care of, can you take me to where you lived and show me the special thing your master had?"

"Woof!" Ranger started back toward the house with a spring in his step.

Pandora followed him, glancing back at the partially uncovered column. She was sure it had been used to kill Bruce Norton and probably held a clue as to the killer's identity. But, the police had already searched here and she doubted they'd be back, which left her with only one solution. Somehow, she was going to have to lure Willa into these woods so she could discover the weapon and hand it over to the police.

CHAPTER EIGHT

I woke up wondering about the murder weapon. Striker wouldn't tell me what exactly it was, but obviously, Bruce had been hit on the back of the head. Striker alluded to the fact that the blow had killed Bruce, so I imagined it must have been something large and heavy. A shovel, baseball bat, or board maybe? Not that I was trying to solve Bruce's murder ... I had enough problems trying to solve Van Dorn's.

I made it in to the bookstore early so I could get a jump-start on inventorying some new books. Ranger listlessly sniffed the purple sofa and chairs, then curled up in a corner. He seemed incredibly tired and still a little depressed, but I took solace in the fact that he'd eaten a little bit of the food in his bowl and had at least sniffed the furniture—maybe he was starting to feel better.

I slipped behind the counter and Pandora jumped

up on it, taking an unusual interest in the blue and white stoneware mug that held my pens and pencils. She sniffed the sides, then stuck her face into the middle, pushed the pens aside and sniffed some more. Finally, she looked straight at me, shot her paw out and pushed the mug off the counter. It smashed to the floor in a clatter of ceramic shards, pens and pencils.

"Pandora!" I leaned over the counter to see pens rolling every which way.

Pandora calmly jumped down from the counter, padded over to her cat bed in the windowsill and curled up.

What the heck had gotten into her? I wondered if it was her way of protesting Ranger's presence. Funny, though, she didn't seem to mind him ... she hadn't really hissed at him or anything. It actually seemed like they were getting along and I could have sworn they exchanged a *look* right after she pushed the mug off. That was probably my overactive imagination. I was pretty sure dogs and cats didn't exchange 'looks'.

Whatever the reason, I noticed they were both fast asleep before I finished picking up the mess. Both of them seemed to be unusually tired today. I resumed my activities behind the counter and was engrossed in adding up my sales for the week when the regulars came in.

"Morning, Willa." Bing slid a Styrofoam cup across

the counter toward me. "Have you been back to Van Dorn's?"

"I went back last night." I raised the coffee cup up. "Thanks for the coffee."

"And?" Bing's left brow ticked up a notch.

"I didn't find any journals." I considered telling him about the letters but that didn't seem right. The more I thought about it, the more I realized those letters were personal to Charles. He'd hidden them for a reason and it wasn't for me to be blabbing it all around town.

"Did you meet the nephew?" Hattie asked from where she was perched on the edge of the purple sofa.

"Yes. He was ransacking the kitchen for stuff to sell on eBay."

"I saw an old ashtray from the Van Dorn estate going for over two hundred dollars this morning!" Cordelia said.

"Really? Why so much?" Bing asked.

"Well, it's a big deal, what with the curse and all." Hattie sipped her tea. "And, of course, that nephew is taking full advantage. He's even providing a letter of provenance and everything."

"If you ask me, it's all in poor taste." Cordelia pursed her lips.

"Some people will do anything for money," Josiah said. "I'm surprised the police are letting him in there like that, since it's the scene of a murder."

"Oh, I have a lead on that, too." Cordelia's blue eyes sparkled. She loved having information she could enlighten the rest of us with.

"Do tell," I prompted.

"It seems Bruce got into a fight with some stranger at the Mystic Cafe the night before he was murdered."

"Stranger?" I leaned my elbows on the counter. "Do you think it could have been the nephew, Steve Van Dorn?"

Cordelia shrugged. "I don't know. Myrna didn't know who he was, but she said Bruce saw him writing something in a notebook and he got all mad and started yelling."

"That was probably due to his dementia. People with dementia act all funny and unpredictable." Hattie turned to Cordelia. "Remember how Daddy used to act toward the end?"

"You don't think this person would have killed Bruce because of that, do you?" Bing asked.

Hattie and Cordelia scrunched up their faces in thought.

"That hardly seems likely," Josiah said. "I mean, who kills someone over a few heated words in a cafe? It didn't come to blows or anything, did it?"

"Oh, no," Cordelia said. "Myrna said Bruce yelled and the other guy yelled back and then it was over real quick."

"Well, I assume the police will look into it." Josiah spread his hands. "It won't take them long to find out about the fight since news spreads like crabgrass in this town."

Hattie slid her eyes over to me. "Maybe you should tell Gus, Willa. Just in case she doesn't find out."

"Or that nice young man of yours." Cordelia raised her brows at me. "I heard he was at your house last night."

My cheeks heated up a notch. Was nothing private in this town?

"Now, now, I'm sure the police can do their own job without us butting in," Josiah said.

"I guess you're right. The fight in the cafe probably didn't mean anything anyway." Cordelia shrugged. "Bruce might have been off his rocker."

"Probably," Hattie said. "But I know one thing. If I were Augusta, I'd be putting that nephew at the top of my suspect list."

"Why's that?" Josiah asked.

"Why, isn't it obvious?" Hattie wrinkled her face at Josiah. "The killer is usually the person who has the most to gain, and judging by the prices that nephew is getting for his stuff on eBay, he's making a bundle over the renewed interest in the Van Dorn curse."

Lunchtime rolled around and I realized I was craving a tuna on rye with extra pickles, just the way Myrna makes it. Not only that, but I was dying to find out about the fight Cordelia had mentioned.

Maybe the fight had nothing to do with Bruce having dementia. Maybe he knew something about Van Dorn or the Van Dorn curse. He might have heard Steve planned to sell off Van Dorn's stuff and had it out with him.

If Bruce knew something that could be a clue to Charles Van Dorn's murder, I needed to find out ... and if I happened to find a clue to Bruce's murder, that would be an extra bonus. Not that I was actively looking for such a clue. I was leaving that up to the police, just like Gus had asked me to.

I grabbed my keys and flipped the sign to 'Closed'. A quick glance back into the shop as I backed out the door revealed Pandora and Ranger, both lying calmly in their spots, each with one eye open watching me.

Dare I leave them alone in the shop?

I didn't have much choice if I wanted to question Myrna about Bruce's fight, so I locked the door and stepped into the hot summer day. *The Mystic Cafe* was several stores down on the opposite side of the street. Traffic was light, so I hurried across, my flip-flops slapping against my heels.

Main Street had recently been renovated and I felt a swell of pride as I walked past the freshly painted storefronts. Though they were updated, they still kept their original, early 1900s architectural charm. Most of the stores had hanging plants or window boxes brimming over with colorful flowers—purple petunias, pink, white and red impatiens and a variety of pansies, their face-like petals smiling at me as I walked down the street.

The flowers added ambiance for the many tourists who pumped money into the summer economy. I noticed with dismay that most of these tourists happened to be inside *The Mystic Cafe* right now. I pulled the door open, the buzz of conversation vibrating in my ears as I made my way to the counter to order.

I caught Myrna's eye and her lips ticked up in a smile. She pulled a pencil out of her gray bun and produced a pad out of the vintage cherry print apron that barely covered her wide hips, then ambled over to stand on the other side of the counter from me.

"Hey, Willa, nice to see 'ya. What can I get'cha?"

"The usual." After having had lunch here for the past two years, I didn't need to specify. Bud, who made the sandwiches, knew exactly what to put in mine—lots of extra pickles, chopped up and mixed in with the tuna. My mouth was practically watering as I envisioned biting into the thick sandwich.

Myrna smiled and scribbled on the pad, ripped off the piece of paper and clipped it onto a round metal holder, which she twirled around so Bud could see the order.

Myrna moved to the register, her fingers poised over the keys. "You need a drink? Chips?"

"Yeah, I'll get an iced tea and some chips." I paid and glanced behind me to see if anyone was in line. No one was, so I leaned across the counter toward her and whispered. "Do you have a sec?"

She narrowed her eyes at me then glanced around the store to make sure no customers needed her. "Sure."

I jerked my head toward the drink cooler that was in an out of the way corner and she stepped out from behind the counter and met me over there.

"What's up?" She peered up at me from under the blue frames of her cat's-eye glasses.

"I heard Bruce Norton got into a fight in here the other night." I stood in front of the cooler, surveying the iced tea selections.

"Yep. He was quite loud about it, too."

"So you heard what they were arguing about?" I turned hopeful eyes to Myrna as I slid the cooler door open.

"Well, I try not to eavesdrop, but you could hardly help it."

"What was it about?" I picked a peach iced tea and slid the door closed. "I mean, I know Bruce wasn't really 'with it', and I was wondering if it was just gibberish or if it was something important ... you know, considering what happened later."

Myrna scrunched up her face. "Not with it? I don't know about that. Bruce came in for sandwiches and coffee sometimes, and he seemed 'with it' to me."

"Oh?" My brows shot up. Maybe whatever it was that made Bruce so mad really did have something to do with why he was killed. "So, then, what was the argument about?"

"Why don't you ask the guy he was arguing with? He's sitting right over there." Myrna pointed behind me and I whirled around, confused, because I hadn't seen Steve Van Dorn when I'd come in. I followed her finger to a corner table where a small, pinch-faced man sat.

"That's not Steve Van Dorn," I said.

Myrna glanced at the counter where a customer was standing, head tilted back as he mulled over the menu hanging above.

"I don't know who Steve Van Dorn is, but that's the guy Bruce was arguing with in the corner booth," she said as she made her way over to wait on the customer.

I grabbed my sandwich and small chips from the counter and headed toward the corner booth. The man had a notebook open on the table in front of him with a half-eaten pastrami sandwich next to it. He was so engrossed in what he was writing, he didn't notice me approaching until I was standing at the end of his table.

He looked up, his startled, brown eyes distorted behind thick lenses. He covered the grease-smeared, mustard-dotted pages protectively. "Can I help you?"

"Hi, I'm Willa Chance."

He blinked at my extended hand, then extended his slim, pale one for a limp handshake. "I'm Lester Price. But you can call me Les."

"I own the bookstore down the street and couldn't help but notice you writing. Are you a writer?" I'd learned early on that asking people about themselves was a good way to break the ice.

"Why, yes, I am." He clicked his vintage, Waterman cherry red mechanical pencil proudly. My lips quirked up in a smile. Like most writers, I had a favorite pen I always used—mine was a Mont Blanc Meisterstuck roller ball. It had come in a set with a fountain pen and mechanical pencil like most vintage pens, but I liked the rollerball the best. I guessed the Waterman was Les' favorite and decided it wouldn't be such a bad idea to use our common calling as writers to get him to open up.

"I'm a writer, too. I was a crime journalist before I came up here to take over my Gram's bookstore." I nodded at the notebook. "Are you doing a piece on Mystic Notch?"

"Sort of." Les hesitated, apparently sizing me up to see if I could be trusted. I must have passed muster, because he added, "Actually I'm writing about Charles Van Dorn."

"Charles Van Dorn?" I didn't bother to hide my surprise. "That's a strange coincidence. Are you writing a book?"

"It's no coincidence, really. My father was the journalist who wrote a series of articles about Van Dorn back in the sixties. You may have heard of him—Sal Price?"

I nodded, even though I hadn't heard of him. Couldn't hurt to butter the guy up.

"He started writing a book just before Van Dorn killed himself, but he never finished. Anyway, my father passed away recently and then I heard about the house being sold, so I figured I could honor my dad and come out and finish the story."

I narrowed my eyes. That sounded noble, but if he were writing a book, the renewed interest in the Van Dorn curse would surely make the book much more desirable to publishers. "So then, you must know about the Van Dorn curse and the symbol that Lily Johanson had on her forehead."

"Of course. That's a big part of the book, but the curse was just part of Charles Van Dorn's persona. Did you know that he used to have séances and try to raise the dead? He was into the occult and, well ... who knows what really happened to Lily."

"Is that what you and Bruce were fighting about?"

"Fighting?"

"In here the other day, it's all around town."

"Oh." He squirmed in his seat. "Well, I'm not exactly sure what he got all riled up about. He saw me writing and started yelling. I'm not even sure he knew what I was writing about. I don't think he was in his right mind."

"That may be." I studied Les carefully so I could judge his reaction to my next piece of information. "But did you know he was found murdered yesterday at the Van Dorn mansion ... and with the same symbol on his forehead?"

Les' eyes grow wide. "Symbol on his forehead?"

"Yes, the triangle with the dot in it, same as Lily."

Les gasped, slumping back in his seat as if all the air had been knocked out of him. "No, it can't be!"

"It's true."

Les looked terrified, as if he'd seen a ghost ... or worse. His mouth opened, closed and then opened again. "It's the curse! My father was wrong ... it really is real!

"What do you mean your father was wrong?"

His eyes darted around the room as he gathered up his notebook and shoved his pencil in the plastic protector of the breast pocket in his yellow, short-sleeved button-down shirt. "Before he died, he told me all about that last summer here. The summer Lily and Charles died. But he said the curse wasn't real. He told me Charles staged it all for effect ... but now that someone new has been killed up there with the same symbol ... well ... it seems like what he told me might have been wrong."

And with that he pushed up from his seat, darted out of the booth and rushed out the door.

I tapped my finger on the waxed-paper-wrapped sandwich I held in my hand as I watched him disappear into the street. Our conversation had certainly been enlightening. If Lester Price had knowledge from his father about what went on around the time Van Dorn died, he might be able to help me figure out what really happened.

Of course, Les did have a vested interest in reviving the Van Dorn curse since it would help him sell more books, but one thing was for sure. He wasn't the killer. My years as a crime journalist had given me a sixth sense about reading people's reactions and I could tell he was genuinely surprised when I'd told him about Bruce. Either that or he was one heck of an actor.

CHAPTER NINE

$\mathscr{M}$y stomach nagged at me, and I hurried out of the cafe. I was halfway to the bookstore when a prickly feeling on the back of my neck stopped me in my tracks. Turning slowly, I noticed the street behind me was dotted with tourists, but two people stood out like cats in a hen house.

They wore long, flowing dresses of light gauzy material. The redhead's dress was snowy white, which contrasted sharply with the dark glare she was aiming in my direction. I knew her, of course—Felicity Bates—widow of the son of one of the richest men in the area. I couldn't really say we were friendly. In fact, she had pretty much hated me ever since her son had gone to jail for murder. I guess she felt it was my fault since I'd had something to do with figuring out he was the killer.

The woman standing next to her looked to be in her

eighties. She had the same angry glare and wore a similar dress, but in light green. I pictured that was what Felicity would look like in thirty years.

The two women stared at me. Felicity pointed. I was hungry and didn't have time for her crap, so I thrust out my chin and started across the street to my shop.

"*Beep!*"

My heart skidded to a stop and I jumped back as the yellow Dodge lurched past. I'd been so focused on Felicity and her look-alike friend, I hadn't been watching the traffic.

"Sorry!" The driver yelled out the open window as he kept going. I recognized the voice of Steve Van Dorn and chuckled to myself, thinking about how ironic it would be if he killed me before I could figure out who had killed his uncle.

Finally, I reached the safety of my shop, unlocked the door and stepped inside.

"Meow."

Pandora must have spied the sandwich wrapper in my hand. She looked up at me and chattered her teeth together—something she did when watching birds and begging for tuna.

"Okay, hold your horses."

I sat down on one of the chairs and she trotted over, hopped up on the other chair and blinked at me. I ripped off a piece of paper and put a smidge of tuna on it, then set it on the floor.

Pandora looked put out, like I should have been feeding her on the chair, but she jumped down anyway and sniffed suspiciously at the lump of tuna.

I looked around for Ranger, hoping the promise of some of the sandwich would have roused him, but he still lay in the same spot he'd been in when I'd left.

"You want a piece, Ranger?"

He lifted his head and sniffed, but didn't get up.

I shrugged and bit into the sandwich. The zest of the pickles and the tang of the tuna tap-danced deliciously on my taste buds. "Yumm."

I ripped open the chips, took the top piece of bread off the sandwich, stuck some chips in and replaced the bread. The next bite was even better with the added crunch of the salty chips.

Pandora had finished her glob of tuna, so I scooped out some more and put it on the piece of paper. She sniffed, then backed away, wrinkling her nose at the big piece of pickle that stuck up from the middle. To my surprise, she pushed the paper over to Ranger, sliding it right under his nose.

Ranger opened one eye. He sniffed. He thought for a moment, then he stuck out his big tongue and the tuna glob disappeared into his mouth.

"Well, at least he's eating a little," I said to Pandora.

"Maybe I should buy him some tuna for supper—but without the mayo."

She twitched her whiskers at me, then tilted her head to look under the chair. Her paw shot out and a pen rolled out from under the front of the chair. She pounced on it, flinging it up in the air with her paws and then batting it when it fell to the ground. The pen spun wildly and then rolled to a stop at my feet.

Pandora looked up at me expectantly.

"Umm ... thanks," I said, and picked up the pen.

"Mew." She turned, her kinked tail looking like a question mark high in the air and leapt up onto her comfy bed in the windowsill just as the front door opened and Pepper stepped inside.

Unlike me, Pepper always dressed nice. Today was no exception. She wore a lavender tank top that complemented her auburn hair beautifully. Her lavender, navy and gray plaid skirt fell an inch above the knees, revealing legs perfectly shaped by her rigorous daily walking routine. Her hair was piled high on her head. One long strand on the side of her face had escaped, falling past her shoulder. I knew that the rest of her hair fell past her waist, but she rarely wore it down.

Pepper caught the excited look on my face and smiled. "I *thought* you might have something new to share."

She was right, I'd been dying to tell someone about

Van Dorn's love letters but she was the only one I trusted.

"You won't believe what I found over at Van Dorn's." I glanced out the window to make sure no one was coming to the shop as I made my way behind the counter where I'd stashed the notebook with the letters. "But you have to promise not to tell a soul."

Pepper had squatted down next to Ranger to rub his ears. I tried to envision the Golden Retriever taking up residence in Pepper's cozy cottage. She kept everything neat as a pin, but Ranger didn't seem like he'd mess things up too much. I made a mental note to consider Pepper as a potential adopter for the dog.

She looked up at me, her green eyes twinkling with excitement.

"I won't tell a soul, promise." She made 'cross my heart' motions with her right hand just in case I didn't believe her.

I held up the letters.

"What are those?" she asked as we worked our way toward the purple couch.

"Love letters."

"Love letters?" Pepper wiggled her eyebrows. "From Striker?"

I rolled my eyes. "No, I found them at Van Dorn's. They're from him to some unknown lover."

"Really? How romantic." Pepper gently picked up

one of the letters and opened it. Her perfectly arched brows climbed her forehead as her eyes scanned the page. "Wow."

"Yes, apparently this affair was hush-hush."

"Right. Which means he wasn't supposed to be having it." Pepper chewed her bottom lip. "Do you think the person was married and the jealous husband killed Van Dorn?"

"Maybe. I'm definitely going to have to ask him about these, but I don't see how they could have had anything to do with Lily, because one of the letters says, 'Lily must not find out'. I pulled the third letter out of the pile and Pepper unfolded it to read.

"We need a list of the women who hung around Van Dorn back in the day," Pepper said, her eyes still glued to the letter.

"I know. Too bad that was so long ago. I don't know who to ask."

"Maybe Bing knows. He must have known Van Dorn if they were in the same type of business."

"He did say he knew him. He even asked if I would look for some journals with instructions for magic tricks." I made a mental note to ask Bing about the people who hung around Charles Van Dorn.

Pepper leaned back in the chair and picked up another letter. "So, did you find out anything more about Bruce Norton's murder?"

"Not really. I did see Striker looking over the crime scene last night when I was at Van Dorn's."

"Oh?" Pepper's brows ticked up.

I nodded. "He didn't really give me any clues, though. Only that Ruth heard cars going up and down the road all night."

"On that road? No one drives down there."

"I know. But the killer must have, so she must have heard at least one car, and of course she said it was around six and Bruce died around two so that doesn't make much sense."

"Ruth has been complaining about cars going by all day and night since they put that stream gauging station in up the road from her thirty years ago. Plus, she hasn't made much sense in years."

"True. Striker also said that Bruce was hit hard with something. I guess it must have been in the back of his head because I didn't see anything bashed in when I found him face up."

"He was face-up?"

"Yep, that's how I saw the weird triangle mark."

Pepper puckered her lips and squinted her eyes. "Well, if he was hit in the back of the head, wouldn't he have fallen face down?"

I hadn't thought about that. "I guess so. The killer must have turned him to make the mark on his forehead."

"Yeah, I guess. I'm sure Striker and Augusta have thought of that."

"They wouldn't tell me if they had. You know how tight-lipped those two are."

"Yeah, we need someone in that police department that will feed us information," Pepper said.

I looked at her curiously. She was getting more interested in these cases than I was. "I didn't realize you had a hankering for solving murders."

Her face brightened. "Oh, I love to watch murder mysteries on TV. Of course, I don't have the experience you do with your background, but I still think it's fun. We do need an 'in' at the police station, though. What about that new recruit Gus has?"

"Jimmy?"

"Yes! He doesn't seem to have a lot of confidence. I bet we could persuade him to fill us in." Pepper got a dreamy look on her face and I was afraid of what was coming next. "In fact, I bet I could help him out with that lack of confidence"

"Oh, no, don't mess with that poor guy. He's just a kid." I remembered the disastrous consequences the last time one of Peppers herbal teas had backfired and I could only imagine what would happen if she made Jimmy even less confident.

"What?" Pepper blinked at me innocently. "You have to admit, I did help Ophelia."

I nodded my agreement. "But Jimmy will get confidence over time as he gets more experience. Besides, I don't really need information on *Bruce's* murder. I'm leaving that to the police."

"But, don't you think the two are related?"

"Related? No. What makes you say that?"

Pepper shrugged. "Well, it just seems pretty odd that all of a sudden the house is being sold off and Bruce ends up dead in the backyard with that symbol on his forehead."

"Maybe, but I think it's more likely that someone put that symbol there to capitalize on the curse."

"What do you mean?"

"You know how people collect weird stuff, right? Well, it turns out the Van Dorn curse is very collectible. Especially since Bruce was found with that symbol on his forehead. It seems to have rekindled interest in the old curse."

"You think someone killed Bruce to make the curse more popular?"

"According to Hattie and Cordelia, the nephew who inherited the house is making a bundle off the contents on eBay. It wouldn't be the first time someone killed to make more money."

"But why Bruce?"

I shrugged. "Maybe he was just in the wrong place at the wrong time."

"I didn't realize that kind of stuff was so popular."

"I guess so. There's even a guy in town that is writing a book on Van Dorn. Come to think of it, he had a run-in with Bruce the night before Bruce was killed."

"A run-in?" Pepper's eyes lit up. "Maybe he's the killer?"

"I thought about that. I even talked to him down at *The Mystic Cafe*, but judging by the way he reacted when I told him about Bruce's body being found, he probably isn't the killer."

"Maybe he's just a good actor. I mean, the killer would hardly want to let on that they knew about it already. And it sounds like a book on the curse would surely be profitable."

I thought back to Les' reaction. "I don't think he was that good of an actor. His father covered a lot of the stories about Charles Van Dorn fifty years ago. He'd even started, but never finished, a book on him. His father recently passed away and I guess he wants to finish the book to honor his dad. I don't think he'd be strong enough to club Bruce—he was just a little guy."

"You might want to team up with him, then, because he might know a lot about what went on fifty years ago. He could be a good resource to help you figure out what happened to Charles."

I pressed my lips together. She did have a point, and I didn't have too many ideas on other places to find information. I made a mental note to become friends with Les Price.

Pepper fluffed the letters gently into a pile and stood. "I have to get back to *The Tea Shoppe*. You'll let me know if you get any more clues, right?"

"Sure." I picked up the letters to hide them back in my notebook. "But, like I said, I'm not investigating Bruce's death, just Van Dorn's."

"Right. That's what I meant." She pulled the door open, then turned back to face me. "And Willa ..."

"Yeah?"

"I think you'd be smart to stay away from that nephew. If your suspicions are correct, he could be the killer and if he's killed once, he might not think twice about killing again."

CHAPTER TEN

I spent the rest of the afternoon half-heartedly waiting on customers. Pepper's parting words echoed in my mind. I had planned to go back to Van Dorn's after work and try to complete my inventory of his library, but if my suspicions were correct and Steve really was the killer, that might not be very smart.

I had been so busy with customers and so deep in my own thoughts, I didn't notice the storm rolling in. Suddenly, the street outside the shop was dark. Pandora and Ranger shifted their positions restlessly. The leaves twisted furiously on the trees. I angled my head to look out the window at the angry, deep purplish-gray sky and then saw something else that made me pull back sharply from the window.

Felicity Bates and the silver-haired woman were on the sidewalk looking in at me!

The door blew open with a loud bang, filling the shop with the scent of ozone, and the two women sashayed in as if they were out for a Sunday afternoon stroll on a sunny day.

Pandora jolted out of her cat bed, took one look at Felicity, arched her back and hissed loudly. Then she scrambled off the window seat and ran into the back.

I remembered Felicity didn't like cats. Apparently, the feeling was mutual.

"Can I help you?" I reached down to massage the dull throb in my leg.

"Hello, Wilhelmina," Felicity looked at me as fondly as she would look at a cockroach in her salad. "This is our family friend Claire Smith-Baker."

I turned to the silver-haired woman, who nodded a greeting. At least she wasn't looking at me with distaste. Instead, she was looking at me with a keen interest, like I was science experiment.

"Nice to make your acquaintance." She nodded her head at me.

"Same here." *I think.*

I raised my brows expectantly, hoping they'd get to the reason for their visit. I knew it couldn't be social, given the history between Felicity and me. And I figured it had to be important for that same reason—there was no way Felicity would come into my shop unless she absolutely had to.

"We heard you were selling off the books from the Van Dorn estate." Claire glanced at the rows of bookshelves and I followed her gaze, my heart jumping when Robert Frost's ghost peeked out from the end of one of the rows. Claire did a double-take, squinting in that direction.

Had she seen him?

I felt a momentary panic, but then she turned back to me with a smile on her lips.

"I'm not actually selling them off," I said. "I'm just inventorying them for the estate. I suggested they sell them at auction. There are so many books in the collection."

Claire leaned over the counter, her light gray eyes, sharp and clear, drilled into mine. "I'm interested mainly in some handwritten journals that I believe Charles Van Dorn kept."

An invisible hand squeezed my heart.

Bing had asked me about handwritten journals, too. Why was everyone suddenly so interested in them?

I studied Claire. She seemed harmless enough. Her silvery hair was swept up in a barrette in the back from which a thick, lustrous fountain of hair fell halfway down her back. The pale green dress hung on her thin frame. My eyes fell to her neck where she wore an unusual silver necklace—double serpents intertwined with light green chalcedony stones.

LEIGHANN DOBBS

She stared at me intently, but her gaze didn't feel menacing. If it weren't for the fact that she was hanging around with Felicity, I probably would have just thought she was a nice old lady who dressed oddly.

But she *was* hanging with Felicity, which made her request all the more suspicious.

"I haven't come across any journals," I said sweetly.

Felicity pressed her lips together. "I told you she wouldn't help."

Claire shot her an angry look out of the corner of her eye.

"Now, now. If she hasn't seen them, she hasn't seen them." She turned back to me, her face transforming from angry to sweetly smiling. "But if you come across them, I do hope you will let me know."

She produced a business card from her pocket and slid it across the counter, the scent of patchouli drifting across along with it. My eyes widened as I read it —'Claire Smith-Baker - Spiritual Medium'.

"You're a medium?"

She nodded. "Yes, dear. I talk to dead people."

I glanced nervously at the area where Robert Frost had been, relaxing when I noticed he wasn't there. I didn't want Claire to know I had ghosts in my store or that I talked to them.

I slid the card into my pocket. "I'll let you know if I find anything."

"Excellent." She turned to leave, pulling Felicity along with her. "I'm staying at the Bates Mansion and my cell phone number is on the back of the card."

The Bates Mansion was a monstrosity on the outskirts of town, high up on the mountain. It loomed over the valley with its spiked roof lines and black metal wrought iron fence. The side of it had been blown off in an unfortunate incident that I'd injured my hand in earlier in the summer, but I imagined they had probably fixed that by now. I had made it a point not to drive by and check. But if Claire was staying there, it meant she must be a good friend of the family. My lips quirked up in a smile as I wondered if ornery old Idris Bates, the family patriarch, had gotten himself a girlfriend.

The two women exited the shop, Felicity spearing me with a hate-filled glance before she slammed the door shut.

I stared at the door, listening to the rain drum on the window. What was so special about this hand written journal? It seemed like quite a few people were after it and I had to wonder if the journal had anything to do with Van Dorn's murder fifty years ago. Where had it been all these years and why all the sudden interest?

I blew out my cheeks, slipping Claire's card out of my pocket for another look. I shouldn't be surprised that she claimed to be a medium. Felicity claimed to be some sort of witch and Idris had an evil disposition, so it stood to reason they'd have a friend that could talk to the dead.

Maybe Pepper was right and Bruce's murder *was* related to Van Dorn's. Maybe they both had something to do with these journals everyone wanted, and if I followed the clues to Bruce's murder I would figure out what happened to Van Dorn. It sure would be easier to follow fresh clues than ones that were fifty years old. Then again, my main suspect for Bruce's murder was Steve Van Dorn and he was too young to have killed Charles.

As I stared out the window, the drumming rain tapered off. Pandora came out from the back of the store and reclaimed her spot at the window. Ranger sighed and rolled on his side. The sun came out and a colorful rainbow appeared in the sky.

The sidewalk filled with tourists who had taken refuge from the rain inside the various shops and I noticed a familiar figure struggling down the sidewalk with a large bag.

The shop door opened and Jimmy Ford lumbered in, dropping the huge, twenty-five pound bag on the floor with a thud.

Ranger lifted his head and sniffed.

"I brought some of Ranger's food from Bruce Norton's house." Jimmy bent down to pat Ranger, who had walked over to sniff the bag. "I figured he should have what he was used to eating."

"Thanks. Were you there looking for clues?" I must be slipping because I hadn't thought that there could be a clue to Bruce's murder at his house. Then again, I reminded myself that I wasn't really investigating Bruce's murder.

"Yep."

"How is the case coming?"

Jimmy looked startled, then glanced at the floor. "I'm not sure if I'm supposed to say ..."

"Oh, I wouldn't tell." I leaned toward him. "Maybe I can even help."

Jimmy looked at me hopefully. "Well, I really could use some help. I don't feel like I've contributed much and—"

The door burst open and Pepper came rushing in carrying a large tray loaded with cookies, porcelain teacups and saucers, a steaming teapot and handmade tea bags.

She zoned in on Jimmy. "Hi, Jimmy. Would you like some tea and oatmeal cookies? They're fresh out of the oven."

I frowned at her. Had she been hovering in her store window, waiting for him to walk by so she could fix him with one of her herbal teas? It surely seemed that way.

Jimmy's face lit up. "Oatmeal cookies are my favorite."

Pepper ignored my frown and invited Jimmy over to the sofa. Ranger flopped down beside it, one eye on the bag of food. Pepper started her pouring ritual. First putting the tea bags in the cups, then pouring the steaming water over them.

"Lemon?" she asked Jimmy, who shook his head.

She put a cookie on a napkin and handed it to Jimmy while the tea steeped.

"Milk?" She pointed to a tiny silver creamer on the tray. Jimmy nodded and she poured a dash into a blue and white porcelain cup, then handed it to Jimmy.

"Jimmy just came from Bruce Norton's with some dog food for Ranger." I skirted around the counter and stooped to snag a cookie from the tray.

"Oh, really?" Pepper turned inquisitive eyes on Jimmy. "Did you find anything at his place that could lead to arresting his killer?"

Jimmy's eyes shifted nervously from Pepper to me and back again.

"It's okay. You can tell us," I encouraged him. "I know how Gus can make it hard on new recruits and I still remember a few investigative techniques from my former job, so maybe I can help you out."

"Would you?" Jimmy brightened. "Augusta said you

used to be a crime journalist. She raves about your investigative techniques. I could learn a lot from you."

·I paused, momentarily taken aback. Gus raved about me? I had no idea my sister was proud of my former career. She usually acted like my investigating habits were a nuisance.

"Sure, I could help you," I said. "Tell me what you've learned."

Jimmy slurped the last of the tea from his cup and I noticed Pepper had a satisfied smirk on her face. He grabbed a cookie and bit in.

"Well, we didn't find anything at Bruce Norton's house."

Ranger let out a pathetic whine at the mention of his former master's name and Jimmy leaned over, gingerly giving him a few pats on the head. I mentally considered adding Jimmy to my list of potential adopters for Ranger, but then dismissed the thought. He seemed a bit afraid of the dog and I had my doubts as to whether he could handle him properly.

"Really? What did you see? Was there anything amiss?"

"Not really. No signs of a struggle or anything to indicate he had an ongoing disagreement with anyone." Jimmy chewed his cookie thoughtfully. "There was one thing that seemed odd, but I'm not sure it meant anything."

My gut started to tingle. "That's good. As an investigator, you need to go with your instincts. What was it?"

"He had a folder full of pictures, documents and newspaper clippings open on the dining room table, like he was studying or something. But they were old and yellowed, from a long time ago."

"Really?" I mumbled, trying to choke down the cookie that had turned to a lump of paste in my mouth. I had a sneaking suspicion those pictures had something to do with the murders of Charles and Lily. Maybe there *was* a connection between the two murders. Bruce had been friendly with the Van Dorn crowd back then so maybe he knew something about the murders. Or maybe *Bruce* was the killer, but if he was, then who killed *him* and why? I needed to get to Bruce's place and take a look for myself.

"Do you think that's relevant? I wasn't sure if I should mention it to Augusta."

"Meow!" Pandora jumped onto the counter and skidded down the length, flipping a yellow highlighter off the top. The highlighter clattered on the floor and rolled under the couch.

"What's with her?" Pepper asked.

"She's been acting strange all day. I think having a canine guest is affecting her behavior." I fished under the couch to retrieve the pen, then returned my attention to Jimmy. "That could be an important clue or maybe not. I wonder if I could get a look over there and then I could let you know if you should mention it to Gus."

"Oh, I don't know if Augusta would like it if I just brought you over there." Jimmy shook his head, his face turning pale.

"Well, I do need to go and pick up some of Ranger's things ..." I let my voice trail off.

"Oh, right. I guess maybe there'd be no harm in that. But right now I have to get back to the station. I'll be in touch about going to Bruce's."

He stood to leave and I rushed over to the counter to grab one of my business cards.

"Here's my cell phone number if you want to get in touch." I shoved the card at him, making a mental note to keep my cell phone turned on—I considered it an intrusion and rarely used it. I had one more question I hoped to have answered. "Did you find the murder weapon?"

He shook his head. "Nope. We're not sure what it was, exactly. Some type of heavy, blunt instrument. We set up a search grid in the surrounding woods, but found nothing. Augusta said we may have to widen the grid, but she's afraid the killer took it with them."

"Meow!" Pandora leaped onto the coffee table and Pepper had to react quickly to keep the teapot from spilling to the floor.

"Pandora cut it out!" I swiped at the cat who deftly avoided my grasp, then retreated to the counter to glare at me, her tail high above her head, the kink at the end making it look like she was pointing outside.

"I'll be in touch about going to Bruce's." Jimmy swung the door open, then turned back to look at me. "Oh, there is one other thing you might be interested in."

"What?" I tried not to sound too eager.

"That symbol on Bruce's forehead ..."

"Yeah?"

"I don't think it was done by any kind of ghost or part of any fifty-year-old curse. Not unless the ghost went to a craft store recently."

"Why do you say that?"

"That symbol was written with alcohol-based markers like artists use. I do some drawing myself and use them. They didn't exist fifty years ago. The lab was even able to nail down the exact make and color of marker." He pressed his lips together, squinted his eyes and looked up at the ceiling for few seconds. "If memory serves me right ... yes ... it was a Copic Y28 Lionet Gold marker, to be exact."

CHAPTER ELEVEN

*T*hat night, my mind whirled with questions as I drove to Van Dorn's. Why was everyone after the journal? Who was Charles' lover? Who killed Lily? Did Bruce's murder have anything to do with Charles' murder fifty years ago? And last but not least, where was the murder weapon?

Not only that, but I was becoming increasingly concerned about Pandora's behavior. She'd been acting so wild at the shop that I almost didn't want to bring her in with me the next day. I'd taken her and Ranger home and fed them dinner after work. When I'd left on my way to Van Dorn's, she'd tried to sneak into my car.

I'd finally had to lock her cat door as well as the door to the basement—I knew she had a secret exit down there that I hadn't been able to figure out yet. I'd driven away to the sound of her wailing inside the house. I was afraid that Ranger's presence was driving her over the edge and figured I'd better find him a new home soon.

I parked behind Steve's yellow Dodge, a tingle of doubt running through me. I felt funny about being in the house alone. What if he *had* killed Bruce? I didn't relish the thought of being alone in a remote house with a killer, but if he really was the killer, surely Gus would have figured it out and had him arrested by now. I had to finish cataloguing the library, so I shrugged it off and climbed the porch steps, taking care not to step on the rickety boards that had come loose.

I hesitated at the front door, unsure if I should just walk in. Even though Steve knew I was coming, it felt odd to barge in unannounced.

"Hello! It's me, Willa!" I yelled into the house.

"In here." Steve's voice sounded like it was far away—he must be in the back.

I walked down the hall toward the library, stopping short when I reached the doorway and saw Steve inside, rummaging through one of the shelves, a stack of books piled on the floor beside him.

"What are you doing?" My heart sank looking at the mess.

"Hey, Willa. Have you seen any hand-written journals in here?"

"What? No."

"Oh." Steve looked disappointed. "Some old biddy came by and offered me a lot of money for them."

"Did she have long, gray hair and a mean-looking redheaded side kick?"

"Yes." Steve looked at me surprised. "How'd you know?"

"She came to my store, too."

"Huh! Those must be mighty important." Steve rubbed the two-day-old stubble on his chin. "I should charge more. I bet she'd pay twice what she was offering."

I didn't reply, choosing to start putting the books neatly back in their place instead. "I need to keep these shelves the way they were so I can keep track of the books I've catalogued," I explained.

"Sorry." Steve stepped over the pile of books and headed to the door. "I have more eBay pictures to take. If you find the journals, set them aside for me, will 'ya?"

"Okay." I turned my back, glad he was leaving the room. I finished putting the books back, then picked up my notebook, intending to start cataloguing where I'd left off. I scanned through the book spines, carefully looking for more hollowed out books with love letters or other clues inside.

A few strangely shaped spines caught my eye—not a hollowed out book—a photo album! My pulse raced as I reached for it. Surely, Van Dorn would have included photographs of his closest friends, and surely, one of them would be the person with whom he exchanged those love letters.

The book was loaded with old photos. Some of them were black and white, but most were in that strange, yellowish color that early photos had. They were mostly taken in and around the house, which looked pretty much the same now as it had back then, except for the dust and disrepair.

Most of the people were dressed up, the men in suits and the women in full-skirted cocktail dresses. I recognized Charles right away, but didn't know who any of the others were. One woman was particularly beautiful and photogenic, and I guessed her to be the tragic Lily Johanson. In several of the pictures, a man stood off to the side, staring at her with intense longing on his face. Lily didn't seem to return the emotion, though, and I wondered who he was. Could he have been her killer?

There was another woman, too, very young and very pretty. Charles was in many of the pictures with her. They seemed to be quite chummy, though I couldn't get a sense of any feeling between them. She was different from the other women—her clothes not as fancy and her demeanor not as frivolous.

As I flipped through the pictures, my eyes keep going back to the other woman. Was she the one in the love letters? The only thing I knew for sure was that Lily was not the woman Charles had been having the affair with.

But why even have an affair? Charles was single and an adult, he didn't need to hide from anyone ... unless the other person was married. Fifty years ago, that would have been quite scandalous.

I squinted at the picture of the pretty girl. She had a ring on her left hand. Was it a wedding ring?

I had too many questions, and the only person who could answer them was Charles. Where was he? If he wanted me to solve his murder, he'd better show up.

"Charles," I whispered, then looked around for the misty swirl that usually happened when a ghost appeared.

Nothing. Not even a teensy drop of condensation or a small chill in the air.

"Hey, if you're here, I have some important questions."

"Were you calling me?"

The voice startled me and I spun around. It wasn't Charles, though—it was Steve.

Had he been lurking there watching me?

"Oh, no ... I was just talking to myself," I stammered.

His eyes fell to the photo albums. "Oh, I see you have some photos. Are those of my uncle? I don't suppose my dad is in any of them ..."

A look of sadness passed over his face and I felt a tug at my heart. I knew his father had just died and, while I hadn't pegged him as the sentimental type, the look on his face suggested that I might have been wrong.

He walked over and looked down at the pictures. Reaching out a scarred hand, he flipped the pages. "Yeah, I recognize some of these. My dad had some duplicates of them."

"I thought your dad and Charles didn't get along."

"Oh, they did at first. At least, that's what my Dad told me." A pained look crossed his face. "But I guess they had a falling out. I was too young to remember. I only have a few vague memories of Uncle Charles."

"Your father didn't approve of Charles being a medium?"

"That's right. But before Charles got famous, we spent a lot of time here." A wistful smile tugged at the corners of his lips. "Those were good times."

"So, I guess this is Lily Johanson." I pointed at the picture, hoping Steve would know who at least some of the people were.

"Yep." He scowled. "She was the one who was murdered."

I nodded. "Do you know anything about that?"

"That all happened after my father and Uncle Charles had the falling out. He didn't believe in all the ghost stuff and didn't talk about Charles much." Steve's face turned hard. "I lost my mother around that time. I think I was around ten or eleven. Anyway, I couldn't have cared less about some uncle I hadn't seen in years. After Mom died, I kind of lost my way."

"Oh, I'm sorry." I meant it, too. I still thought Steve was an opportunist taking advantage of Bruce's death to make more money, but I could see he hadn't had it easy.

I returned my attention to the photo album, pointing to the guy longing for Lily. "Who's the guy?"

He squinted, then shook his head. "No idea."

I flipped to a picture of the pretty, young girl. "How about this woman?"

Steve snorted. "Oh, yeah, her I know. That's Gladys Primble."

"You knew her?"

"Sure. She was Uncle Charles' housekeeper. She used to make the best cookies and took care of me lots of times when I came here to visit. She used to watch me when I was a baby and my father came to visit Uncle Charles. But, in the end, I guess she must have pulled a fast one."

"Pulled a fast one?" My brows mashed together. "What do you mean?"

"Uncle Charles left the house and its contents to my father." Steve gestured toward the rest of the house. "My father thought that a slap in the face because he didn't approve of Charles' séances and stuff. Dad said the house was cursed, which is why he never did anything with it. Charles also left some money in a trust to pay the taxes for the house. He actually didn't have a lot of money in the bank when he died, but according to my Dad, the real slap was that Uncle Charles left a big chunk of that money to Gladys Primble."

I STARED AT STEVE. "Why would he leave money to his housekeeper?"

Steve shrugged. "Who knows? As I said, Dad hadn't talked to Uncle Charles for some years by then. We didn't know what was going on with him."

"Was it a lot of money?"

"About twenty-five grand. Not that much. Of course, back then that was worth a lot more. Anyway, it pissed Dad off big time."

My investigator's intuition was starting to work over-time. I knew some people left money to loyal servants back a hundred years ago, but in the 1960s I didn't think that was very common. But if Gladys had been Charles' lover ...

"I gotta get back to my listings." Steve turned and headed toward the hallway.

"Was Gladys Primble married?"

Steve stopped and cocked his head to the side, pressing his lips together. "Yep, she must have been because I called her *Mrs.* Primble."

That was it! Gladys must have been Charles lover and they had to hide it because she was married.

But, what did that have to do with Charles' murder?

Steve went back to his eBay listings and I tried to continue cataloguing the books. My mind spun with this new information. Was Gladys Primble Charles Van Dorn's secret lover?

Maybe Gladys knew Charles was going to leave her the money and *she* was the one who killed him? Or perhaps there was some kind of a love triangle between her, Lily, and Charles and she killed them both in a jealous rage. Maybe Bruce was involved, somehow. I wondered if those old photographs Jimmy had seen at Bruce's had to do with Charles' murder. Maybe Bruce was looking into it for some reason and suspected Gladys.

A shiver danced up my spine as I glanced out the window toward the place where I'd found Bruce's body. Was it possible that the two of them met here, and Bruce confronted her with his theory and she killed him?

I needed to go to Bruce's and look at those old pictures *and* I needed to talk to Gladys Primble. It was looking more and more like the two murders were related.

I picked up the pace. I wanted to make it to the end of the row of books I was working on before I called it quits. Plus, I was hoping Charles would show up—I had a lot of questions for him.

Twenty minutes later, I was done with the section of books I'd wanted to finish, but still hadn't seen Charles. It was just like a ghost to pester you when you didn't want to see them and then vanish when you had questions.

I gathered up my notebook and, after wrestling with my conscience about stealing from a client, slipped a photo out of the album and tucked it inside the notebook. I knew Charles wouldn't mind if taking them meant solving his murder.

Closing the library door quietly, I started down the hall, wondering if I should say good-bye to Steve. I probably should. It would be rude to just leave, and I wanted to let him know I'd have to come back tomorrow night.

Sounds of hushed talking filtered out of a room on my left. I remembered seeing an office down there which, I assumed, had been Charles' office. Steve must have moved his eBay operation from the hotel and set it up in the comfort of Charles' old office.

I tiptoed toward the open doorway, stopped just outside, and flattened myself against the wall so I could hear what he was saying. Guilt gnawed at my stomach, but the hushed tones sounded suspicious, and even though I'd just made the discovery about Gladys, Steve was still one of my main suspects since he was benefitting financially from the renewed interest in the Van Dorn curse.

"I told you the money will be there." Steve's voice was barely above a whisper. "See if you can hold them off ... I'm waiting on some eBay sales ... it could mean the end of everything if you can't hold them off, but we're so close to ..."

Steve's voice got even lower and I leaned closer. A floorboard creaked sending my heart into a tailspin.

"Who's out there?" Steve's voice was louder now.

I popped my head into the doorway as if I'd just been walking down the hall, instead of eavesdropping outside the office. "Hi, I was just taking off."

"Hold on," Steve said into the phone, then put his hand over it and looked up at me. "Did you find the journal?"

"No. Sorry." I glanced down at the desk and noticed he had official-looking papers spread out with a bold, fancy font and gold seals affixed to them.

He followed my gaze. "These are my certificates of authenticity for eBay for the Van Dorn collection."

He held up a thick piece of paper and I could see it had a ribboned title across the top, the gold seal, then a picture of the item and the date with some text below, which I assumed was some sort of jargon letting the buyer know it was the real deal. On the bottom, it was signed Steve Van Dorn in gleaming, gold ink to match the stamp.

I stepped inside the office to get a closer look and caught a whiff of alcohol. *Had Steve been drinking?* Something niggled at my memory as I stared at the paper.

"That's nice," I said.

"They sure do help boost customer confidence," he said. "Are you all finished cataloguing the books?"

"No. I need a few more nights of cataloguing, but I'm finding some valuable books." I tapped my notebook, then brought it back to my side quickly before the picture could fall out. "I'll type everything up for you when I am done."

"Great," he said, then held up the phone. "I gotta get back to my call."

"Right, I'll be back tomorrow night."

He nodded and turned away, speaking into the phone in a normal tone. "Jeff? Yeah, like I said, a couple more days ..."

I backed out of the room slowly, trying to hear as much as I could of his conversation. On his desk, I noticed a strange-looking, large white round pen—it must have been the one he was using to sign the certificates, but it wasn't like any normal pen I'd even seen. My eyes fell to the name on the side "Copic."

My heart stuttered in my chest when I noticed the

A SPIRITED TAIL

marking on the very end of the pen—Y28. It was the same type of pen that had made the marking on Bruce Norton's forehead.

I practically ran for my car, pulling my cell phone out of my pocket as I went. My fingers fumbled the keys for Gus' number.

Wait. I couldn't call Augusta—she'd want to know how I knew about the marker and Jimmy might get into trouble. He was a good source of information and I didn't want to risk that—you never knew when an 'in' at the police station might come in handy.

I slipped into my car and turned the engine over, the phone still in my hand. Maybe it was just a coincidence. How many people used those Copic markers?

My eyes slid to Steve's yellow car parked next to mine and something clicked into place in the back of my mind. Ruth Walters had seen a yellow car drive by that morning. That was one coincidence too many. Steve *had* to be Bruce's killer.

I dialed the police station, tapping my fingers impatiently on the steering wheel as I listened to it ring.

"Mystic Falls PD."

"Hi, this is Willa Chance. I need to speak to Jimmy Ford right away!"

CHAPTER TWELVE

I couldn't tell if Jimmy was excited or terrified, but he told me to get out of there in case there was trouble and I complied. We worked out a plan where he would go up on the pretext of looking for the murder weapon and stumble across the markers, then bring Steve in. It would work out perfectly since Jimmy would get the credit and I wouldn't get into trouble with Gus and Striker. I just hoped Jimmy didn't get hurt.

I was probably supposed to keep it all a secret until Steve was officially arrested, but I had to tell *someone*, so I called Pepper. Besides, I knew she could keep a secret. She'd been keeping some of mine since kindergarten.

"I think I found Bruce Norton's killer," I announced as soon as she answered her phone.

"What? Who?"

"Steve Van Dorn."

"So it *was* him!" she said. "Wait, how do you know for sure?"

"Remember how Jimmy said the symbol on Bruce's forehead was drawn with a certain type of marker?"

"Uh huh."

"I saw Steve with that same exact marker *and* he is driving a yellow car."

"Yellow car?"

"Striker said Ruth Walters claimed a yellow car drove by early in the morning when I found Bruce."

I could hear Pepper thinking on the other end. "But Ruth says a lot of things that aren't right—"

"I know, but the two together are too much of a coincidence. Plus, he's profiting big time on that eBay stuff *and* I heard him saying that he needed money bad for something." I realized I hadn't told Jimmy about that, but I guess it didn't matter. Whatever he was into would surely come out after he was arrested.

"Willa, he could be dangerous. I hope you're not thinking about confronting him." Pepper's voice was laced with concern.

"No, of course not. I called Jimmy and he's going to be the one to figure out the evidence and make the arrest."

"You mean he's going up there to confront Steve by himself?"

"Yep, as far as I know."

"Oh, that's wonderful." Pepper was practically squealing. "If he's confident enough to do that, that means my tea is working."

Or maybe he's just doing his job.

"Right, well, let's hope so. I haven't told anyone, though, so keep this to yourself until Jimmy brings him in."

"Mum's the word," Pepper said, and we disconnected just as I pulled into the driveway of my house. A small, beige car that had been behind me slowed as it passed my driveway. I tensed, my nerves on edge.

Had the car been following me?

I adjusted the rearview mirror just in time to see a redheaded passenger and a gray-haired driver and I relaxed back into my seat. It was only Felicity and Claire —probably following my every move, just in case I acquired the journals.

I turned the car off and glanced at my house. Pandora had her face pressed to the window and she looked mad. No telling what she'd done to express her displeasure. A hairball on my pillow? A dead mouse hidden under the couch that I would only discover once it started to stink? My curtains in shreds?

I sighed and made my way inside, knowing I'd have to face her wrath sooner or later.

I opened the door to loud hissing. Pandora looked at

me reproachfully, then walked stiffly around the kitchen, her kinked tail pointing toward the cellar door.

"I know you have a secret exit down there," I told her. She turned slitted golden-green eyes on me and scampered into the living room, where I figured she'd left my punishment.

Ranger was more friendly. His sad, brown eyes looked up at me and I bent down to pet him.

"Don't worry. You're not in trouble."

He thumped his tail once on the floor and I took that as a good sign that he was starting to release some of his grief.

Pandora must have noticed the attention I was paying to the dog because she suddenly appeared beside me, purring and rubbing her head against my arm.

I gave her a quick scratch behind the ears, then turned back to Ranger. "Good news. I think we got the guy that killed your master."

The fur on Ranger's forehead crinkled and his eyes slid over to Pandora. Pandora's eyes narrowed to slits as she looked at Ranger, then up at me. I could have sworn the two animals were communicating with that look. Nah, that was crazy ... I'd been living alone too long.

I pushed myself up from the floor. It was late and I was hungry. I opened the fridge and took out the cottage cheese that Striker hadn't used the night before, then grabbed a peach from the windowsill and some honey from the cabinet.

Pandora and Ranger watched me while I cut up the peach. "Of course, now that I know Steve killed Bruce, I still have to find Charles' killer because it couldn't have been Steve. I guess the two murders weren't related after all."

I put the peach slices in a bowl, dumped in the cottage cheese, poured some honey on top, then sat at the table to eat. My leg started to burn and I propped it up on the chair next to me.

My thoughts drifted to Eddie Striker and a little hollow feeling of longing lodged in the pit of my stomach. I hoped I wasn't starting to fall for him—I was too old for that, wasn't I? I told myself that I wasn't at all upset that he hadn't called since he'd been here the other day. Sure, he produced a good meal and gave a nice massage, but my honey peach cottage cheese porridge was delicious and I could massage my leg myself just fine.

Leaning forward to press my thumbs into the injured area, I caught a glimpse of the round paperweight in the living room. It was glowing cherry-red, probably reflecting something from the room. It was a simple, but beautiful, piece of glass—round and thick—and reflected all kinds of lovely colors that reminded me of Elspeth. I knew I should stop over for a visit.

A quick glance at the clock told me it was too late for that tonight. I finished off my supper and put the bowl in the sink. Pandora and Ranger were watching my every move.

I decided to turn in early so I could get an early start tomorrow. I wanted to do some computer research on Gladys Primble to see if she lived in the area. I also planned to pay a visit to the writer, Les Price. If he was finishing his father's book, he might have some knowledge about Charles and Gladys. And, of course, I still had a business to run.

Pandora weaved back and forth in front of the cellar door, her tail up high, the kinked end bobbing up and down.

"Meow!"

"Yes, I know you want the door open so you can go down there and catch mice." I walked over and unlocked it, knowing that if I didn't she'd meow at me all night.

She thanked me by rubbing her head on my ankle. "Spoiled."

I tugged the rope through Rangers collar. I really did need to get to Bruce's and pick up some of Ranger's stuff, not the least of which was a leash. The big dog was obedient and I was sure he would stay with me outside, but I didn't want to take any chances. I took him outside for his nightly business and then kissed both animals good night and headed into the living room to see if

Pandora had left me any nasty surprises. She hadn't, which in itself was mildly suspicious. Perhaps there would be a surprise for me somewhere else.

The sun had set and the paperweight on the table was colorless. At a quick glance it almost looked like there was a handwritten note inside, but when I took a second look, I saw it was reflecting the print from the newspaper it had been sitting on. Odd, it looked like the blue ink from a fountain pen when I'd first glanced at it.

My eyes must have been playing tricks on me. It had been a long day and I noticed they got more tired at night lately. Pandora and Ranger were still in the kitchen, staring at me.

"Are you coming?" Pandora usually slept in the room with me, and Ranger had been sleeping up there with us curled in the corner, but tonight the two of them made no move to follow me. Maybe they thought it was too early.

"Suit yourselves." I flipped off the living room light and headed up the stairs by myself, sending a curious glance back at the dog and cat and wondering just what the two of them would do in the kitchen while I was upstairs sleeping.

PANDORA CRANED HER NECK, *peeking around the corner*

to make sure Willa was going upstairs. "Is she going to bed this early?"

"Seems like it." Ranger got up and sniffed the cabinet Willa had put his dog food in. His appetite was starting to come back, especially since he'd helped to find Master's killer.

Pandora looked from the dog to the cabinet. The dog food bag Willa had put inside had been very large. She hoped that wasn't an indication of how long the dog was staying, but she couldn't worry about that right now. There were more important things to consider.

"We have somewhere to go tonight."

Ranger whipped his head in her direction. "Go?"

Pandora flicked her tail at the basement door. "Yes. I need to tell the wise ones about the special place. They may have questions that you can answer."

"But Willa said they found Master's killer."

A strange feeling passed across Pandora's whiskers as she batted the plastic ring from a milk jug across the floor. She was glad they had found the killer, but couldn't imagine how they'd found the murder weapon without her help.

Maybe she wasn't giving the humans enough credit. They'd probably searched the area again and found it or figured out who it was some other way ... in which case they'd still need the murder weapon. She made a mental note to check if it was still there tonight, after she completed her task.

"This isn't about the killer. At least I don't think so. There's something at the special place you showed me ... something that has to be protected and I need to consult with others about it."

Ranger's ears perked up and he started panting, a happy smile on his face. "Ranger good dog. Ranger protects."

"Yes, that's right." Pandora started toward the cellar door "Follow me."

They took the same route out of the house as they had the night before, but this time they headed through the woods behind Willa's to the barn where Elspeth kept her brood of cats.

Pandora's heart warmed thinking of the old woman. She had a fondness for cats and did what she could to provide warm homes for several of them. Her barn was the perfect place for those who didn't care to stay in the house, as was the case with most of the elite cats Pandora was going to visit.

Of course, Elspeth didn't know that her cats were an elite species sworn to help humans keep the balance between good and evil since ancient times. Or did she? Pandora wondered sometimes because the old lady seemed to know a lot more than most humans should.

The night was warm and Pandora drank in the smell

of the forest. Pandora and Ranger ran side by side, the bright moon lighting the way. When she came to visit Elspeth with Willa it usually took ten minutes to get there, but she and Ranger could run at full speed and they arrived at the small barn next to the gingerbread-trimmed Victorian house in only two minutes.

Pandora paused outside the barn, a flitter of anxiety tickling her tummy. She didn't know how the others would respond to her bringing a dog. "Stay behind me and don't make any sudden moves. Some of these cats are very nervous around your kind."

Ranger frowned at her. "Ranger doesn't chase cats."

"I know that, and you know that, but they don't know that. Just follow my lead."

Pandora flicked out a gray paw and pushed the door open. She slipped inside. Ranger lingered just outside the door.

Pausing in the doorway, she blinked to allow her eyes to adjust to the dark interior. Several pairs of eyes watched from the dark, then as Ranger pushed in behind her, she heard claws scrape against wood as some of the cats scrambled behind the bales of hay that were stacked around the barn.

"Hiss!" Pandora swung around to see the fat calico, Otis, arching his back and swiping his claws toward Ranger's face. She jumped between them just in time, knocking Otis's claw away with smug satisfaction. There was no love lost between her and Otis—he was one of the old ones—an ancient feline who had served many humans, and he didn't like Pandora's modern ways. Although she'd tried to make friends with him several times, there was always a combative rivalry between them.

"This is an outrage! She's brought a canine here!" Otis screeched, his back still humped.

"Oh, come on. He won't hurt anyone." Pandora gestured to Ranger who was standing calmly behind her. "See? Besides, he has important information about something you will be very interested in."

Their ears perked up. Sasha, a sleek Siamese, ventured forward, sniffing Ranger from all angles. To his credit, Ranger stood stock still, his nose twitching furiously, but he made no move to sniff back.

"Why do we need a dog?" Sasha asked.

"I brought him in case you had questions I could not answer. He led me to the house where his master was killed and I know there is something inside that needs our attention."

"How would you know?" Otis had jumped on a tall hay bale to groom his fur.

"Just a feeling. Don't the rest of you get them?"

Several heads nodded and a white cat with thick, lustrous fur came forward.

"Where is this place?" she purred.

"The Van Dorn Mansion."

Several cats gasped.

"Wasn't he—" Kelley, a Maine Coon who had remained in the background started to say.

"The keeper of secrets." A deep baritone cut her off from the back of the barn and a large, black cat emerged from the darkness. His name was Inkspot and he had a tendency to be overly dramatic.

"Secrets?" Pandora asked.

Snowball, the white cat, answered. "Yes, now I remember. He could talk to those who had passed over and gleaned important information on how to move things from this plane to the next ... information that could be deadly if it fell into the wrong hands."

Pandora felt a chill flick across her whiskers. She actually didn't know for sure who 'the wrong hands' were, but she knew that the results of them getting ahold of this information would be disastrous for both the humans and the cats of Mystic Notch.

"I guess that must have been what I sensed in the house," she said.

Snowball nodded. "It's been protected in that house for decades."

Pandora felt a jolt of electricity—it had been protected because no one had been in the house, but that had all changed now. "The house is being sold and all the contents are being sold off, too."

Snowball's whiskers twitched and her eyes darted around the room. "That means anyone could find it ... even the wrong people."

"We must take measures to secure that information!" Inkspot turned to Ranger. "Tell us what you know."

Ranger glanced at Pandora who nodded. "Well, I don't know much. The house has been empty a long time and Master would take me there. He longed for the good times he used to have there. But then one day, another man was there and he fought with Master and then Master was dead."

Ranger hung his head and Pandora felt that annoying tug at her heart again. She turned away, admonishing herself for getting all sappy and sentimental and wondering if it was because she'd been hanging around with humans too much. She hoped it was only temporary —the sooner she got Ranger out of Willa's house the better.

"That's right." Otis looked down at them from his high perch with superiority. "Van Dorn died long ago. But he had the information well hidden. I'm a bit disappointed it's still in the house—he was supposed to make provisions for it after his death."

Pandora narrowed her eyes at him. "How do you know?"

Otis's eyes got misty and his whiskers drooped. "I used to know his cat. Sadly, she only had nine lives—much less than we do—and she's parted the curtain now."

Pandora almost felt sorry for him ... almost.

"I felt something in there." Pandora said. "This information must still be in the house ... and now that the house is being sold ..."

"We must go and remove that information from the house and put it in a secure spot!" Inkspot declared. "Do you know where it is, Otis?"

Otis shook his head.

"We'll have to get into the house and find it." Sasha's luminous, blue eyes turned toward Ranger. "Do you know any easy access routes?"

Ranger's face crumbled. He dearly wanted to be helpful, but he didn't know how to get into the house. "I never went in."

"That won't be a problem," Pandora said. "When I was there, I saw many ways in ... but the house is big, It could take days to find this thing and it may be crawling with police now."

"Then we need to get in and out quickly," Inkspot rumbled.

Kelley groomed the long, white fur on her chest. "It would help if we knew exactly where this information was stored."

"Maybe I can help," Pandora said hopefully. "I could sense it was in there, so maybe I can hone in on its location."

Otis snorted from above where he was hunkered

down, his front paws tucked under his chest. "Now, that would be quite a feat."

Ranger let out a low growl at the offensive Otis and Pandora felt a swell of warmth in her chest.

Was the dog coming to her defense?

It had been a long time since another furry creature had stuck up for her—not since she was a tiny kit with litter-mates to defend her. She stuck her paw out to shush him. She didn't want to see a fight break out between Ranger and Otis. Not that she really cared that much about either of them, or so she told herself. She just didn't want to clean up the mess.

Truffles, the small, black and orange tortoiseshell, trotted into the center, her greenish-yellow eyes glowing in the slit of moonlight that filtered in from the door Pandora had left ajar. "Finding its location may be easier than we thought ... I have a friend that has knowledge of the goings on there."

Inkspot turned his green eyes on the petite feline. "A friend? One of the feral cats?"

The feral cats were a colony of wild cats that lived in Mystic Notch. It was rumored that they descended from an ancient clan. Most of them answered to no human, but even so, the humans helped provide shelter and food for them. Pandora felt a swell of pride knowing that her human, Willa, was one of those.

"No, but I can ask them, too. They have eyes and ears

everywhere," Truffles answered. "This cat has been with the people who served the Van Dorn family for decades. She might know where this information is kept."

"Very well, then, find out what she knows." Inkspot nodded at Truffles, then turned to address the rest of the cats. "In the meantime, let us prepare. We will voyage to the Van Dorn mansion under the cover of darkness tomorrow night."

CHAPTER THIRTEEN

I had just finished looking Gladys Primble up on the internet when Bing, Hattie, Cordelia and Josiah filed through the door with their Styrofoam to-go cups from *The Mystic Cafe* in hand.

"Did you hear the news?" Cordelia's eyes twinkled as she handed me a coffee.

I raised my brows. "About?"

"Why Steve Van Dorn, of course," Hattie said. "Turns out I was right."

Cordelia nodded in agreement. "It almost always comes down to money."

"Meow!" Pandora frowned up at Cordelia and Hattie.

"Don't mind her," I said. "She's been acting strange lately. I think she's unsettled because of Ranger."

Pandora scowled at me, then leapt onto the counter

and batted my purple Sharpie around like a hockey player until it rolled off onto the ground. I bent to pick it up. It reminded me of the Copic marker that Steve had—the one that had provided the clue to his guilt.

Had Pandora been trying to give me a hint all this time?

I scratched her behind the ear. "It's okay, Pandora, we already figured it out."

"Figured what out?" Bing scratched his chin.

"Oh, nothing. Just cat talk."

"I don't know." Josiah had plunked down in one of the chairs and held his coffee cup on his knee. "It seems like an awfully big risk for money, especially when the house and contents are already worth a lot."

The door opened and tiny, gray-haired Emma Potts came in. The elderly woman was the church secretary, but also held a much more important position. She was the one who coordinated the feral cat housing and feeding in Mystic Notch.

I'd been introduced to the gangs of wild cats earlier in the summer and found them charming. Unfortunately, there were many others in town who didn't agree and wanted to stamp them out, no matter how inhumane the method. Needless to say, Emma kept the location of the cattery secret and it was known only to the few volunteers, myself included, who came out to feed and check on the cats.

"Hi, Emma." Cordelia waved from her position on the purple sofa. "Did you hear the big news about Bruce?"

"Yes, so terrible, and right here in town." Emma shivered. "It's hard to imagine a killer lurks among us."

"Not anymore," Josiah said. "Steve Van Dorn's been arrested for it."

Emma's mouth flew open, then snapped shut. "Steve Van Dorn! No. I don't believe it."

My brows puckered together in confusion. Bing, Cordelia, Hattie and Josiah mirrored my look. How did Emma know Steve? Of anyone, Steve Van Dorn would be the most believable, because he was a stranger and obviously benefitting financially, not to mention he had the pen that wrote on Bruce's forehead.

"Why is that?" Josiah asked.

"I ... well ..." Emma looked from me to Hattie to Josiah. "It's just that he seems so nice and he's a friend of ... well ... I just don't know."

And with that she turned and rushed out of the store.

"Well, I'll be." Hattie craned her neck to stare at Emma rushing down the sidewalk. "What do you think that was all about?"

"I don't know." My eyes followed Hattie's. Did Emma know something about the Van Dorns? Maybe she had some information about Charles. She would be about the same age as him. I made a mental note to stop by the cattery later on ... I had some cat food donations to drop off anyway.

"Well, I guess that's one mystery solved," Bing said. "But now I wonder what will happen to the house and the belongings."

"Good question." I hadn't thought about that. I'd spent several nights cataloguing that library and with Steve in jail, that effort would be wasted. Not to mention that I might not be allowed back into the house, and I still had questions for Charles.

"Did you ever find that journal?" Bing's blue eyes drilled into mine and I got the impression the journal had something more important in it than just some instructions for magic tricks.

"No, but it sure seems to be popular. That must be a really great magic trick in there."

Bing's eyes sharpened. "Who else was looking for it?"

"Claire somebody," I leaned over the counter, grabbed the card I'd stuck under the corner of the cash register and glanced at it before handing it to Bing. "Claire Smith-Baker."

Bing frowned at the card. "I've never heard of her."

"She came in with Felicity."

Bing's eyes widened. "Felicity Bates? If she's hanging around with the Bateses I certainly hope you won't give the journals to her."

"Why not?"

"Well, you know ...they're bad news. It wouldn't be in the best interest of ... anyone." Bing gave me a look as if I should know what he was talking about. I didn't. My gut told me he was right, I just didn't know *why*. Anyway, I had no intention of giving the journal to anyone who hung around with Felicity.

"I don't even know if I'll be going back there," I said. "If Steve goes to jail, then I'm not sure what will happen to the property."

"I wonder if it will be closed up for another fifty years," Cordelia mused.

I wondered that, too. And if so, would Charles' ghost leave me alone or, now that he had my attention, would he follow me around until I found his killer? I figured it was in my best interest to find out as much as I could about whom he hung around with back then. "Bing, did you hang around with Charles back in the day?"

"Well, I wouldn't say I hung around with him. I did a lot of traveling back then so I wasn't in town much. But, of course, I knew him since we were in similar business-es." He narrowed his eyes at me. "Why do you ask?"

I shrugged, trying to seem like it wasn't that big of a deal. "Oh, no reason. I'm just curious about the man. He had an interesting taste in books."

"Well, if you really want to know about him, you should ask Elspeth," Hattie said.

"Yes, she was quite friendly with that crowd back then, as I recall." Cordelia added.

"Oh, I was planning on checking in with her anyway."

"Well, don't go today." Hattie chugged the rest of her coffee and stood. "She's going to Noquitt, Maine, to visit some great grand-nieces of hers. Won't be back 'til tomorrow."

"I didn't know she had family in Maine," I said.

"Yes, I guess they are distant relatives, but Elspeth said they had some sort of family tragedy ... an aunt died or something and she wanted to go back and make sure the girls were okay. Something about passing on some family traditions or knowledge."

"Well, I guess this whole thing with Steve Van Dorn is going to be good for that writer." I headed behind the counter, hoping the four of them would get the hint. I needed to get some work done if I was going to close up shop to visit Gladys Primble.

"Writer?" Hattie and Cordelia wrinkled their gray brows at me as they brushed cat hair from their matching, purple polyester pantsuits. They usually knew everything that was going on in town and I was surprised they didn't know a writer was visiting.

"Yeah, I guess he's writing a book on the Van Dorn curse. He's the son of some journalist who used to write publicity stuff for Charles Van Dorn."

"Oh, that must be the stranger staying out at the Moonlight Motel." Josiah slid his eyes over to Hattie and Cordelia, a sly, satisfied look on his face.

As former postmaster, he still kept in touch with all the goings-on in town and was almost as knowledgeable as Hattie and Cordelia. Sometimes, it even seemed like they had an ongoing contest to see who could be the first one to find out the new gossip.

Hattie frowned at Josiah. "I didn't hear about any stranger at the motel. Did you, sister?"

Cordelia shook her head, eyeing Josiah suspiciously. "No."

"Yep, it's true. I was down there just last night with Vern Bosch and Frank Delaney. We have a standing poker game with Mabel and Bert. Anyway, they mentioned this stranger who didn't follow the typical tourist pattern—you know, the type that goes out sight-seeing and hiking. This guy just mostly stays in his room. I bet that's your writer guy."

Bing chuckled at the look on Cordelia and Hattie's faces. "Looks like the Mystic Notch grapevine has a break in it."

Hattie and Cordelia exchanged a glance.

"Well, I guess we need to get down to the beauty salon and find out where the problem is." The two women power walked to the door while Bing and Josiah stood up.

"I hope you get back in that library, Willa. I sure would like to get that journal ... and I hope you'll steer clear of this Claire person," Bing said.

"I gotta mosey along, too." Josiah rubbed his chin. "You know, there's somethin' bothers me about this Steve Van Dorn guy being the killer. I mean, it's an awful big risk and he was already going to be wealthy even without this new interest in the curse. Just seems like an unnecessary risk to take."

Pandora flicked a few more pens off the counter and I made a mental note to get a new penholder as I watched the four of them leave. A hollow feeling settled on my stomach. Something bothered me about Steve killing Bruce, too. I glanced down at Ranger who was sleeping soundly next to the couch. I remembered how protective he'd been of Bruce's body when the police had arrived.

He hadn't growled at me and had even let me approach, but I assumed that was because he sensed I was an animal lover and meant no harm. It was only when the police wanted to mess around with the body that he got protective. Which made me wonder, if he got that protective over the police touching the body, why hadn't he attacked Steve when he'd killed his master?

GLADYS PRIMBLE LIVED in a modest house off Forest Road. I didn't know what to expect as I pulled into her driveway, but I certainly wasn't expecting to see the seventy-year-old woman chopping a pile of wood in the backyard.

I approached warily, watching her muscled arms flex under her plain, gray tee shirt. She was pretty buff for an old lady.

Gladys noticed me and turned, a frown creasing her face. "Help you?"

I pasted on a friendly smile. "Hi. I'm Willa Chance ... Owner of Chance Books."

"Mew." I looked down at the most unusual cat I'd ever seen. It was a bright ginger color with long wavy fur. I'd never seen fur like that on a cat. It looked more like lamb's wool than cat hair.

"Oh, that's Euphoria, she's a Selkirk Rex." Gladys bent down and the cat trotted over to her, submitting to a few scratches behind the ear before she feigned disinterest, turning her attention to the logs of wood.

Gladys stood and brushed cat hair off her white painter's pants. "Anyway, what can I help you with?"

"Well, I've been commissioned to catalogue the library of Charles Van Dorn and was wondering if I could ask you a few questions. I heard you used to be his housekeeper." My cheeks burned and my mouth felt dry. I was never good at telling lies. Of course, I wasn't actually lying; what I'd said was true. I just neglected to add in the part about how Steve was in jail and I probably had no business with the Van Dorn library anymore.

Her eyes sparked at the mention of Charles Van Dorn and she narrowed them at me. "Cataloguing his library? ... I thought the contents of the house were held up in some issue with his brother or something."

"Oh, it was, but the brother died and the estate passed to Charles' nephew."

Her eyes widened. "You don't say! When did this happen? I'm afraid I don't get TV or newspapers here and I don't go into town much. We're pretty self-sufficient."

"The new owner flew in a couple of days ago and opened the house. He's already sold some of the contents."

Gladys cheek ticked. She took a red and black bandana out of her back pocket and wiped her brow with shaky hands.

"I guess you and Mr. Van Dorn must have been very close."

Her brow creased. "Why do you say that?"

"I found a photo album and you look quite friendly in the pictures. Actually, he had quite a lot of pictures of you in there, which is pretty unusual. I mean, people don't usually have a lot of photos of their housekeepers in the family photo albums, do they?" I shrugged. "That's why I figured you guys were so close."

More sweat beaded on her brow and she swiped at it with the hanky. Her eyes darted around the yard.

"Yes, I guess you could say we were close. Now if you'll excuse me, I just realized I'm late for an appointm—."

"Hey, Ma—" A tall, thin man with graying hair came careening around the corner, looking from Gladys to me inquisitively. "Oh, sorry. Didn't realize you had company."

"This is Willa Chance from the bookstore downtown." Gladys waved a hand at me. "She was just leaving."

"Oh? What does she want?" The man looked down at his mother who simply turned him around and pushed him toward the house.

"Sorry, Willa," she shot over her shoulder. "Maybe we can talk some other time, but right now I'm late."

And with that, she shut the door just as the curly orange cat slipped inside through the crack.

I walked back to my car feeling somewhat dejected. I hadn't found out much about her relationship with Van Dorn, but I had discovered one thing. After Gladys found out Van Dorn's house was for sale, she was pretty eager to get rid of me, which made me wonder ... did Gladys Primble have something to hide?

CHAPTER FOURTEEN

I was still thinking about Gladys' odd behavior as I bent down to put the key in the lock of my bookstore. A swirl of snowy white and pale green material caught my eye, and I looked up in time to see the gauzy skirts of two dresses disappearing around the corner to the alley—Felicity and Claire.

"That's it, I've had enough!" I ran to the mouth of the alley to tell them off, but the alley was empty. They must have run the length of the alley and were already out onto the other street. If it had just been Felicity, I might have considered that she'd made the quick getaway by flying off on her broomstick, but my jury was still out on Claire.

"I know you guys are following me and I want you to stop now!" I yelled into the empty alley, then trudged back to open my shop.

Pandora and Ranger eyed me lazily as I unlocked the bookstore and opened for the afternoon's business.

"I'm glad Steve got arrested, but that means I won't be able to go to Van Dorn's to talk to Charles," I said out loud. "And it makes me wonder what will happen to the house now."

"Mew." Pandora stretched in her cat bed, her back humped like a horseshoe.

"Maybe I don't need to find Charles' killer at all. I mean, he hasn't bothered me in a few days and I don't think he'd venture from the mansion."

Pandora leapt onto the counter, staring at me with her greenish-gold eyes as if she was hanging on my every word.

"And really, who cares about a fifty-year-old murder, anyway? The important thing is that I helped find Bruce Norton's killer."

"Meow!" Pandora shot her paw out, knocking several pens to the floor.

"Okay, well, if you *were* giving me hints about the pen—which I'm not convinced you were—you can stop now because we caught the guy."

She swatted more pens to the floor.

"Sure, I get it. You want me to keep investigating Charles' murder." I bent down and picked up the pens. "I do have to admit, I am curious as to who did it. My money is on Gladys."

"Meow!" Pandora head butted my chin.

"You, too? But what I really want to know is what is in that journal everyone seems to be looking for."

"Brrill." Pandora made a vibrating meowing noise.

"But I guess that will probably stay locked away at the Van Dorn Mansion for another fifty years. If only Charles was here so I could ask him."

"You rang?"

The voice startled me and I dropped the pens, whirling around to see none other than Charles Van Dorn's ghost proving that he did, in fact, leave the mansion, which probably didn't bode well for me.

"So there you are. Where were you when I had questions?" I bent to retrieve the pens again.

"Sorry, I was off in the nethers. But don't you worry. I'm going to be close by your side from now on ... at least until you solve my murder. I have a very good reason now to pass to the other side."

"Oh? And what might that be?"

He wagged his finger at me. "Never you mind. You just focus on finding out who killed me. Do you have any leads?"

Pandora jumped to the floor, batting at the swirling mist flowing around Charles' feet. He glanced down with a smile, then bent down to pet her, his hand passing right through her and causing her to shiver. Ranger seemed oblivious to the whole interaction, making me wonder if other animals could see ghosts, or if it was a talent only Pandora possessed.

I watched him pet the cat and wondered if he was the type to have two lovers. Maybe he had been having a fling with both Lily and Gladys and Gladys had found out and killed them both.

"I might have a couple of leads," I said. "Like maybe it was a jealous lover."

Charles bolted up from his crouched position, looking rather indignant. "What? I never!"

"I found the love letters."

His face, usually an opaque swirly white color, turned pink.

"Those are not what you think," he sputtered.

"You don't think your secret lover could have killed you?"

"No."

"Was there some sort of lover's triangle with you, Lily and someone else?"

"Certainly not!" Charles boomed. "Lily did have someone interested in *her,* though ... a secret admirer of sorts, but not the kind anyone would want to have. This one sent her creepy letters and notes. *That's* who I think killed her. In fact, I was gathering my evidence when I was killed, probably by the same person!"

"Or maybe someone was jealous of your attention to

her and killed you both," I interjected. "A spurned lover, perhaps?"

"What? I didn't have any spurned lover."

"What about Gladys Primble?"

"Gladys? She was married, for goodness sake."

"All the more reason to keep it hush-hush," I pointed out.

"You think I had an affair with Gladys and she killed me?"

I shrugged. It was a good theory and there were several reasons that Gladys fit the bill. They could have had a lover's quarrel. Maybe he paid too much attention to Lily and she got mad?

I remembered Gladys' son. He would be in his early fifties—just about the right age to be Charles' son. Maybe she got pregnant, Charles spurned her, and she killed him in a fit of rage.

But that didn't fit because Charles' murder was premeditated and set up to look like a suicide on purpose. Maybe they weren't even having an affair and she killed him simply because she knew he was going to leave her money when he died.

But *why* would he leave her money in the first place?

"If you weren't having an affair, then why did you leave her money?"

"Harumph." Van Dorn's bushy eyebrows pinched and wiggled together, like two caterpillars fighting.

"That's none of your concern. Gladys was a valued employee and she did me a great service while I was alive and some of that extended after I died."

"What? What do you mean she did you a service *after you died?*"

"Never mind, it has nothing to do with my death. Aren't you going to follow the trail I was already on?"

"Okay, I'll bite. What evidence did you find?"

"Lily was found murdered with one of my favorite cufflinks in her hand. That was a setup. My cufflinks had gone missing earlier that weekend. Of course, the police didn't believe me, but you can ask anyone who was at the house. Anyway, there was one other thing that the police never thought was important, and I think that's the clue to the real killer."

"And what was that?"

Van Dorn leaned toward me. "There was talcum powder in her hair."

"Talcum powder?"

"Yes. And quite a bit of it, too. Lily didn't use it. She didn't have any in her room. It was as if the killer sprinkled it there on purpose, or it fell from them onto her."

My brows knit together and I pictured the deep crease that was going to become permanent in between them if I kept frowning like this. This was his big clue? I didn't want to insult him, but I couldn't see how talcum powder would help us solve the murder.

"Why would the killer do that?" I asked.

"That's for you to figure out," Charles said. "And I'm going to stick to you like glue until you do."

Great. I could hardly wait to have an annoying ghost tagging along everywhere I went. I tilted my head and looked at him. He was looking back with his most sincere face, but I had to wonder if he was hiding something or lying to me. I didn't think so—my investigator's intuition told me he was telling me what he knew.

But why wouldn't he tell me who those love letters were to? I was just about to ask when the bells over the door jingled, pulling my attention away long enough to see Pepper rush in, waving her hands, her face flushed.

I turned back to Charles, but he was gone.

"Did you hear the news?" Pepper asked.

I swung my attention back in her direction. "What?"

"Steve Van Dorn has been released." Pepper's green eyes looked huge in contrast to her peaches and cream complexion. "He didn't kill Bruce."

"What? That can't be right. He had the pen and a motive."

"Mew!" Pandora batted a pen out from under the chair as if to accentuate my words.

I picked up the pen and held it up. "See, even Pandora agrees."

Pepper frowned at the pen, then at Pandora. "Okay,

well, I'm telling you he was released. It turns out he has an air-tight alibi."

I let that sink in for a few seconds. Steve wasn't Bruce's killer? That changed things.

But, if Steve didn't kill Bruce, then who did? I thought the motive was the extra money Steve would be making with the renewed interest in the Van Dorn curse because of the marking on Bruce's forehead.

Who else would have motive? Bruce had argued with the writer, Les Price, but surely a little argument in a diner wouldn't have amounted to murder. Even if it did, you'd think the murder would have happened in the heat of the argument at the diner.

Maybe there was something from Bruce's past that had gotten him killed?

The image of Gladys Primble chopping wood flashed into my mind. She had the strength to do it even at her age, and she'd acted strangely when I told her about Van Dorn's house being for sale. Who better to have talcum powder than the housekeeper?

"I think I might have another suspect." I told Pepper about my visit to Gladys and Van Dorn's strange clue. "She was around during the time of Charles' murder and so was Bruce. Maybe Bruce knew something that she didn't want him talking about."

"But, why would she wait all those years to silence

Bruce? I don't think that's it, but ..." Pepper chewed her bottom lip, her eyes narrowed in thought.

"What?"

"Maybe Charles fathered Gladys' son."

"Maybe. I could see why she wouldn't want that discovered, and it could be the reason that Charles left her the money." I looked over to where Charles' ghost had been. "But, Charles swore he wasn't having an affair with her and I don't think he was lying."

"I just hope this hasn't shaken Jimmy's confidence. He was pretty pumped up when he brought Steve in."

As if on cue, the door opened and Jimmy shuffled in. His shoulders were slumped, his face long.

"I guess you guys heard."

"Yeah, sorry." Pepper's face was etched with concern. "What happened?"

"It turns out Steve wasn't even in town at the time of death."

"Really?" I scrunched up my face. "But I saw him that morning at the house."

"Yep." Jimmy sat down on the couch. "He got in around six thirty a.m., but Bruce was killed around two a.m., so Steve couldn't have done it. He was on an airplane, and that's been confirmed."

"But he had the pen!"

Jimmy rolled his eyes. "You won't believe his story. He says he got off the plane and went right to the house.

Bruce was already dead. He claims he tried to revive him. He didn't want to call it in, being the new guy in town and he's had a checkered past. Claims to be all rehabilitated and all that, but didn't want to risk it. The weird thing is he says he did write on the forehead."

"What?" Pepper blanched. "Yech."

"He seemed pretty embarrassed about it," Jimmy continued. "He said he only wanted to increase the value of his possessions and then had the audacity to claim he wasn't being greedy!"

"Sheesh."

Jimmy looked at the floor, his face splotched with outbreaks of acne that hadn't been there yesterday. "Needless to say, Augusta and Striker are a little put out with me."

And probably with me, too, I thought.

"But I overheard Steve say he needed money bad." I tapped the pen against my lips. "Maybe he had an accomplice and they set it up this way so as to confuse the police?"

"Do you think he would be that clever? And who would be his accomplice? He doesn't seem to know anyone here," Jimmy said.

"Oh, yes he does."

"Who?" Jimmy and Pepper asked in unison.

"Emma."

"The church lady?" Jimmy looked at me like I was crazy. "She wouldn't kill Bruce."

"I know, but when she was here this morning and heard Steve was arrested, she got all flustered and ran out."

"Well, that's weird," Pepper said. "Why do you think that would be?"

"I have no idea," I answered aloud, which was true, but I knew one way to find out that I didn't want to mention out loud.

It was time to pay a visit to the cattery.

CHAPTER FIFTEEN

The cattery for the feral cats was located on a tract of land that the church owned. It was hidden off the beaten path. There were many opposers in town and we didn't want to advertise where the cattery was, which was also the reason I couldn't talk about it in front of Jimmy—I didn't know if he was friend or foe.

I made it a point to pick up some extra cat food when I went shopping to donate to the feral cats. So, even though the church was within walking distance, I got my jeep from the town parking lot and drove to the church, parking near the edge of the lot near the cattery. I figured the fewer people who saw me lugging stuff from my car into the woods, the better.

I got out and popped the back of my jeep, grabbed

the two cloth grocery bags, snuck a furtive look around the parking lot and headed down the trail.

The canopy of trees in the woods lowered the temperature by a couple of degrees, which was most welcome on the hot summer day. Sunlight filtered through the dense foliage, sparkling dots on the trail in front of me. Birds chirped and flew from branch to branch.

As I reached the cattery, the peaceful sounds of the forest were broken by voices inside. Two voices—a man and a woman. My heart clutched as I recognized them. Steve Van Dorn and Emma.

I stood outside the building, my muscles tense.

Was Emma in trouble?

Listening to the conversation, I could tell by the low tones there was no conflict going on. It appeared they were just having a friendly chat, but I couldn't hear what they were saying. I relaxed and pushed the door, listening to it creak open.

The conversation stopped and Steve and Emma both turned to look at me. I felt a tingle of nervousness as I wondered if Steve knew I had given Jimmy the tip on the marker.

"Oh, Willa, did you bring more food? Thank you so much." Emma rushed over to take the bags from me. "You two know each other, right?"

"Yep. Hi, Steve."

I looked quizzically at Emma, wondering just what Steve was doing there.

"Steve is a friend of our cause. He's helping me capture some of these cats so we can get them spayed and neutered," Emma explained.

I noticed several cat carriers on the floor with their doors open. Insuring the feral cat population didn't run unchecked was important, so getting them spayed and neutered was a critical part of our program.

The cats, though, weren't as excited about it as we were and it could be impossible to coax them into the crates. Every month, we tried to take at least a few to Doc Evans, who donated his time and medical supplies for the job.

Steve squatted down next to a crate and extended his hand toward a black and white tuxedo cat that he was trying to coax inside the crate with a treat. I marveled at the way the cat responded to him. Apparently, Steve had a way with animals. Most of the feral cats weren't fit for adoption. They distrusted humans too much. But some could become housecats and find their forever home... maybe this tuxedo cat was one of the lucky ones. But, even though the cat seemed to like and trust Steve, *I* still didn't.

He looked up at me sheepishly. "I suppose you heard what happened."

He didn't seem mad at me, so I figured he didn't

know I was the one who had tipped off the police, which was good. Even if he wasn't a killer, I still didn't want to be on his bad side.

I nodded.

Steve looked down at the floor and shifted his position. "I feel embarrassed about it now. I mean, it was a dirty thing to do. I guess I just wanted what was best for the cats."

"Cats?"

"Steve has his own feral cat rescue back home," Emma cut in.

"You do?" My first impression of Steve was that he was trouble. I couldn't picture him catering to cats, but with the way he was gently coaxing the little tuxedo cat, I had to admit my first impression might have been wrong.

Steve nodded. "Yes, but it's in trouble. We need to raise money fast or the building is going to be condemned and the cats will be taken to shelters. Some of them will likely be euthanized because they aren't fit for adoption."

My stomach twisted at his words. I hated the thought of cats being euthanized, especially if it could be prevented.

"That's why I wrote on that man's forehead. I had just flown in and came up to see the house first thing. I didn't even get inside and I heard the dog crying and saw that man lying there. I rushed over, thinking he needed help, but he was already dead. And then I got the idea to write the symbol. I'd been reading up a lot about the curse and planning on using my uncle's past and the curse to spur interest in the items and..." Steve shrugged. "I guess it was bad judgment."

"Wait. You heard Ranger? He was there?"

"The Golden? Yeah. Nice dog."

"He let you touch Bruce?"

"Yep. He seemed nervous. I got the impression he wanted me to help, but I couldn't and then he sniffed me and we made friends."

"So, then what did you do?"

Steve's face turned red. "I went home and waited for someone else to discover the body. I couldn't call it in with my past, and there was no helping the guy anyway. I'm not proud of it."

"Now Steve, that's nothing to be ashamed of. You had good intentions," Emma clucked.

I wasn't sure what to say. He *did* have good intentions but it was still creepy. I had to admit I did feel a little sorry for him ... *if* what he said was true. But why would he be at the cattery if it wasn't?

"You didn't see anyone or pass anyone on the road? Or see any evidence?" I asked.

"Nope. The police asked all that." Steve narrowed his eyes at me. "Are you with them?"

"Oh, no. She just has a habit of butting in," Emma cut in.

Out of the corner of my eye, I saw several of the cats converging on the corner of the barn, leaping and batting at something invisible ... no, not exactly invisible. The swirling mists of Charles Van Dorn solidified for a second and he looked at me pointedly—a reminder about researching his murder.

"Do you know a lot about your uncle's past?"

Steve shook his head. "Just that he was some kind of psychic and there was a big to-do about his death and he killed some girl he had staying there."

"He was a nice man, your uncle," Emma said. "I don't think he killed anyone."

"You knew him?" I said incredulously. I couldn't picture little mousy Emma hanging around with the Mystic Notch celebrities.

Her mouth straightened into a prim line. "Well, I went to a few parties up there."

I slipped the picture of the guy staring at Lily that I'd taken from the Van Dorn photo album out of my pocket. "Do you know who this is?"

"Oh, sure, he's that writer guy, Les' father."

"Sal Price?"

"Yes, that was his name." Emma shivered. "I never much liked him, but Charles said the press coverage helped him make a big name for himself so he invited him to everything."

Could Sal Price have been involved? Maybe his son, Les, would know something. I made a mental note to visit him out at the Moonlight Motel.

"What do you know about Lily Johanson and Charles?" I asked Emma.

"Not much. I think Lily was sweet on him." Her face turned pink. "I can't say I blame her. He was a handsome man. It's such a shame he decided to take his own life."

Over in the corner, Charles' ghost puffed up and swirled at the compliment.

"He didn't return her affections?" I persisted.

"No. He was entirely focused on his career."

"What about his housekeeper?"

Emma's brows mashed together. "Gladys?"

I nodded.

"Oh, I've known her for years. They were very close and she was broken up badly when he died."

"You don't think Charles and Gladys could have been ... you know." I wiggled my eyebrows and Emma looked at me funny, then her eyes went wide.

"Certainly not. She was married to a very nice man. Charles was too much of a gentleman to fool around with a married woman. They *were* very close, though. I remember she wanted to go back into the house and collect some memorabilia after Charles died, but the police had it shut up tight." She tilted her head and looked up at the ceiling. "I don't think anyone was ever allowed in after that until Steve inherited it. She still lives right here in town."

Emma looked at Steve. "I guess you didn't realize that house had such an interesting history."

Steve's brown eyes were alive with interest. "I didn't. You know, I never actually thought much about it, but I guess Uncle Charles did live an interesting life."

"Do you know why Charles left Gladys money?" I asked Emma.

"He left her money?" Emma looked from me to Steve and we both nodded. "I didn't hear that. But I do know one thing ... I'm not sure Gladys would have still worked for him much longer anyway."

"Why?"

"She was about six months pregnant when he died."

CHAPTER SIXTEEN

ow that Steve was in the clear, my job of cataloguing the library was back on, so I headed to Van Dorn's after work. Ranger had eaten a full supper and Pandora had made a lot of discontented mewling sounds as I left home.

I was looking forward to finishing up with the books and hopefully finding those journals.

Steve pulled in the same time I did and we greeted each other in the driveway. I still thought what he did to Bruce was creepy, but I kind of had a soft spot for him now that I knew he was a cat lover.

"I hope you won't tell anyone my little secret," Steve said.

"That you're a cat lover?"

"Yep." He smiled and, for the first time, I noticed he had a nice smile that transformed his face.

"Nah, don't worry, your secret is safe with me," I said. "I was wondering, though, how do you know Emma?"

"The feral cat network on Facebook."

"There's a network?" I asked as we walked up onto the porch together and Steve unlocked the door.

"Yeah, it's like a closed group. We help each other out." Steve unlocked the door and gestured for me to precede him inside.

"Huh."

"So, why do you think this Norton guy was killed?" he asked. "At first, I thought maybe he just had a heart attack, but I guess not, considering all the interest from the police."

"It wasn't a heart attack. It's a mystery as to why he was killed."

Steve scratched his head. "Is that why you've been asking all those questions? You think it has something to do with my uncle, don't you?"

"I ... well ... " I stammered. I was never very good at lying.

He pressed his lips together, scanning the house. "You know, this whole history is really interesting. Maybe I shouldn't be selling this stuff off in such a hurry. And the interest in those journals, what do you make of that?"

"Good question. I don't know, but more than one person really wants them."

"Yeah, we better be careful with those. Do you think this Bruce guy was after the journals?"

"That's a good question." I hadn't considered that angle. Bruce knew Charles and hung around here back in the day. Maybe he had come here that night for the journals ... but why wait all this time?

Steve's eyes turned sad. "I wonder what happened to the dog?"

"Ranger? I have him temporarily. I couldn't let him go to the pound and I was thinking I would see if any of Bruce's relatives wanted him, but Bruce didn't have any." I shrugged. "So, I guess I'll keep him until I find the right master."

"Oh? He was a real nice dog. I'm glad that you have him. I would have hated to see him go to the pound."

We proceeded down the hall toward the library and office. About halfway down, Steve slowed his step. He put his hand out to stop me. "Wait here. Something's not right."

I felt a prickle of adrenaline as Steve took off down the hall. I didn't notice anything ... maybe Charles was here and Steve was picking up on it.

"Crap!" Steve yelled from the office and I rushed toward it, skidding around the corner to see Steve standing in front of a large, mahogany cabinet.

"What happened?" I asked.

He stepped aside, revealing a thin crack in the cabinet.

"What's that?" I asked.

"Apparently, this cabinet had a secret compartment." He motioned me over. "Check it out."

I walked closer to inspect the cabinet. It was ingenious, really. There was a hidden compartment on the side, which was made to look like part of the molding. It now hung open, the small interior compartment dark and empty.

"Do you think someone came in and opened this?" I remembered Charles didn't like people going through his things and wondered if maybe the ghost had been playing a joke on Steve.

"It sure looks that way." Steve glanced around the room, then went out into the hall. I could hear him checking the windows and doors. "There's no sign of a break-in."

Charles appeared in the corner and I raised my brows at him then pointed to the cabinet. He shrugged and shook his head. I guess it wasn't him.

Had someone been in here, or did the cabinet pop open on its own? I glanced out the window and did a double-take. Was that a pair of cat ears peeking up from the tall grass? It was just getting dark and I squinted my eyes to get a better look, but when I looked again all I saw was grass. Great, now I was seeing cats everywhere I went along with Charles' annoying ghost.

"Maybe the door just cracked open, you know, with the heat and all?" I suggested.

Steve came back and stood in front of the cabinet, rubbing his hand over his face. He looked down, his eyes narrowed, and then he bent down and picked something up.

"I don't think so. I'm pretty sure someone was in here and it looks like they left this clue."

He held out his palm and I gaped at what was in there—a clump of curly orange cat fur.

STEVE CALLED the police and Gus, Striker and Jimmy showed up. We met them in the foyer and none of them looked too happy to see me there.

"Willa, why am I not surprised to see you here?" Gus asked.

"Well, I *am* cataloguing the library, so I guess that would be why..."

I glanced uneasily at Striker. I hadn't heard from him since the other night when he'd been over to my house. Was he mad at me? I couldn't tell. Of course, we didn't actually have that "call each other all the time" kind of relationship, so it was probably just that he was busy with the case. Come to think of it, I was kind of busy myself.

As if reading my mind, Striker winked at me and I berated myself for feeling a flitter in my stomach.

Jimmy stood off to the side, shoulders slumped, his face red and blotchy. My stomach twisted at his dejected look—it was all my fault. I'd given him the tip about the pen and now it looked like he'd screwed up.

Gus got down to business. "So, where did they break in?"

Steve scratched his head. "See, that's the thing. It doesn't seem like they exactly did break in."

Gus' left brow shot up and she looked from Steve to me. "You called about a break-in, right?"

"Yeah, I'll show you," Steve said.

We all clomped down the hall to the office and Steve pointed out the hidden drawer.

"So, let me get this straight. No signs of entry. Nothing is stolen that you know of, and all you've got is an open drawer?"

"And this." Steve held up the cat fur.

"Hair?"

"Well, actually I think it's cat fur." Steve held the clump up in front of his face. "Looks like a rare breed, the Selkirk Rex."

"Are you guys serious?" Gus whirled on me. "You had something to do with this, didn't you?"

I held my hand up in front of me. "I ... no. I mean, I was just here to catalog the books."

"I hope you guys aren't wasting the taxpayers' money on some kind of wild goose chase."

Or wild ghost chase.

Steve held up his hands. "No, I swear. I know someone broke in."

Gus rolled her eyes. "And what do you want me to report? A break-in where nothing was stolen? That some cat hair was left here? Or maybe you want me to think a cat broke in?"

"Well, now that you mention it, I guess it does sound kind of lame."

She gave him a stern look and nodded, then turned her glare on me. "And *you* ... can you at least *try* to stay out of trouble?"

Then she spun around and marched out of the room, her blonde ponytail swinging like a metronome behind her.

Striker shrugged, winked at me again, and followed her.

Jimmy grimaced and trudged out behind them, leaving Steve and me staring at the empty drawer and wondering if the thief had gotten what they wanted and what, exactly, that was.

～

"SOMETHING'S WRONG." *Pandora peered through the blades of grass at the Van Dorn mansion, her heart sinking. "I don't feel it anymore."*

"It can't be," Inkspot growled, his green eyes glowing in the moonlight. "We must secure it."

"Well, I'm telling you someone else must have gotten to it."

"She speaks true," Snowball hissed. "There is no secret in there. It's gone."

They sat stock still in the grass, staring at the lights coming from the house. A face appeared in the window.

Willa!

"Duck!" Otis hissed, but with their cat instincts they didn't need the warning, they had already crouched down so as not to be seen.

Pandora was thankful she hadn't brought Ranger this time. He wanted to come, but Willa had closed the cellar door and the dog couldn't fit out the cat door, though he did try.

Pandora's lips quirked into a smile at the memory of him trying to wriggle through the small door and getting stuck halfway. She hoped he'd been able to pull his front half back in—the last she'd seen of him, it had been sticking out the door and he'd been barking at her to come back and help him.

It was a good thing he hadn't fit. He did not have their feline reflexes and would surely have given them away.

"So now what?" Kelley batted at a firefly blinking in front of them.

Everyone turned to Inkspot.

"We must find the journal and see it is protected from the evil ones," Inkspot growled.

Otis chuffed. "I told you it would do no good to trust the modern cats, with their new ways and sensitive 'feelings'. This has gotten us nowhere. We don't even have any proof that the item we seek was ever in there."

Pandora felt the hairs on the back of her spine stand on end and she humped her back, getting ready to lash out at the disagreeable Otis, but Sasha stopped her with a thrust of her paw.

"We must all get along," Sasha reminded her. "You two remember we have a higher purpose."

"Yes." Inkspot turned. "We must work together, Otis and Pandora, you two especially ... you are more alike than you think."

Pandora looked at Otis out of corner of her eye.

Alike?

She didn't think so. He is a pompous jerk and I certainly wasn't anything like him, *she thought as she pounced on a white moth, stilling its flutter. She lifted her paw and the moth flapped its wings and flew up in front of her. They watched it land on a tall blade of grass.*

"Come," Inkspot said as he started back toward Elspeth's house. "We must meet with Truffles and see if she found anything out from her contact before we make an alternate plan."

CHAPTER SEVENTEEN

*D*espite all the questions circling in my mind, I'd made good headway with Charles' books while his ghost watched me from the leather sofa in front of the stone fireplace. Every once in a while, he would blurt out missives such as 'be careful', 'don't rip the pages' and other annoying advice that I could have done without.

Charles' unwanted attention was unsettling, but we got into a rhythm and I was able to ignore him. He evaded my questions about Gladys and pretended like he didn't know anything about someone breaking in earlier in the day, claiming he must have been 'out' talking to me at my shop at the time.

It was well past suppertime when I packed up my stuff and said goodbye to Steve. I had to admit, he was starting to grow on me, especially since I'd seen him at the cattery, but I still had my suspicions. He could still be involved. Maybe he and Gladys were in on it together. Though he *had* seemed upset that Charles left Gladys money, but that could have been a cover. His alibi of being on the airplane was good, but he and Gladys could have set things up beforehand so as to have the perfect alibi—Gladys murders Bruce and makes the clues lead to Steve who has the perfect alibi in order to throw the police off and confuse them. But why? And how would Steve and Gladys have known each other in the first place? Maybe there was a Facebook group for this sort of thing just like there was for feral cats.

The whole thing about Steve drawing on Bruce's forehead was weird. Why would he do that and incriminate himself? Then again, maybe the whole plan was for the police to pull him in, so they could discover his airtight alibi. But had Ranger really stood by and let that happen? I had one way I could find out - bring Ranger over and see his reaction. I felt sure if Steve were the one who killed Bruce, Ranger would react negatively to him.

I drove home with my head spinning. I felt certain that Bruce's murder was related to both Charles' and Lily's murders, but I needed more information on their deaths before I could figure out how or why.

How could I get that information?

And then the perfect solution popped into my head. Jimmy. He'd have access to those old files and it would kill two birds with one stone. I felt responsible for the screw-up with Steve and if I could help Jimmy redeem himself by solving the case, plus the fifty-year-old murders, then all the better. I decided to tell him everything I knew.

Rummaging in my hobo bag, I pulled out my cell, then turned it on. I hated the darn thing interrupting me all the time, so I usually kept it off, but I had to admit, it sure was convenient when I wanted to interrupt someone else.

The phone lit up with a text from Striker: *'Dinner Friday?'* I felt foolishly giddy and replied *'yes'*, and then I looked up Jimmy, who I'd entered into my contacts earlier and called him.

"Hi, Willa. What's up?" I cringed at the uncertainty in his voice. I hoped he still trusted me and wanted to investigate the case with my advice.

"I have some ideas I want to run by you regarding the case," I ventured.

"Oh ... I don't know if that's a good idea."

"Why don't you just hear me out? Meet me at my place in fifteen." My stomach grumbled loudly. "And pick up pizza on the way—I'll pay."

Five minutes later, I pulled into my driveway to see the cat door slightly askew. Apparently, Pandora *had* been out. Was it her I had seen at Van Dorn's? No, that couldn't be possible. His house was miles away and besides, what would she be doing there?

I pushed the cat door back in. It did get stuck open sometimes and I didn't want to leave it that way or mice would come in by the droves. As I adjusted the door, I saw some golden fur on it. Had Ranger tried to follow Pandora out? I smiled at the image of the large Golden Retriever trying to fit through the small door.

Inside, Pandora blinked at me innocently from atop the kitchen table.

"Hi, guys." The cat didn't make a move, but Ranger hoisted himself up from the floor and walked over to sniff at my pants.

I fed them, and just as I finished, Jimmy arrived, filling the house with the smell of dough and tomato sauce.

I slid some paper plates on the table and pried the lid open, my mouth watering at the cheesy slices topped with green pepper and onion.

I gestured to the table and Jimmy pulled out a chair and sat.

"Something to drink?" I asked.

"If you have some hot water, that would be great." He pulled a tea bag out of his pocket, then noticing my frown, added, "Pepper gave me these tea bags and it's really tasty. I have to admit, I'm almost addicted to it."

"I'll bet," I mumbled, shoving a mug of water in the

microwave for him and getting myself a tall glass with ice.

Ranger ambled over to the table, his eyes glued to the pizza.

"Can I give him some?" Jimmy asked.

"Sure."

Jimmy broke off a tiny piece of crust and fed it to the dog, who inhaled it. Pandora craned her neck to see what was going on, then turned her back on us, flicking her kinked tail in disdain. She didn't like pizza.

"So, what did you want to talk about?" Jimmy folded his pizza and shoved the end in his mouth.

"Well, I feel kind of bad about the whole pen incident with Steve ... it *was* a good lead, though."

"It was. It's just a fluke thing that he wrote on the guy after he was dead." Jimmy grimaced. "I mean, who would have expected that?"

I nodded. "Right. So, to make up for it, I wanted to share some of my ideas with you. Maybe they'll help solve the case for real."

"Why me?"

I shrugged. "Gus and Striker don't take me seriously."

"Really?"

"Yep."

"Join the club." He raised his teacup and we clinked rims.

I studied Jimmy while I figured out where to start. I

didn't want to tell him about the love letters, and certainly couldn't tell him I talked to ghosts. I decided to play up my journalistic intuition.

"I have a feeling that Bruce's murder has something to do with the deaths that happened at Van Dorn's fifty years ago and I think I have a likely suspect."

His gray eyes sparked with interest. "Really?"

I nodded and wiped the grease off my mouth. "Apparently, Charles Van Dorn left a sum of money to his housekeeper."

Jimmy's left brow ticked up as he bit into another piece. "Why?"

"I'm not sure, but I think they might have been having an affair," I said.

Jimmy's eyebrow ticked higher.

"Or, there was some sort of love triangle with Charles, Lily and Gladys," I added.

"And you think she killed them?" Jimmy asked. "I thought Charles committed suicide."

"Yeah, that's what everyone thought." A misty form in the corner of the kitchen caught my attention and I glanced over to see Charles shaking his head. I guessed he was making good on his threat to stick to me like glue until I found his killer. I hoped he wasn't planning to sleep over. There was nothing worse than waking up to a cold, wet ghost face staring at you.

"So, you think Gladys killed Lily and then faked Charles' suicide because she was jealous?"

"That's the thing. She might have killed Lily because she was jealous, but Charles' murder was premeditated and made to look like a suicide. The pre-meditation doesn't fit with a crime of passion."

Jimmy scrunched his face up. "But what makes you so sure Charles' death wasn't suicide?"

"Just intuition. Anyway, Gladys might have been jealous or maybe she knew Charles was leaving her money and wanted it then instead of waiting thirty years for him to die."

Jimmy looked up at the ceiling, chewing his pizza thoughtfully. "And you think she also killed Bruce?"

"Maybe."

"But she'd be seventy years old!"

"Trust me. She's more than capable of doing the deed."

"But *why* would she kill Bruce?"

"I think she might have gone to the house to get something and Bruce just happened to be there, so she had no choice. Also, Bruce might have suspected her, too. You said he had those photos at his house. Maybe he had an investigation of his own and came to the same conclusion I did and confronted her."

"Hmm ... maybe."

"When I told Gladys the house was being sold, she

seemed really surprised. Maybe she was just acting, or maybe she really didn't know the house was being sold. If there was something in that house she wanted—maybe something that incriminated her in the murders—and she went there and ran into Bruce and had to kill him, she might not want to go back too soon afterward. Especially if she really didn't know it was being sold, because she'd figured she could go back any time. But once I told her Steve was selling everything off, she realized she *had* to get in there to get what she needed."

Jimmy looked at me doubtfully. "That seems kind of farfetched and I don't think Gus was convinced there really was a break-in."

"I know she wasn't, but that piece of fur ..."

"What about it?" Jimmy slurped his tea and I wondered about those herbs Pepper had put in. Hopefully it wouldn't backfire and make him less confident like some of her teas had done in the past. Then he'd never want to help me!

"It was from a rare cat, one that Gladys just happens to own."

"But *why* would she need to break in to Van Dorn's?"

"That's a good question." I didn't feel like it was my place to tell him about the love letters—that was Charles' secret to share. "I think there may have been some sort of evidence of their affair she wanted to keep buried. She probably had a key to the house and that's why there was no evidence of a break-in."

"But, why after all these years? I mean who would care now if she had an affair with Van Dorn fifty years ago?"

"Gladys has a son that is the right age to be Charles' son. In fact, she was pregnant when Charles died. Maybe she was trying to protect him somehow. Maybe she didn't want him to find out Charles was really the father."

"So, why wouldn't she have gotten what she wanted back then after he died?"

"I don't know. The house was secured by the police after he died so she probably couldn't get in. Then after that, it was locked up. Maybe she felt that since the house was locked up, whatever she wanted was safe. It was after I told her about Steve selling stuff off that she got agitated."

"It does sound like there could be a lot of reasons Gladys could be the killer, but I can't picture anyone going to all that trouble." Jimmy sipped his tea. "Although it is almost perfect. Kill Lily, frame Charles, then kill Charles and have him confess to killing Lily in a suicide note. And then collect your inheritance. Case closed. The police wouldn't even investigate Charles' death and would likely stop the investigation on Lily's."

"Exactly," I said, letting Jimmy continue with his own conclusions.

"And no one would even question why Charles left Gladys money." Jimmy sighed. "Maybe Gladys really is that devious, but we can't just go on a hunch."

"Right! We need proof."

"How do we get that?"

"I need to look at all the files from Charles' and Lily's cases and get into Bruce's house to see what he had." I gave Jimmy my most earnest look. "Will you help me do that?"

Under the table, Ranger, who had been flicking his eyes back and forth between us as we ate the pizza, whined at the mention of getting access to Bruce's.

Jimmy pursed his lips, and reached down to pet Ranger on the head. "Okay, but we have to be careful. We were wrong before and I don't want Augusta to get madder at me."

As if to emphasize Jimmy's words and taunt us for our error in having Steve brought in, Pandora leaped on the table with a blue pen in her mouth, then proceeded to drop it right in the middle of the last slice of pizza.

CHAPTER EIGHTEEN

$\mathcal{D}$uring my crime journalist days, I had developed a gut instinct about crimes, and it was usually right on target. Right now, my gut instinct was telling me that Bruce Norton's murder was directly related to the murders of Charles and Lily fifty years ago.

The only people—and ghosts—who were still around from back then, didn't seem to want to give me straight answers, but I knew one person who might have them. Les Price.

Even though Les hadn't been around, his father had, and since he was continuing his father's book, I figured he'd have plenty of information about the goings on back then.

So, the next day, I headed over to the Moonlight Motel before work to bring some fresh baked muffins to Mr. Price. In my experience, baked goods usually worked pretty good to get people talking and I was hoping Les Price was no exception.

The Moonlight Motel sat just off Route 302 in the White Mountain National Forest. The motel, a small, one-story building with about twenty rooms and an office, was nestled in a forest of dense pine trees. I breathed in the fresh, pine-scented air as my tires crunched over the white stone driveway.

Having grown up in town, I knew Mabel and Burt, the owners, so I used two of the blueberry muffins to bribe them into pointing me toward Les' room. I knocked on the door, holding the bag of muffins up in front of me as if it was a ticket for entry.

The door opened slowly and Les peered out, blinking and squinting as if he hadn't seen sunlight in days. I glanced inside the room. Les' laptop sat open on the round table, papers were strewn about on the bed, and piles of clothes on the floor.

"Oh. Hi. What are you doing here?" he asked.

I held up the muffin bag. "I just thought I'd stop by and bring you some of the best muffins in New Hampshire."

Les looked from the bag to me skeptically, then over his shoulder into the room. "Well, I'm kind of busy writing ..."

"That's what I want to talk to you about. The Van Dorn stuff," I said quickly.

"Oh?"

"Yeah, I have a theory and I'm wondering if your dad's notes might help."

He hesitated, looking from the messy room to me.

"It could be beneficial to both of us. Plus, these muffins are still warm." I dangled the muffin bag in front of his face.

"Okay." Les stepped aside and I squeezed in, wrinkling my nose at the smell of burnt coffee and ketchup.

Les gestured to the messy room. "Sorry, I've been on a writing tear ... well, you know how it is."

I nodded. I did know how it was, or used to know, back when I made my living by writing. Les pushed a pile of clothes off the chair and we sat at the small round table under the window, the bag of muffins between us.

"Coffee?" He pointed to the coffee maker sitting on the table. I wasn't sure how long the coffee had been in there, but it looked like mud.

"No, thanks." I angled the bag at him, giving him first choice. He reached his hand in and came out with a muffin, then I took one for myself and placed it on the table in front of me.

"So, it looks like you've been hard at work." I nodded at the pile of papers on the bed. "Have you been out to Van Dorn's?"

"No. After what you told me about the body, there was no way I was going up there to be the next victim of the curse. Anyway, I heard that Van Dorn guy got arrested for killing that old man, so I guess the house must be locked up again." Les slid the glass carafe out of the coffeemaker and poured himself a mug of thick sludge.

"He did ... but then he was released. I guess it wasn't him." I peeled part of the paper cup off the bottom of my muffin carefully.

"What?" He looked up at me, the movement causing him to dribble thick dots of coffee on the table.

"Yeah, I guess he had an alibi. He was on an airplane. The weird thing is, he confessed to being the one that wrote on Bruce's forehead, but I guess he wasn't the one who killed him."

Les stopped dabbing at the spilled coffee and squinted up at me. "Why would he do that?"

"To make more money. He figured the items in the house would be more valuable if there was a renewed interest in the curse."

"Oh." He sat back in his chair with a sour look on his face, flicking his pencil on the notepad in front of him. "Are there any leads to the killer? What about the murder weapon?"

I shrugged, brushing crumbs off my finger neatly into the paper muffin cup. "The cops don't share with me. I did find out the murder weapon was some kind of club or blunt object, but they haven't found it yet. But, I have an idea about the murder and I think it's related to what happened fifty years ago."

Les stopped tapping and stared at me. "Really?"

I nodded and told him how Charles left Gladys money, how she was strong enough to clobber Bruce, and how she seemed quite agitated when I visited her and told her the house was being sold.

"I think she might have been after something in the house. It's possible she went there to get it the morning of Bruce's murder. Bruce just happened to be there and she had to kill him. I was wondering if there was anything in your father's notes that might support my theory," I said hopefully.

Les pressed his lips together. "The housekeeper ... yes. He did talk about her. She was always around. So, you think she had something to do with the murders back then?"

"Yep. Maybe she was jealous of Lily or something ..." I let my voice trail off and shrugged. I didn't want to tell him about the love letters.

"Huh, that could be. I remember my father saying something about her acting suspicious. It's in his notes somewhere, I think." Les jumped up and sprinted to the bed, then started rummaging around in the stacks of papers.

"Did your father write anything about Lily's death ... or Charles' suicide?"

"Well, he always thought Charles killed Lily. I mean, because of the mark on her head and such. Plus, he did say they had something going on." He stopped rummaging, pushed his glasses up on his nose and looked at me. "Yes, that's right. There *was* something. Maybe there was something between Charles and Gladys at the same time, and then Lily got angry and they had it out? It could have happened that way."

"Maybe. If you have notes from your father, that might help us prove it." I wondered if what Les was saying could be true. According to the letters, the affair had to be hidden *from* Lily, but what if that was because Charles was also having one *with* Lily. If Les' father thought something was going on between them, maybe Charles had lied to me. But why?

He looked down at the mess of papers. "I can't find the exact note, but I believe he said something about seeing Gladys come out of that stream gauging station—you know, that little building in the woods just up the street from the Van Dorn's? She denied it when he confronted her. He always thought she hid some evidence there."

A feeling of excitement sprouted in my stomach. This could be the lead I was looking for. "You mean evidence on Lily's death?"

"I think so."

"If she is the same killer, she might have left the weapon that killed Bruce there, too."

"Exactly what I was thinking." He started pacing the room, which I found to be a little unnerving. I twisted in my chair, to face him.

"What about Charles' death? Did your father have notes about that?"

"What?" He looked at me distractedly. "Oh, no. My father had already left on the train earlier that day, so he didn't know a thing about Charles' death. He never went back after that."

He started pulling some clothes out of a drawer and I wondered what the heck he was doing. "Do your father's notes mention anything about a hand-written journal?"

He looked up from his task, his brows knit together. "Journals? No, why?"

"Oh, a few people have mentioned them and I was wondering what they were. I haven't found them in the library."

"Well, I don't know anything about that." He looked pointedly at the digital clock on the bedside table. "I just remembered I have an appointment, so if you'll excuse me ..."

"Oh, right." I shoved the rest of the muffin in my mouth and brushed the crumbs into the bag. "Well, thanks for the info. Let me know if you remember anything else."

"Right. You do the same. This could be a great addition to the book."

I left the muffin bag on the table and took my exit, feeling a little more hopeful and making a mental note to check the gauging station ... if Gladys had hidden something there once and it was never found, she might think it was the perfect place to hide a murder weapon.

CHAPTER NINETEEN

$\mathcal{I}$ went home to collect Pandora and Ranger after my visit with Les. I wasn't back at the bookstore for more than an hour when the door opened and Jimmy Ford hurried in, clutching a plastic bag as if he was hiding a stolen treasure.

He looked around furtively. "Do you have a back room?"

"Sure. Why?"

He leaned across the counter toward me. I noticed he seemed taller somehow, his shoulders broader and his face less blotchy. Or maybe it was just the uniform.

He cut his eyes toward the bag and whispered, "I have the files from the old Van Dorn cases."

"Great! Let's look at them right here." I gestured to the sofa.

He frowned. "I'm not sure I want Striker or Augusta to know I'm looking into this. These are old cold case files. They were pretty easy for me to check out of storage, but after the whole thing with Steve ..."

"Right." I rushed to the door. "I'll close the store while we look at them."

I flipped the sign and locked the door while Jimmy settled on the couch. He opened the folders and spread the contents on the coffee table.

Charles' ghost hovered near Jimmy's elbow, looking down at the pictures and scowling.

Jimmy rubbed his elbow. "Is it just me or is it chilly in here?"

I exchanged a look with Charles. "The air conditioning vent is blowing on you there."

Jimmy scooted over a few inches and I repressed a smile, which quickly faded as I looked at the pictures.

Pandora and Ranger came to join us, and Jimmy petted Ranger's back, then stroked Pandora behind the ears. Pandora must have liked that because she jumped into his lap and started purring loudly. Jimmy's face lit up and he rubbed her neck and belly.

The pictures were old eight-by-ten's, shiny and aged with curled edges. Most were black and white but a few were color. They had that yellow tinge typical of colored photos from the 1960s.

One of the pictures showed Lily lying on her back, her eyes staring blankly, the strange triangle mark on her forehead. She was in a bedroom, which I assumed was one of the guest rooms at the Van Dorn mansion. It was lavishly decorated in a 1940s style. I realized I'd never been upstairs at the Van Dorn's and wondered if I should check out the room.

Jimmy pointed to a stack of yellowed papers filled with old-fashioned typewriting. "According to the file, Lily was hit on the back of the head with a blunt instrument."

My eyes widened. "Just like Bruce."

He nodded.

Remembering what Charles had said about the talcum powder, I grabbed a magnifying glass from behind the counter and trained it on Lily's hair. Sure enough, I could just barely make out tiny, white flecks in her hair.

"Does it say anything about the powder in her hair in the report?"

"Huh?" Jimmy grabbed the magnifying. "Wow, how did you notice that?"

"Good eyes." I shrugged, sliding my eyes to Charles.

Jimmy flipped through the papers. "Here it is. It says that was calcium carbonate on the lab results."

"Is that what talcum powder was made of?"

"I don't know."

I reached for the stack of papers and thumbed through them, quickly reading the notes on Lily's investigation. "Looks like they didn't do much investigating."

Jimmy nodded. "All the clues pointed to Charles."

"Or were set up to point to him." I put the report down and started on the other stack, the one about Charles' death.

The first picture was of Charles slumped over his desk, which I recognized as the very room from which Steve was running his eBay business. I wondered if he knew his uncle had died in that room ... or if he cared.

Charles' ghost glanced down at the photo, then gasped and swirled agitatedly. I noticed Robert Frost and Franklin Pierce poking their heads out from one of the rows of bookshelves. Frost waved to Charles who squinted, then widened his eyes in recognition and waved back before gliding over to them. The two men shook hands like long lost friends, which I guess they were, considering that Charles used to channel Frost. As I turned my attention back to the gruesome picture, I heard Frost introducing Van Dorn to Pierce.

Charles had been shot. A second picture revealed the gun on the floor under his dangling hand. Switching back to the first picture, I could see his head had fallen on the desk blotter and a dark puddle spread out under it, the strangely tinted, colored photo, showing reddish-orange edges in the puddle.

The suicide note, written neatly in fountain pen, was conveniently at the corner of the desk, just a corner of it resting under the top of his head. The orange fountain pen lay uncapped on top of the letter, as if he'd written it then shot himself, not even bothering to care if the ink dried up on the nib. I thought it was pretty convenient that no blood got on the note so the whole thing could be easily read.

The transcript of the note was in the files. It was short and sweet—a simple confession of how he killed Lily and then couldn't live with himself.

"Look at the placement of the suicide note. Isn't it convenient that no blood got on it? That note would have been directly in front of him on the desk when he was writing it. Do you think he would have had the presence of mind to move it to the side in his despondent state?"

Jimmy frowned at the picture. "It doesn't seem like he would, but then maybe he realized there would be a ... err ... mess, and he wanted to be sure they read the confession."

Pandora meowed and jumped down from Jimmy's lap.

With a chill, I noticed the desk in the picture was the same one Steve had been using. Had there been a stain on the top? In the picture, Charles had a blotter which I assume had since been removed, but I made a mental note to check the room anyway—not that I wanted to see the bloodstains, but there could be other clues.

Pandora trotted back over, dropping a pen on the floor in front of Jimmy.

"She's not going to let us forget the pen incident with Steve," Jimmy said, rolling his eyes.

I picked up the thin file on Charles. "There're hardly any notes on Charles' death, either."

"Once it was ruled a suicide and the note was his confession for Lily's murder, they stopped investigating both cases," Jimmy said.

"The *police* stopped investigating. But maybe not everyone else did." I tapped the pile of typewritten papers. "We need to go check out Bruce's place. He may have a clue the police never found."

WE CLOSED up the bookstore and headed to Bruce's, despite the protesting squeal of Pandora. Ranger wanted to come, too, but wasn't nearly as annoying as Pandora about it.

I hated to leave the shop closed during the day. I did, after all, have a business to run. But something told me we should get to Bruce's right away and I was getting tired of seeing Charles' ghost glaring at me at every turn. I was just glad I had inherited my house and didn't have a mortgage. As it was, I'd probably have to eat ramen noodles all next week.

Bruce lived in a secluded area. We drove down a meandering dirt road about a half-mile past the Van Dorn place, and came out in a peaceful clearing where Bruce's cottage peeked out from behind a stand of tall pine trees.

The exterior was freshly painted—red with white trim. A rocking chair sat idle on the porch, and window boxes with dried-up flowers that must have added a spark of color at one time hung below the windows. I looked at the dead flowers with a heavy heart. Bruce obviously took pride in his place, but he wasn't around to water the flowers anymore and they'd suffered without his attention.

Jimmy took a key from his pocket and unlocked the door. "Remind me to lock up when we leave."

Inside, the cabin was as neat as the outside. An old sofa sat against the wall in the living room, a crocheted afghan in greens and oranges draped over its back like a shawl. Next to the living room was a small kitchen with knotty pine cabinets and old appliances. The dining room had papers and photos spread all over the table.

"These are the photos." Jimmy pointed to the dining room table.

I looked down at the glossy photos, newspaper clippings, and what looked like some old ticket stubs. A cherry red fountain pen sat on the table next to a strange, white oval object in a plastic bag. The object had apparently deteriorated over the years and some white powder had caked the inside of the bag.

"What's that?" I pointed to the white object.

Jimmy wrinkled his face at it, then picked it up and studied it. "Huh, that's weird. It's a cuttlebone."

"Cuttlebone? What the heck is a cuttlebone?"

"It's for birds. They sharpen their beaks on it. It's actually the spine of some type of squid - cuttlefish."

I was kind of grossed out about the whole squid spine thing. "Did Bruce have a bird?"

Jimmy looked around the room. "I didn't see one when we were here before."

I made a quick survey of the house, my gut churning at the thought of finding a cage with the fragile body of a parakeet or canary dead on the bottom. It didn't take long. The cabin was small, just one floor, and the only door, besides the front door and the one in the kitchen was a door off the dining room leading to a crawlspace under the cottage. I was glad I didn't find a dead bird, or a birdcage. My search brought me back to the dining room where I looked down at the photos again.

In one of the pictures, I recognized the bedroom in

which Lily had died. This one had no body, though. This picture must have been taken after ... or before.

"Didn't Gus and Striker think it was odd that Bruce would have these pictures of Van Dorn's?" I asked. "Some of these look similar to the police photos.

"Well, that's just it. We didn't know these were of Van Dorn's—none of us had seen the other photos from the old case."

He had a point. None of them had been in Van Dorn's until *after* they'd been to Bruce's, so they wouldn't recognize the interior of the house in the photos and besides, why would Striker and Gus care about an old solved case anyway?

I turned to the pile of newspaper clippings, all from the month of Charles' death. There were articles about parties and some of the attendees. Then, of course, several about Lily's death and Charles' alleged suicide. Something in one of the articles caught my eye.

"Check this out. It says Charles had a rival. Someone named Claire Voyant ... it sounds like they were real enemies."

"Bad enough enemies that she would have killed him? And what kind of name is Claire Voyant, anyway?" Jimmy asked.

"Yeah, it is kind of a silly name. She must have been a medium or wanted people to think she was. Maybe Charles and this Claire Voyant were battling over customers. Maybe she thought if she got Charles out of the way, there would be more customers for her."

"Money *is* one of the common motives for murder," Jimmy said.

"And so is jealousy. Maybe there was a love triangle between *her*, Charles and Lily," I added.

"Or her, Charles and Gladys," Jimmy mused. "You keep going for this love triangle angle, but I'm not so sure about that."

I didn't want to have to tell him about the love letters in order to get him to see why I was so sure about that. "Well, it makes sense, and Les Price seems to think it could be Gladys, too. She'd fit the bill for the older crimes as well."

"Les Price? The writer? How does he know?"

I told him about my talk with Les and how he'd said his father's notes also indicated there might be something funny going on with Gladys. My mind drifted to the stream gauging station but I didn't tell Jimmy since I didn't want to send him on a wild goose chase and get him in trouble with Gus.

"What do you make of all this?" Jimmy asked me, indicating the table full of notes and pictures.

"It looks like maybe Bruce wasn't satisfied with the way things were handled back then and had been investigating it himself all these years."

"For fifty years?"

He had a point. Fifty years was a long time to investigate something. "Maybe not all this time. It could be that the recent events with Charles' brother dying and Steve selling stuff off brought it all up again and he decided to look into it."

"Maybe he was looking into it because *he* had something to hide," Jimmy suggested.

"He might have had something to hide from fifty years ago, but he certainly didn't bash himself in the back of the head, so even if Bruce Norton *did* have a secret, there's someone else out there now who has one, too."

WE GOT BACK to the shop with a few hours to spare before I had to head out to Van Dorn's. When I opened the door, something caught my attention behind me. I looked over to see a black car and I got the distinct impression the driver was watching me, even though I couldn't see through the dark windows. Had it been following me?

I shrugged and entered the shop. I wasn't worried. Felicity and Claire must have changed cars—didn't they think I would know it was them?

Ranger greeted me as soon as we stepped in. He sniffed me thoroughly and barked loudly.

"Shhh..." I stroked his ears and he calmed down. "Good boy."

Ranger must have been coming out of his funk. He'd greeted me in a similar manner when I'd gone to pick the two of them up at my house after my trip to the Moonlight Motel this morning. Except at home, he'd seemed very agitated and barked much louder. I hoped he wasn't becoming too attached to me and showing some sort of separation anxiety. I needed to find him a new home and quick.

"Ranger must smell his old home on me. He needs to find his new forever home." I glanced slyly at Jimmy but he wasn't paying any attention. He was busy petting Pandora, who had ignored me entirely and was now lying on her back while Jimmy rubbed her belly.

"Yeah, poor guy." Jimmy stood up amidst a cacophony of protesting mewls from Pandora.

The bells over the door jangled and Pepper rushed in, tea bags in hand.

"I saw you guys come in. Did you get any more clues?" She looked hopefully from me to Jimmy.

"You might say that." I filled her in on everything that had happened since I last talked to her

"Wow, you've been busy." She turned to Jimmy. "I made you some more of my special tea bags."

She handed the tea bags to Jimmy, winking at me over his shoulder when he wasn't looking.

"Thanks." He beamed at her and I noticed her looking at him approvingly like he was some sort of successful experiment. I had to admit, he did seem more confident, and looked it, too. His shoulders weren't slumped now as if he was trying to disappear, which made his chest seem broader, and I noticed how he looked me in the eye more instead of always avoiding eye contact. Of course, I liked to think his newfound confidence was due to me passing along some of my investigative skills, but maybe Pepper's teas did have something to do with it.

"So you really think Gladys is the killer? Isn't she kind of old?" Pepper's question pulled me out of my thoughts.

"I can think of several motives for her and Les Price seems to think she could have been the killer fifty years ago. I saw her chopping wood and she could definitely club someone to death."

"This Claire Voyant person ... if she really had a rivalry with him, she would have had a good motive, too," Pepper said.

"But what would her motive be to kill Lily?" I asked

"And what about Steve? Does this mean he's all in the clear now?" Pepper flopped down in one of the purple chairs. "This is getting complicated."

"Steve has an alibi for Bruce's death and he was only

a child when Charles and Lily were killed," Jimmy pointed out.

"I still don't understand why Bruce would be involved," Pepper said.

"Well, he hung around there back in the day. Maybe he didn't think the investigations were done right and wanted to make sure he did right by his old friends," I answered

"For all we know, he was involved with Lily," Jimmy added.

"Or maybe he killed one of them," Pepper said.

I hadn't thought about that, but didn't have time to mull it over, because just then, the shop door opened and Emma came in, carrying a plastic cat carrier. Ranger ran over, vacuuming his nose across the entire area of the cage while something mewled inside. Pandora looked at it quizzically, then turned and curled up in her cat bed.

I peeked inside to see the black and white tuxedo cat from the cattery.

"I was just picking up Scooter from Doc Ellis and thought I'd stop in here," Emma said, looking at Pepper and Jimmy nervously. I figured the nervous look was because she didn't know if Pepper and Jimmy would be friends of the cattery and didn't want me to say anything, so I kept my mouth shut.

"Scooter?" Jimmy poked his finger into one of the crate openings and I tensed knowing that most feral cats don't like to be poked at. Luckily, Scooter didn't seem to mind and I was surprised to see the cat butting his head up against Jimmy's finger through the holes. Emma looked a little surprised, herself.

"Scooter's looking for a good home. He's been neutered and has all his shots." Emma looked at Jimmy hopefully.

"Aww, well, I hope he finds one." Jimmy straightened. "I have to get back to the station. I'll talk to you guys later."

"Bye, Jimmy," Pepper said.

Jimmy paused at the door and gave me a pointed look. "Willa, you let me know if anything comes up."

"Will do."

"Well, I should be going back to my shop. I saw Jimmy and wanted to drop those tea bags off. Don't you think Jimmy seems more confident now?" Pepper asked.

"He does," Emma said. "Is it something in your tea or is he just a late bloomer?"

Pepper shrugged, her cheeks pink. She started toward the door, shooting me an I-told-you-so look over her shoulder.

"Well, I need to be going, too." Emma picked up the cat carrier. "I was just bringing Scooter back to the cattery from his overnight stay with Doc Evans and I wanted to be sure to stop in and talk to you about Steve Van Dorn."

"Oh, why?"

"Well, I know you thought less of him because of the whole thing with Bruce Norton." She shivered. "It is reprehensible what he did, but he's not that bad, really. He's actually quite nice. You have to understand his mother died when he was very young and he's had a hard life."

I nodded. "Okay, I'll take that into consideration."

Emma opened the door, backing out with the cat carrier in front of her. "Give him a chance," she said and then closed the door.

I thought about what she said. If Steve was devoted to cats, he couldn't be all that bad, but I still thought writing on a dead guy was creepy and I wasn't convinced he had nothing to do with Bruce's death. Luckily, I had a secret weapon I could use to test out that theory. If Steve had something to do with Bruce's death, I felt certain that Ranger would act accordingly. Either he would bark, or growl or do something to indicate that Steve was up to no good. That's why I was bringing Ranger with me to the Van Dorn's.

Too bad I wasn't taking Pandora. I knew she was going to be mad, but I couldn't very well take a cat with me.

I threw some cat treats in her bowl.

"I'll be back to get you in a few," I yelled. I expected a lot of angry mewling and hissing, but instead there was silence. She must have sensed I was leaving her here and taking Ranger and had gone off somewhere to sulk.

I hooked Ranger's leash to his collar, grabbed my leather hobo bag and jangled my keys at the door. Pandora must have been really mad, because I locked up and then glanced back inside through the window as I walked by and she was still nowhere to be seen.

CHAPTER TWENTY

O n my way to Van Dorn's, I thought about the stream gauging station that Les had mentioned. Had Gladys hidden some sort of evidence there fifty years ago? Could Bruce's murder weapon the police had been looking for be there now?

I drove past Van Dorn's driveway to take a peek. The stream gauging station was just a small, brick structure filled with pipes and meters. I guessed it was used for measuring the flow or level of the stream that led to the larger river. I'd actually never seen it. Driving by now, I could see why—there was only an overgrown dirt trail in the woods to mark its presence. The structure itself was hidden inside the wood, and a small plaque at the head of the trail with letters and the identification number for the station—SGS 17 06-82—was the only thing that marked its existence.

Beside me, Ranger started whining, his gaze intent on something in the woods.

"You know something's in there, don't you?"

I was dying to get out and see for myself, but if I did find something, how would I explain that to Gus and Striker? They were already suspicious enough of my involvement. I turned the car around and headed to Van Dorn's.

"Don't worry, I'll think of something," I promised Ranger.

A prickle of worry settled in my stomach as I pulled into the Van Dorn driveway next to Steve's yellow Dodge. I glanced over at Ranger, who squirmed uneasily. Would he have an adverse reaction to Steve ... and if he did, what would I do?

"Looks like we're going to find out," I said aloud and Ranger looked at me quizzically as I led him toward the house.

Steve must have seen us coming, because he greeted us at the door. I tensed as he squatted and fluffed Ranger's fur, but Ranger didn't bark or growl—he went willingly to Steve, wagging his tail so hard that his rear end wriggled back and forth as Steve petted him. I guess he harbored no ill will toward Steve, but did that really prove Steve wasn't involved with Bruce's murder?

After a few minutes of mutual adoration, Steve looked up at me. "I was just taking some of the sheets off the furniture and setting the house up proper. I guess Uncle Charles deserves at least that much."

He held the door open and I stepped inside. The living room had been transformed. With the boards off the windows and the sheets removed, it looked as it must have in Charles' day. I felt as though I'd stepped through a time portal and traveled even further back than the 1960s because Charles had furnished the house in antiques.

"Wow, it looks great," I said.

"Well, I've only done the living room so far." Steve's face softened with pride as he looked around. "You know, I'm starting to get interested in Charles' story now. My father always painted him to be a bad guy, but maybe he wasn't so bad. He sure was interesting."

"Yeah, he was a celebrity in his day. Do you think he really had psychic abilities?"

Steve frowned. "Well, I don't know. But if he did, it sure would be nice if he came and told us what really happened fifty years ago."

"Indeed." I glanced around for Charles' ghost, suppressing a smile.

"I did find another photo album under the coffee table in here." Steve pointed to a two-tiered table where I could see a leather album sitting on the bottom tier.

"Let's check it out. Maybe we can get some insight into Charles' life."

"Sounds good. I'm beginning to question if Charles really did kill Lily ... or himself."

"Actually, we might be able to find some clues about that right here in the house," I said, glad to have an opening to make my case for searching the house.

"Really? Wouldn't the police have found all the clues back then?"

"Not necessarily. Once Charles died and left that note, they stopped looking into both the deaths and closed both cases." I told him about the pictures and files I'd seen, taking care not to mention that it was Jimmy who had provided them.

"He died in my office?" Steve grimaced. "That's kind of creepy."

Yeah. I thought it best not to mention he died on the very desk Steve was using, even though Steve's earlier actions with Bruce proved he didn't have any qualms about dead bodies.

"Have you looked upstairs yet?" I asked.

"I went up and looked around the other day, but didn't delve into each room. Do you think you would recognize the one that you saw the pictures of Lily in?"

"I think so." I had a pretty good memory for that kind of stuff and it had served me well down South. I just hoped I hadn't lost too much of it to middle age. "Let's start in the office."

Steve headed down the hall, with Ranger trotting

alongside him. We got to the office and I felt a chill. I hadn't thought much about the office before, but now that I'd seen the pictures of Charles dead in it, the room made me feel a little light-headed. I glanced at the desk surface, my mind conjuring up the picture of Charles, his head slumped on the desk, the note off to the right ... and the dark stain.

There was only slight evidence of that on the desk now. The blotter had stopped the blood from staining the wood except for a few spots. I didn't point them out to Steve.

Steve had pretty much taken over the room with his printer, computer, shipping boxes and a pile of items, which I bent down to inspect.

"I was gonna list those on eBay." He glanced at the computer. "But now I kind of feel like a heel, selling his stuff off like that."

"Well, I guess you'd have to sell it sometime, unless you plan to move in and live here."

"Oh, no, I couldn't afford the upkeep, plus I have responsibilities at home." He leaned toward me and lowered his voice. "My feral cats and all."

I nodded, bending down to look under the desk where I noticed a small stain that marred the Oriental rug. But no clues. "Did you look in the desk drawers?"

"Yeah, nothing in there but pens and paper."

I opened them one by one. Old roller ball pens of

good quality and writing paper. I fingered the sheaf of thick, manila writing paper, embossed with Charles' initials. Probably the same paper used to write his suicide note.

I sighed. The room didn't have any clues as to who had been here the night Charles died, or if it did, I couldn't find them.

"Let's look upstairs," I suggested.

The three of us ascended the ornate stairway. At the top, a wide hallway led off in both directions. I turned right, peeking into the rooms to see sheet-covered furniture. I passed several bedrooms, then a bathroom in black and white tile with an old, claw foot tub. I remembered the fireplace in Lily's room—rounded, white marble with a cherub in the center—and stopped in front of a room that fit the bill.

"I think this is it, but I need to uncover the furniture to see for sure."

"Okay." Steve pulled the cover off the bed to reveal that it was still fully made with silver satin bedding. The dresser and vanity were next and sparkled with 1930s splendor, as if they had just come out of the factory. They were the same as the furniture in Lily's picture.

"This is the room." I angled my head to inspect the Oriental rug. I could barely discern a stained area, which the pattern did a good job of masking.

We searched the drawers and closet—all empty.

Feeling discouraged, I got down on my hands and knees to look into the dark crevices of the closet. Maybe something had rolled in there? I stretched to reach into the corners, my spirits sinking when I came up empty.

"There's nothing in here." I turned back to the room. From my perspective seated on the floor, I had a clear view under the furniture and a spark of light under the bed caught my eye.

"Wait a minute." I crawled over and stretched my arm under the bed, feeling around. My fingers brushed against something cold and smooth. I inched under a bit more and grabbed it, pulling my arm out to find a small, silver jar in my hand. It was empty with no cap, but a label on the front read 'pounce'.

"What the heck is pounce?" Steve asked. "Is that something for cats?"

I laughed. "No. It's for ink ... fountain pens or quill pens. It helps the ink dry. This one is small so you could carry it in your purse." I looked around the dressers for evidence of fountain pens, but the surfaces were bare. "A lot of people like to dabble with ink and fountain pens and use old school methods, such as helping the ink dry with pounce. I guess Lily must have been one of them. A lot of people used fountain pens back then because roller pens were fairly new."

"Oh. Well, she sure wasn't killed with a pen."

"No, that's for sure. I guess it was a long shot to find a clue here, anyway."

"Yeah." Steve looked as disappointed as I felt. "Hey, we still have the photo album."

I brightened. "Yeah, let's go check that out."

Unlike the album in the library that had informal, candid shots, this album was filled with pictures taken at various parties. The pictures seemed more posed, almost as if they might be for publicity, and the people were dressed to the nines. The photographs were mostly black and white, held into the book by little corner pieces that had been pasted on the thick, black pages. I saw a lot of the same faces—those must have been the 'regulars'. Some of the pictures had handwritten notations in white ink.

I wondered which one was Bruce. Since I'd only seen him in death with graffiti on his forehead, it was hard to tell. I scanned the writing under the pictures and found him—a tall, handsome man in a nicely tailored suit who appeared with Charles a lot. They must have been good friends. No wonder he was looking into his murder.

"Looks like they had some fun parties," I said.

"Yeah. Very fancy." Steve pointed to the full-skirted cocktail dress on one of the women.

"Is that Emma?" It was hard to think of the tiny, old church lady as ever being young.

"I don't know, but here's Gladys." Steve pointed to a

woman in a plain dress standing in the background of several of the pictures.

"And this looks like Lily." She was much more beautiful in this picture as compared to the one I'd seen at my shop.

Another woman who appeared in many of the pictures stood out. She wore extravagant flapper-style dresses, even though they must have been out of style when the pictures were taken fifty years ago. I noticed she also had an armful of bracelets and several necklaces.

I did a double-take and brought the photo closer to my face. I recognized one of those necklaces—intertwined serpents with a chalcedony stone in the middle.

My eyes flew to the handwritten note under the photo naming the people. My heart skidded in surprise when I saw the name 'Claire Voyant' and then I recognized who she was.

Charles' rival, Claire Voyant, was actually Claire Smith-Baker.

"THIS WOMAN here was your uncle's rival back then." I pointed to the picture of Claire.

"Why would he invite his rival to his parties?" Steve asked.

I pressed my lips together. "I was wondering that

same thing. I saw a newspaper article about them, but maybe the party was before they became rivals. They might have been friends who had some sort of falling out."

This sure did add a twist to the story. Could Claire have had something to do with Charles' death? She was in town ... maybe she'd even been here when Bruce was killed.

I didn't have time to think about this new twist, because just then Ranger started barking like crazy at the window.

"What's that about?" Steve jumped up and ran to the window.

I joined him and looked out to see Pandora in the side yard, chasing a butterfly.

"Oh, it's just a cat," Steve said.

"Not just any cat ... *my* cat," I said, wondering how Pandora had gotten all the way out here. Had she stowed away in my jeep? I guess that explained why she was nowhere to be found when I left the shop.

Ranger looked up at me, panting and wagging his tail.

I narrowed my eyes at the Golden Retriever. "Did you know about this?"

"Woof!"

"I had better go get her." I wasn't sure what I was going to do with her when I got her. Drive her back to the store and make sure the cat door was locked, I supposed. I didn't want to leave her loose here for fear she would wander out into the woods and get lost.

"I'm good at catching cats," Steve said, and the three of us headed out the front door.

Pandora was in midair when we spilled out onto the porch and she turned her head in our direction, then landed on all fours, facing us. Ranger trotted over to her and the two of them sniffed a greeting.

"Pandora, come," I commanded.

She looked at me, flicked her right ear and then turned her back, flitting off to smell a tall weed, her tail up straight like an exclamation point, the kinked end pointing toward the woods up the road.

"Let me try." Steve slowly walked down the porch steps toward Pandora, who blinked at him inquisitively. When he got within three feet of her, he crouched down, holding his hand out. "Hi, Pandora."

She inched forward, cautiously sniffing his hand, but when he made a move to scoop her up, she darted away, shooting me a reproachful look.

Steve stood up. "We may have to try to corner her."

At those words, Pandora let out a haughty meow and flounced away toward the end of the yard, Ranger following behind her.

"Pandora! Ranger! No!" My heart plummeted. They were heading toward the road, and even though there wasn't any traffic to speak of, I still didn't want them out there.

My shouting only made them go faster and I bolted off the steps after them with Steve following behind. They ran to the road and took a right, almost as if they knew where they were going.

"Crap," I said and started running faster. The woods were deep up here. Panic lapped at my gut as I realized that if they got lost in there, we might never find them.

They had turned into the woods near the pumping station and were headed to the west, Pandora in the lead, her kinked tail bobbing up and down as if pointing the way. Ranger followed happily with his nose to the ground. Steve and I navigated the woodsy terrain, cursing loudly. Finally, I could hear the sound of the river. Pandora slowed her pace to a trot and we were able to catch our breath, but not catch up to the animals.

"Pandora, please stop!" I gasped, trying to suck enough air into my lungs to keep me powered.

And then, mercifully, she stopped. She and Ranger looked at the ground and then at each other. Pandora stuck out a paw and batted some leaves around, revealing the ground beneath which had been freshly dug.

"Meow!" Pandora put on her cutest look and rubbed against my ankles, then trotted back to the leaves and then back to me.

"What's that?" Steve asked between breaths from his bent over, hands on knees position.

"I'm not sure." I squatted to get a closer look. A long, wooden piece was halfway buried under the leaves. My heart stuttered as I brushed the leaves aside and recognized what it was. A board, but not just any board. One of the porch columns from the Van Dorn house ... and, if I wasn't mistaken, the end was covered in blood.

"Is that what I think it is?" Steve squinted down at the piece of wood.

"Yep. This could be the weapon that killed Bruce Norton."

"Meow!" Pandora purred proudly.

I reached out to pet her and this time she didn't dart away. "Yes, you did good."

"How strange," Steve said, stroking Ranger. "It's almost as if they led us to it."

"Yeah. Weird." I eyed Pandora suspiciously. "We need to call the police."

I pulled my cell phone out of my pocket and checked for a signal. No bars. "There's no signal here, let's go back to the road and see if we can call out."

I looked around to get my bearings so I could lead the police back to where the column was. On the right, I could see the gauging station about three hundred feet away. That would be my landmark. We headed out of the woods, this time with Ranger and Pandora trotting beside us obediently. As we approached the road, I saw a black car lurking on the side.

"Hey!" I broke into a run, intending to yell at Felicity and Claire and tell them to stop following me, but the car sped off as soon as it saw me coming out of the woods.

"Who was that?" Steve asked as we watched the car disappear in a cloud of dust.

"I'm not sure, but I think it's Felicity Bates—she's been following me."

"Why? And who is she?"

"I'm not sure why. We've had sort of an ongoing feud. And not only that, but she's been hanging around with your uncle's rival, Claire, except she calls herself Claire Smith-Baker now."

Steve's brow wrinkled. "The lady from the pictures? Why would she change her name and what would she be doing around here?"

"I have no idea, but she just earned a spot on my suspect list." I glanced down at my cell phone. Three bars. I punched in Augusta's number, bracing myself for the onslaught of her disapproval.

We brought the animals back to Van Dorn's and put them in the house, then waited at the end of the road for Gus. I figured Pandora could keep herself busy sniffing around inside the house and hoped she wouldn't get out and wander off.

It didn't take long before the brown Sheriff's car turned the corner, with a black SUV behind it that made my heart flip—Striker.

Gus got out of the driver's seat, scowling in my direction. She was all business. "Okay, where is this murder weapon?"

"We're not sure that's what it is," I pointed out.

"Right. Well, show me where it is and we'll figure that out."

Striker had gotten out of his SUV, his brows raised at me.

"Chance, how come you always seem to be finding dead bodies and murder weapons?" He teased me good-naturedly and I just shrugged as we all started off toward the road. Jimmy jumped out of the passenger seat and bounded over to join us. It might have been my imagination, but I thought he shot me a conspiratorial wink behind Augusta's back.

We followed the tamped-down undergrowth and easily found the spot in the woods.

"You guys stay back." Augusta barked the order toward Steve and me while she squatted to inspect the board. Jimmy whipped out a camera and took pictures from various angles. Striker stood beside me, watching.

"So what were you two doing way out in the woods,

anyway?" Striker's left brow ticked up as his gray eyes drilled into mine.

I felt my face flush. What was he getting at?

Steve chuckled. "Nothing like that. We were chasing Willa's cat and Ranger. They're actually the ones that dug this up."

Augusta frowned at me. She was hard to please. Here I'd delivered the murder weapon practically to her front door and she was still giving me a sour face.

"You don't seem very happy about finding the murder weapon," I said.

"I'm happy the murder weapon was found, just not that *you* were the one to find it." She motioned to Jimmy, who carefully picked up the weapon with latex-gloved hands. It was about twice the thickness of a baseball bat and about three feet long—large enough for even a small person like Gladys to get enough momentum to swing and crack a skull.

"We need to section off the area and do a grid search," Striker said. "There could be other clues and they're going to be hard to find with all this undergrowth."

"Maybe we could just have Willa lend us her cat," Gus said sarcastically.

I laughed along with everyone else, but I had to wonder ... this wasn't the first time Pandora had led me to a vital clue in a murder case.

"I'll need statements from the two of you." Gus

gestured to Steve and me. "Jimmy, maybe you can drop the evidence back at the car and get their statements."

"Sure thing." Jimmy made an 'after-you' gesture with his free hand and we started toward the road.

Jimmy separated us as per police protocol and I waited in the driveway while he took Steve's statement inside. Steve stayed in the house and Jimmy came out, notebook in hand.

"That was pretty good work," he said. "How did you know the murder weapon was there?"

"Well, actually, I didn't. Not really. Les Price had told me his father thought Gladys hid something at the gauging station back fifty years ago, and I figured if it worked back then, she might think it would work now."

Jimmy glanced up the road in the direction of the station. "So we might find some evidence for Charles' and Lily's murders there, too?"

I shrugged. "Maybe."

Jimmy nodded, then narrowed his eyes at me. "But how did you find exactly where it was? That's a pretty big area and the police have already done a search here."

"Oh, that really *was* Pandora. She must have stowed away in my car or something and I saw her here out in the yard. When I came out to capture her, she ran off. I chased her and she and Ranger stopped at the weapon to sniff it." I realize that Pandora had unwittingly given me the perfect excuse to find the murder weapon ... sometimes her disobedient behavior did come in handy.

Jimmy frowned. "That's what Steve said."

"Yes, it's true," I said. "So, now what?"

"We'll take it in, test it to see of that dark stuff is Bruce's blood and see if we can get any DNA. Then, hopefully we can use that DNA to find the killer."

"How are you going to do that?"

"Well, normally, we have the suspects give us samples ... but we haven't done that with Gladys." Jimmy glanced uneasily up the road. "Gus doesn't even know she *is* a suspect."

I pursed my lips. "Right! I doubt she is going to listen to me. So without a sample from Gladys, how are we going to prove that it was or wasn't her?"

Jimmy looked down at his notebook, his lips moving as if he was having a silent argument with himself. Then he looked up, a light blazing in his eye that I hadn't seen before.

"I might have to get creative. Leave that to me."

CHAPTER TWENTY-ONE

I got home right around supper and fed the animals, then laced up my white Keds and headed out on the shortcut through the woods to Elspeth's. The sun was low in the sky with only a few hours of daylight left and it slanted through the trees, leaving long shadows and flickers of golden light.

Pandora usually accompanied me to Elspeth's—she liked to hang around with Elspeth's many cats. Tonight was no exception, and she trotted along happily beside me. Ranger, not wanting to be left out, came along as well. I let him off the leash after a few minutes and he obediently stuck with us.

The shade of the dense forest cooled the hot summer night and perfumed the air with the smell of pine needles and damp earth. As I picked my way along the barely visible path, I thought about the murder weapon and the pictures I'd seen with Claire Smith-Baker. I didn't think it was any coincidence that she showed up in town now under a different name. Why the change of name? Did she have something to hide? And why was she following me?

Could *she* have been the one those love letters were written to? She was pretty keen to get those journals. She didn't mention the love letters, but what if that was what she actually meant? Or maybe there was something in the journals that linked her to Charles.

Still, that didn't make much sense. Why would she care about some old love letters ... unless they incriminated her in Charles or Lily's death in some way? And if so, could she have killed Bruce? Maybe Gladys wasn't the killer after all, though Les had said his father mentioned her suspicious activity near the stream gauging station. We'd only found the porch piece that looked like it was the weapon used on Bruce. Oddly enough, it looked like it had been buried and then dug up again, which was weird. Maybe the police would find more evidence in there that linked the two murders and, hopefully, reveal the killer.

I came to the edge of the forest, my head full of questions. Maybe Elspeth could answer some of them and once the police looked at the murder weapon, it might answer the rest. I couldn't help but smile as I looked at Elspeth's house. The old Victorian always reminded me of the gingerbread house in Hansel and Gretel, with its large wrap-around porch, intricate gingerbread molding decorating the roofline and wedges of filigree at the corners of the porch posts. The porch railings had been taken over by meandering rose bushes and were alive with lush, fragrant pink roses. To make it even more enchanting, Elspeth had it painted in pale green with pink and white trim, and she kept it neat as a pin.

As I approached, I could see Elspeth coming up from her garden, a basket overflowing with plump, red tomatoes dangling in the crook of her arm. My mouth started to water at the sight of them. She spotted me and waved, her face youthful even though she was in her eighties. Or even older. I realized I didn't actually know how old Elspeth was—it seemed like she had been 'old' since I was little and hung around with her and Gram, but of course, when you are a kid, anyone over the age of twenty seems old.

My mind drifted to the photo albums I'd seen at the Van Dorn's. Bing had said Elspeth knew him well. Had she been in some of those pictures? I hadn't recognized her if she was.

"Hi, Willa. How are you?" She'd stopped at the porch steps, waiting for me to complete the trek across her yard.

"Great. You?"

"Wonderful." She bent down and rubbed Pandora

behind the ears, then turned to Ranger. "And who is this?"

"This is Ranger, Bruce Norton's dog."

Ranger gave a little 'woof' and Elspeth patted his head.

"I heard about Bruce. Such an awful thing." Elspeth shook her head, a snow-white wisp of hair falling loose from the braid that crowned the top. "He was a nice man."

"Meow!" A fluffy Siamese appeared at the door.

"A new cat?" Elspeth had quite a brood of cats, but I'd never seen this one before.

"Yes. That's Lewis." Elspeth started up the steps. "Come on in and you can fill me in on what's been going on in town."

We went inside and Elspeth led us through the living room, with its overstuffed sofas and chairs, and into the old-fashioned kitchen.

"Sit." She gestured toward the chrome table and I slid into one of the matching yellow and white Naugahyde chairs while Elspeth set a large, juicy tomato on a cutting board and sliced it.

Lewis wound figure eight's around her ankles, looking up at her and mewing softly.

Pandora eyed the cat curiously for a few seconds, then ventured forward for a few sniffs which earned her a whack of Lewis's paw. Ranger kept a safe distance.

"How was your trip to Maine?" I asked.

"Oh, wonderful. I have some distant relatives out there. Four young girls." Elspeth chuckled, then added, "Well, I guess I should say women. The oldest is in her thirties. But I think of them as girls still. Anyway, they have a wonderful home full of family history right on the ocean in Noquitt."

"That sounds restful."

"Yes. They've had some ... things going on and I just went out to see if I could help them. Hadn't seen them in many years." Elspeth spread the tomato slices on a large plate and sprinkled them with salt, then set the plate on the table and took a seat opposite me.

I wiped the drool from the corner of my mouth, grateful when she slid a smaller plate and fork in front of me, and said, "Dig in."

Nothing tastes better than fresh-picked tomatoes that have been grown in your own garden, unless they're your neighbor's tomatoes and you didn't have to do any of the work of growing them. I slid my eager fork under a slice and lifted it onto my plate. Normally, I would just pick it up with my hands and shove the whole thing in my mouth, but I was trying to be polite. I cut off a wedge and slid it onto my tongue, reveling in how the salt enhanced the slightly acidic tang.

Across from me, Elspeth daintily chewed a slice of tomato. Lewis jumped into her lap, purring

contentedly. Ranger's eyes traveled from the tomatoes to Elspeth to me and he inched closer to
Elspeth, extending his nose toward the table for a
sniff. Lewis must not have been too keen on having a
big dog nose in his face and his paw shot out,
whacking Ranger on the head and causing the dog to
retreat.

"Now, Lewis, stop that." Elsepth's eyes crinkled at
the corners as she looked fondly at him and the cat
answered her with an asthmatic purr. "He keeps hitting
the other cats like that. I think it's his way of keeping
them in line. He has asthma, so I think he might need to
lash out sometimes. Anyway, tell me about the goings on
since I've been out of town."

I told her about Bruce's death and how Steve Van
Dorn was selling off Charles' household items.

"Bing said you were friends with Charles," I added,
reaching for another slice of tomato.

"I was. Actually, I was better friends with Bruce.
We'd gone to school together since kindergarten and I
met Charles through him. 'Course, I hadn't seen much of
Bruce for several decades. He became somewhat of a
recluse after everything that happened with Charles and
Lily."

"Did you ever go to any of Charles' parties?"

"Of course. I wasn't always this old, you know." Her
light blue eyes sparkled with the memories. "Oh, we

used to have a lot of fun. Charles was very talented, you know ... even Bing had to admit that."

"Do you think Bruce's murder is related to the murders back then? He was found in the backyard."

Her eyes turned to steel, her mouth pressed in a grim line. "Why do you ask?"

"Well, it just makes sense. I mean, Bruce hung around there back in the day. The house has been closed up for decades and then, just as it's about to be opened and looked through again, Bruce is found dead in the backyard. Plus, I don't think those older deaths were looked into very carefully."

"Why not?" She narrowed her eyes at me.

I shrugged. "I looked at the files because I got suspicious. You know how I am." I didn't want to tell her I'd gotten it straight from the horse's mouth—Charles.

She chuckled. "Yes, I do. It does seem like an odd coincidence. I never thought Charles killed himself and neither did Bruce."

"No?"

"Oh, no. He was too happy. Not the type."

"Well, apparently he couldn't live with himself after he killed Lily," I said as a way to see what Elspeth thought about Charles having killed Lily.

"So the police said. What reason would he have to kill her?"

It was a good question. Charles' ghost swore he

didn't kill her and I hadn't come across any reason for it. But, then the question was who *did* kill Lily. Maybe Gladys did if Lily found out about their affair ... or maybe it had something to do with the mysterious Claire Voyant.

"Do you remember someone named Claire Voyant from back then?"

Elspeth made a face like she'd just swigged grapefruit juice. "Indeed, I do."

"You didn't like her? I saw her in some pictures at Van Dorn's but I also read an article about how they were rivals, so I couldn't figure out why he would have invited her to his parties."

"Oh." Elspeth waved her hand. "They both were in the same business, you know. Spiritual mediums and such, but also they were both somewhat of a celebrity ..." Her voice trailed off and she gave me a knowing look.

"What's that got to do with it?"

"Well, you know how those show people are. Big egos and bad tempers."

"Do you think she could have had anything to do with Lily and Charles' deaths?"

"Why do you say that?"

"She's suddenly shown up in town with a different name."

"A different name? How odd. Was she here when Bruce died?"

"I'm not sure, but I can find out ... she's staying with the Bateses."

"Idris Bates?" Elspeth's blue eyes grew large on her delicate face.

I nodded.

She frowned down at the table, petting Lewis absently. "You said you were cataloguing Van Dorn's books, right?"

"Yes."

"You didn't happen to find any handwritten journals, did you?"

My brows mashed together so hard it almost hurt. Now Elspeth was asking for the journals, too? What was going on with these, and did they have something to do with the murders?

"No, but several people have asked."

"Who?" Elspeth looked concerned

"Bing, and Claire. She came to my shop with Felicity Bates, actually."

"Well, if you find them, for goodness sake, don't give them to the Bateses."

"Why not?"

"Oh, well ... err... you know how those people are. They're mean and they don't deserve Charles' journals." Elspeth shook her head. "You give them to Bing."

"Okay." I was planning on it anyway because I didn't

like the Bates family. I didn't realize Elspeth felt the same.

"What do you know about Gladys Primble?" If Elspeth knew Charles, she probably knew the housekeeper. Maybe she'd have some insight as to their relationship or why he left her money.

"Gladys? You mean Charles' housekeeper?"

"Yes, they were very friendly, I hear."

"True, they were. She was very good."

"Almost too friendly, though."

Elspeth eyed me curiously. "What do you mean?"

"Charles left her a sum of money in his will."

"Oh, really? That *is* odd."

"I was wondering why he might do that, and the only thing I could come up with was that they were having some sort of affair."

"An affair?" She looked at me incredulously. "Certainly not. Why would you say that?"

"Well, it's odd that he left her money, and I happen to know that he was having some sort of affair he wanted to keep secret. I figured it could be Gladys because she was married so they wouldn't want anyone to know." I leaned across the table. "I heard Lily was sweet on Charles, so I was thinking maybe Gladys didn't like that and confronted Lily. Maybe things got out of hand and she killed her, or maybe she intended to kill her. Maybe Charles found out and she killed him, too. Then when the house was opened up again, she got nervous and went back to make sure there was no evidence lying around. Bruce just happened to be there and she had to kill him to keep him quiet."

Elspeth's lips curled at the corners. "That's a pretty good theory, except it can't be right."

"Why not? Is it because Gladys is too old now? I saw her chopping wood and she's physically capable of hitting Bruce with a club, plus Bruce had a whole file on the Van Dorn deaths fifty years ago at his place, so he might have figured out Gladys did it and confronted her."

"It's got nothing to do with Gladys being old, and you're right, Charles *was* having a love affair that he wanted to keep secret, but it wasn't with Gladys Primble."

"Who was it with?"

"Bruce Norton."

PANDORA SAT *on Elspeth's black and white tile kitchen floor pretending to ignore the humans, but actually taking a keen interest in what they were saying. She hoped what Elspeth was revealing would lead Willa in the right direction.*

"Are you coming, or what?" Tigger, Elspeth's orange

tomcat, sat beside her, glaring at the fluffy Siamese in Elspeth's lap.

"What's with him?" Pandora jerked her head toward the lap cat.

"He's new ... and quite bossy," Tigger said. "As you can see, my human is coddling him because he has asthma and he is taking full advantage of her sympathies."

"I can see," Pandora replied. "He keeps hitting everyone. What a control freak."

"Well, that will soon stop. However, he is of no use to us right now and your presence is requested in the barn."

"Oh, all right." Pandora turned and trotted out of the room behind Tigger to Lewis' victorious meow—apparently, the newcomer saw their departure as some sort of accomplishment. Pandora chuckled to herself as she pictured how Otis would set this cat straight.

They padded over to the screen door at the front of the house. Tigger jumped up, expertly turning the knob so that the door cracked open. He slipped his paw into the crack and opened the door, then they all slipped out and trotted across the yard, Pandora feeling a hot breath on her shoulder. She turned to see Ranger following right behind her.

"You don't have to come this time."

"What? I want to."

"Well, it's not necessary, and I don't think the other cats like you. I'm not even sure I like you."

"But, I helped find the murder weapon."

Pandora narrowed her eyes at him. "As I recall, I was the one that found that."

"No. I don't think so. I led you to the area and told you where the bad man went."

"But I—"

"Stop it," Tigger said. "Let him come. This won't take long."

Pandora shrugged and trotted into the barn, doing a mental eye-roll. Was the creature going to follow her everywhere now? She certainly hoped not; having a dog tag along could ruin her reputation. She said a silent prayer to the goddess of cats, Bastet, that Willa would soon find him another home.

Inside the barn, the cats had circled around an orange, curly-furred cat. Inkspot looked up as they entered, his lip curling as his eyes fell on Ranger.

"Euphoria here has some enlightening news," he said.

Euphoria turned to Pandora, her yellow eyes glowing in the dimness of the barn. Pandora noticed with amusement that Otis had come down from his usual high perch atop the hay bale and was sitting next to the curvy feline.

"What is it?" Pandora asked.

"Euphoria's human is the one who served the keeper of secrets," Truffles said.

"Does she know where the important thing is?" Pandora asked.

LEIGHANN DOBBS

Otis smirked. "You mean the thing that you led us on a wild goose chase for?"

"It wasn't wild. There was something there, I tell you," Pandora hissed.

Euphoria reached out to touch Otis' large paw with her delicate one. "She may be right. My human recently came into possession of something of great importance regarding the fight between good and evil."

"You mean you know about that?" Pandora asked incredulously. She thought only the cats that frequented the barn were in on the big secret.

Euphoria nodded sagely.

"So we don't need to worry about this thing anymore?" Sasha's gray-tipped fur furrowed between her eyes.

"That remains to be seen." Inkspot's baritone cut through the air. "We don't yet know what Euphoria's human plans to do with it."

"So what should we do?" Pandora asked.

"We wait. We watch. And we get ready to take action."

CHAPTER TWENTY-TWO

*T*sat in stunned silence on my living room sofa, a salt shaker in one hand and one of Elspeth's plump, juicy tomatoes in the other. I ate the tomato like an apple, sprinkling salt on each bite, hoping it would help me digest the information Elspeth had delivered about Bruce and Charles.

My distracted gaze fell on the glass orb on my coffee table, as the clues whirled around in my head. The orb was glowing red, reflecting the color from the tomato in my hand, only much brighter. I leaned forward for a closer look and it appeared as if snow was falling inside like a snow globe.

That's odd, I thought. Then I noticed the salt shaker in my hand had tipped and was spilling on the table. The falling granules of salt must have been reflected in the orb. I threw some of the spilled salt over my left shoulder and returned to my thoughts. A niggling voice in my head told me something wasn't right ... of course, something wasn't right. My carefully built theory about Gladys and Charles had just been blown to smithereens.

This changed everything, but when I thought about it, it made sense... back then, their relationship would have been less acceptable. It might have even ruined Charles' career. No wonder the letters had sounded so desperate that no one could find out ... especially Lily.

But where did that leave me with my Gladys theory? And how did Lily's murder figure into it? Or Bruce's, for that matter.

I tried to visualize what I'd seen at Bruce Norton's house in my mind. Was there a clue on his table that I'd overlooked? I thought about the cuttlebone. Jimmy had said they were for birds, but there were no birds in any of the Van Dorn pictures. And how could a bird be a clue, anyway? Maybe cuttlebones had other uses?

That brought me back to the link between Bruce's murder and the murders fifty years ago. Maybe Bruce was going back to the house to get the love letters when he was killed? But why kill him? Obviously, whoever killed Bruce didn't want to be seen at the Van Dorn house, so it had to be the killer from fifty years ago. But who else was old enough? The only other people I could think of were Elspeth and Claire.

Elspeth had been out of town when Bruce was killed, so it couldn't be her.

I rummaged in my leather hobo bag that slouched on the couch beside me, pulled out the silver business card holder and slipped out Claire's card. Even though I really didn't want to, I had to talk to her.

Claire was quickly bubbling up to the top of my suspect list. She'd been in town during all three murders, she had a rivalry with Charles and she seemed very eager to get her hands on those journals. I had no idea what was in them, but several people were acting like they were very important and I had to wonder if they were important enough for someone to kill three people over them.

Claire answered on the first ring.

"Hi, Claire, this is Willa Chance from the bookstore."

"Yes, Willa. Did you find the journal?" Her voice raised a hopeful octave at the end of the sentence.

"No. Sorry. No journal. But I did find some photo albums and it looks like you're in them."

"Well, it's no secret I was a contemporary of Charles Van Dorn."

"So, you admit you were around when Lily Johanson and Charles died?"

"Yeees." She drew the word out and I wondered if it

was because she didn't like the direction the conversation was taking.

"And you knew Bruce Norton."

"Of course. Willa, what are you trying to say?"

"It's just that there're a lot of unanswered questions from all the deaths and you're one of the few people who was around at the times of all three of them."

A sigh came over the line. "I don't know why you would care about fifty-year-old cold cases, but if you're implying something wasn't right about them, I would agree."

My brows flew up in surprise. I had expected her to deny any knowledge, or get mad, or hang up on me, or maybe even all three. "You thought something wasn't right back then?"

"Yep. Look, if you wanna talk, I'm at Earline's Diner. They're open until ten. You can meet me here if you want."

It was eight thirty and I could get there in ten minutes. Plenty of time. "Okay, see you in ten minutes."

I snapped the phone shut and sank back into the couch. Maybe it wasn't such a good idea to meet with Claire. After all, she hung around with Felicity Bates and one of the Bates family members had tried to kill me before. Not to mention that Claire, herself, probably had something to hide if she'd changed her name. She could even be the one who killed Charles, Lily *and* Bruce.

But all my clues that had been fitting nicely into place were now torn apart and she was the only one I could think of who might have an answer.

Besides, we were meeting in a diner. What could she possibly do to me in public?

THE NEON SIGN of Earline's Diner cut through the dark night like a beacon. The large glass windows showed two lone customers inside, sitting several booths apart, reminiscent of an Edward Hopper painting.

I glanced behind me as I got out of my Jeep. On the way out, headlights behind me in the distance had mirrored my every turn, making me uneasy. Glancing back, I watched the car drive past the entrance to the diner. I noticed it was black—the same car that had been following me. How could that be possible if Claire was sitting in the diner? Maybe she and Felicity had split up or, it was just my imagination that the car was even following me? Probably my imagination.

Claire looked up and smiled when I entered. She almost looked friendly, but I didn't let my guard down. I still wasn't sure if she was friend or foe—probably foe, considering who she kept company with.

I slid into the booth opposite her, eyeing the

LEIGHANN DOBBS

remnants of eggs, bacon and toast on her plate. "Where's Felicity?"

Claire waved her hand "Oh, I don't spend all my time with her."

"No?" I raised my brow at her. "Only when you are following me around, I guess."

"Following you? We haven't been following you. Well, maybe that one time ... or twice. But you make it sound like I'm a stalker. I'm not."

"But why would you follow me?"

"To see if you have the journal. Anyway, we haven't been following you lately and my association with Felicity is only one of necessity."

"Necessity?"

"Yes, but never mind that. Do you want coffee?" She signaled for the waitress, who came over with two pots.

"Decaf, please," I said and the waitress angled one of the pots at my cup and poured, then sauntered away.

"So, what did you want to know about Charles Van Dorn?" Claire asked after the waitress was out of earshot.

My investigator's instincts kicked into gear and I leaned across the table. "How close were you with Charles?"

"Oh, we were quite close. We were in the same business, so ..." she shrugged.

"And you spent a lot of time at his house?"

"Sure, when I was in town. I wasn't here often,

274

though. I had a lot of engagements around the country, as did Charles."

"I read you were rivals, so your relationship wasn't always friendly."

She scooped some egg yolk onto a piece of toast. "Oh, that? That was all for publicity. We never had an adversarial relationship."

"Really? That's not how the papers made it out."

"Oh, the papers. That's what they do, try to create conflict where there is none. Although I will say Charles and I did encourage that sometimes ... you know, it kept people interested in us." She winked at me.

"So, you didn't have any problems with Charles? Like maybe something you might have wanted to take revenge against?"

"Of course not."

I sipped my coffee and studied her for a few seconds. "Then why did you change your name?"

She blinked. "Change my name?"

"Yes, the article in the paper called you Claire Voyant. I might never have figured out it was you if I didn't see you in one of Charles' photo albums. What are you hiding?"

She laughed—not the witchy cackle I'd expected, but a light melodious sound. "Oh, dear, that was just my stage name. It was perfectly acceptable back then."

I narrowed my eyes. "So you didn't have a falling out with Charles before he died?"

"No, in fact I was there that day."

My brows flew up. She was *there*? That could mean two things: either she might have a clue about who killed him, or she did it herself.

"You were at the house the day he died?" I asked. "Why?"

She shoaled some eggs onto her fork. "We were trying to talk to Lily's spirit, if you must know."

"You were?"

She nodded, swallowed and patted her lips with a napkin. "Yes. As you know, Charles and I were mediums, so it seemed the natural thing to do."

"To do for what?"

"Why, to talk to Lily, of course." She gave me a knowing look and leaned across the table, touching my arm with her hand. "You do know what I mean, don't you?"

I shrank back, squirming in my seat. Did she know about me, or was she just acting cagey, trying to feel me out? I decided to keep quiet—I didn't want the word to get out about my unique talents.

"Why did you want to talk to Lily. Was it about her murder?" I asked.

"Of course. Lily was a dear friend." Claire's face pinched.

"So you thought she'd reveal her murderer? But why not leave that to the police?"

Claire made a face. "The police didn't take the case seriously. I got the impression they thought we were 'outsiders', not worth their time. Plus, I don't think they thought very highly of show-people. They didn't listen to anything we said, so we decided to take matters into our own hands. I knew Lily was being stalked by someone, but the police wouldn't listen."

"Charles?"

"Goodness, no!" She looked at me as if I were crazy. Knowing what I knew about Charles and Bruce, I figured it wasn't him, but I'd wanted to see what Claire thought.

"Who, then?"

"We never found out. There were so many people around in those days. But Lily was terrified. She said she'd gotten some strange notes. Of course, she did have an eye for Charles but he did not return her feelings." Claire gave me a knowing look.

"So, you don't think Charles killed her?"

"No, he was no killer."

"But the paper said she had his cuff-link and that she had spurned his interest."

"The cufflink was a plant. Charles had said his favorite pair had gone missing during the house party that weekend."

I settled back in my seat, my palms wrapped around the mug of coffee in front of me. "Who else was there the night Lily died?"

Claire pressed her lips together and looked up. "Let's see. There was Bruce, me, Bill Parker, Charles, Lily, and that annoying writer."

"What about house staff?"

She shoved her food around with her fork while she thought. "I seem to remember Gladys was there and the cook—Mabel something-or-other. The cook stayed in the kitchen. I didn't know her well but Gladys was always around. She was more like a sister to Charles, especially after he and his brother had a falling out."

"And you didn't notice anyone acting strange or anything weird happening?"

Claire shook her head. "No. We found Lily the next day and she had the cufflink. Charles claimed he was being framed but the police didn't listen."

"And what about the night Charles died? Who was there?"

"The same people ... well, except Lily, of course. We wanted a small group because we were hoping Lily would name her killer and we could try to clear Charles."

"And did she? Did you talk to Lily?"

"No. We couldn't even do the séance because someone had taken Charles' crystal."

"Crystal?"

"Yes, he always used a large, round crystal when he contacted the departed. He couldn't talk to them without it, but that day it was missing, which was odd, because naturally he protected it like gold."

"What about you? Couldn't you talk to her? Your card says you are a medium."

Claire smiled patiently. "Yes, but unfortunately, Lily didn't come to me. I can't just conjure people up at will. They have to come to me. I think you know that not all of us have the talent to manifest at will."

I studied her as I took another sip of coffee. Was she being evasive or telling the truth? I couldn't conjure up ghosts when I wanted to, either, so I had no reason to doubt her. Plus, I'd been peppering her with questions pretty hard and she seemed unfazed. My gut instinct told me she was telling the truth.

"So, you were the last person to see Charles, then?"

"Well, I wasn't the very last person to see him. The usual gang was still there when I left. I had to catch a train that night and couldn't stay over."

"What about Gladys? Was she still there?"

Claire thought for a moment, then shrugged. "I guess she must have been. She was always there."

CHAPTER TWENTY-THREE

I woke up the next day with a headache. The Van Dorn case was getting confusing and I wasn't sure I could trust any of the information I'd gotten from Claire. I hoped Charles would make an appearance today and clear up a few things for me.

I dressed in a silky, black tank top and tan capris. Not that I was dressing for the dinner date I had with Striker or anything, but I did take some extra time to tame my red curls and swipe on mascara.

I got to the shop early and the regulars came in with their coffees. Ranger flopped down in front of Josiah and Pandora shot me a disgusted glance, reminding me I needed to find a forever home for the Golden Retriever or I would soon be too attached and end up keeping him for myself. I had considered Striker but hadn't seen him with the dog enough to try to coerce him into taking him.

LEIGHANN DOBBS

"I see you still have Bruce's dog," Bing commented, as if reading my mind.

"Yep, trying to find him the perfect new home."

Ranger looked up at me, a deep V creased in the area in between his eyes as if he knew what I had said.

I crouched in front of him, rubbing his ears. "I'd love to keep you, but I'm not set up for a dog."

"Meow!" Pandora huffed from her cat bed and we all laughed.

"Well, at least he doesn't seem depressed anymore," Hattie said.

"Yeah, he's a good dog. He'll make a great pet for someone." I raised my eyes at the four seniors.

Bing held up his hand. "Not me, I travel too much."

"We're cat people." Cordelia looked at Hattie and she nodded in agreement.

"I've got a dog and she's very jealous," Josiah said.

I wasn't surprised none of them wanted to take on a large Golden Retriever. I had a couple of good candidates in mind, anyway.

"So what's going on with the investigation? Do you have the inside scoop?" Hattie looked at me over the rim of her Styrofoam cup.

"I heard the murder weapon was found," Bing said.

"Yeah, I guess Gus is analyzing it for clues or whatever she does. I haven't heard anything."

"Hmm. Very unsettling." Josiah rose from the couch

282

and tossed his cup in the trash. "Well, I gotta get on with the day."

The others murmured similar farewells and they all shuffled toward the door. Jimmy came rushing in, just as Bing pulled the door open. He nodded to the four seniors as he squeezed past them in the doorway.

"Willa, I have some news!" he said, then looked back at the foursome who had paused in the door to see what he had to say.

"Oh, err... we'll see you tomorrow, Willa." Bing ushered the others out reluctantly.

"Did you find anything on the murder weapon?" I asked as soon as the door closed.

Jimmy's eyes sparkled with excitement. "Yes, that *was* Bruce's blood on the end. There was also some hair which was not Bruce's and a partial fingerprint."

"Whose fingerprint?"

Jimmy's face fell. "That's the problem. AFIS didn't come up with a match, so it's someone who has never been in the system. We don't know who it is."

"And you think the hair was from the killer?"

"Well, it could be."

I chewed my bottom lip. "But if the fingerprint isn't in the system and all we have is some hair, how can we find out who the killer is?"

Jimmy shuffled his feet, darting a nervous glance out the window. He leaned toward me and lowered his voice.

"Yesterday, after I saw the hair, I did something to help the case that I probably shouldn't have done."

My eyes widened. "What?"

"You can't tell Augusta. She won't like it."

I made a zip-your-lip motion. "I promise."

"I figured your theory about Gladys was a good one, so I went out to pay her a visit. The hairs on the club were gray. Gladys has gray hair." He shrugged. "So, I simply got a sample of hair to match it."

"That doesn't sound like anything bad."

"Well, it's not really. Except it was without her permission."

"You stole her hair? How did you do that without her knowing?"

Jimmy smiled proudly. "I took a look around her place and happened to find some on her hairbrush. Saw that on TV once."

I noticed Jimmy was standing taller, his shoulders no longer slumped. Apparently, he had gained some confidence and I felt a rush of pride that I had helped him a little with that. "But will that stand up in court?"

"No, but I just did it to prove or disprove it was her. I figure if we can prove the hair is hers we can have probable cause to get her fingerprint and match it to the one on the murder weapon, and then we can arrest her."

"Well, that was very clever!"

"Yeah," Jimmy said proudly. "She wasn't very

friendly, either, which makes me believe that your theory about her is correct."

"Oh? She wasn't unfriendly to me, but she did kind of brush me off."

"She seemed really put out when I was there. She said she didn't like visitors and now she'd had three in two days."

"Three?"

"You, me and Les Price."

I narrowed my eyes. "Les Price? I guess he must have gone right after I talked to him about Gladys. Probably trying to get a scoop for his book. Well, I suppose I can't really blame him. And that means one thing—Les thought my theory about Gladys could be right, too."

A customer came in and Jimmy looked at him nervously.

"I gotta go." He leaned closer to me and whispered. "Don't tell anyone until I have something official."

Then he winked and disappeared out the door.

I spent the next several hours waiting on customers, my brain whirling with the news. Was it really Gladys? Now that I knew she wasn't Charles' lover, my initial theory about them couldn't be right, but what if she had another motive? Why did Charles leave her money? Was she supposed to do something for him after he died?

Of course, Gladys wasn't the only one with gray hair ... Claire had gray hair and I already knew she was deceitful. She might have even lied to me about the rivalry being just for show and about what time she left Charles' that night. I remembered seeing a ticket stub at Bruce's place. Would that prove Claire had lied or would it prove she had told the truth?

And what about the talcum powder Charles said they found on Lily—could that have come from Claire? Maybe it wasn't talcum powder at all. Claire was known to hang around with Felicity and Felicity fancied herself to be some sort of witch. What if Claire was, too, and had sprinkled some sort of powdery potion on Lily?

None of it really seemed to add up. I was missing something important. I squeezed my eyes shut and tried to picture Bruce's house with his table of clues. I remembered the one odd thing—the cuttlebone. What did birds have to do with Lily and Charles' murders?

The shop was in a lull so I scooted over to my computer and Googled 'cuttlebone'. Jimmy was right. It was the internal structure of a cuttlefish. The picture of them was not appealing and I would probably think twice before jumping into the ocean now that I knew they could be swimming around in the water. The bone was loaded with calcium and used for supplementing the diets of birds, chinchillas, hermit crabs and snails. It could also be ground up and used in toothpaste, (yech) and as a polishing powder, and in antacids, (double yech) or as an absorbent to help dry liquids. Interesting, but how did any of that tie into Lily or Charles' murder?

I had to admit, I was in quite a quandary. Claire's clues could be misdirection. She knew Charles needed the crystal to talk to Lily's ghost. Maybe she didn't want Lily's ghost to speak and took the crystal, then killed Charles later on because he was getting close to figuring out who the killer was.

Of course, the same could apply to Gladys. She'd have access to the whole house and no one would question her skulking around and taking the crystal. Or maybe she was blackmailing him about Bruce. She would have had to have known what was going between them. Maybe Charles stopped paying so she killed him. But if that were true, why would he leave her money? One thing was for sure. It had nothing to do with Gladys' son—Charles was not the father.

My thoughts were interrupted by my phone blaring out the theme from the *Pink Panther* and I pulled it out of my hobo bag. It was Jimmy.

"Great news," his deep voice boomed over the phone.

"What?"

"The hair was a match."

"You mean Gladys is the killer?"

"Well, it looks that way. We're on our way to pick her up now and get her fingerprinted to see if we can match the partial on the murder weapon."

"Wow, that's great. Good work." My heart warmed for him. I hoped he'd get the credit for breaking the case.

"Thanks. Couldn't have done it without you. Gotta run."

Jimmy disconnected and I stood there, phone in hand, daydreaming. It was hard to believe after all this that the three cases were about to be solved.

"Gladys was not my killer!" Startled, I dropped the phone on the counter and whirled around to see Charles' ghost at my elbow.

"Well, it looks like she killed Bruce."

"No, it can't be."

"There's physical evidence."

Charles wrinkled his face at me. "She's no killer. We were as close as peas in a pod. She was a dear friend as well as my housekeeper."

"I hate to tell you, but we found her hair on the murder weapon."

"Pishaw. I don't believe it. And, furthermore, she could not have killed me."

"Why not?

"She was in New York City that day.

"What? Claire said she was at your house."

"Oh, Claire—she has a bad memory. You can't go by what she says. Besides, *why* would Gladys kill me?"

That was a good question. "Why did you leave her money?"

Charles' eyes darted around the shop. "You have to trust me on this. There was a reason ... a reason that is bigger than any of this. But it's got nothing to do with my murder."

I sighed. He seemed like he was telling the truth, but there was one thing that was bugging me. Elspeth had said Charles' suicide note was written in fountain pen but Charles never used fountain pens. Wouldn't Gladys have known that? And if she did, would she have made that mistake? I decided to test Charles out and see if he really did hate fountain pens.

"I heard Gladys bought you a special fountain pen that you used to write the suicide note."

Charles wrinkled his face up. "What? Where did you hear that? It's not true. I hated fountain pens and Gladys knew it. In fact, she hated them, too—ink flying everywhere and splotching up the paper. Oh, I know some people loved using them. Like that writer, Sal Price—always fiddling with his inks and papers and whatnot. I mean, really, why use one of those when you could use a nice, neat, roller pen?"

So, Elspeth had been right. Charles didn't write that note, and if Gladys did, she probably wouldn't have used a fountain pen. I felt a prickle of doubt starting to grow in my chest.

"How can you be so sure it wasn't Gladys? You said you didn't remember."

"I vaguely remember that day. Gladys left in the morning to meet her sister in New York. Back then, the train still stopped at Downtown Station and we all took it."

"So, what happened that day?"

"I only remember we were going to try to contact Lily to see if she could name her killer, but my crystal was missing. I couldn't contact Gladys. There were no easy calling contraptions back then like you have now." He pointed to my cell phone sitting on the counter where I'd dropped it. "And then I don't remember what happened after that."

My stomach sank as I listened to Charles. If he was right, Jimmy was about to make a big mistake that could hurt his career ... and I was partly responsible. Not only that, but my gut instinct told me that Charles was right.

Gladys wasn't the killer.

But if it wasn't Gladys, then who was it? Claire could have been lying about catching the train. Or there could have been another person there lurking about, waiting for everyone to leave so he could do Charles in.

The problem was I had no idea how to make sense out of all the clues I had whirling around in my head and the clock was ticking. I had to do something soon.

"Right, Willa?" Charles was saying.

"What?"

"You're going to find the killer so I can move along my path, right?"

"Oh sure, I just don't know how—"

"Meow!" Pandora let out a screech from the other side of the room as she snaked her paw under the couch and batted at some unseen object. The object skidded across the floor. It spun at my feet, then slowly came to a stop. A silver pen.

I stared at the pen. A light bulb blinked in my head and suddenly all the pieces of the puzzle started to snap in place.

"I know who the killer is and how I can prove it!"

As I headed for the door, my phone broke out in song. I glanced at it as I ran by the counter. It was Jimmy, but I didn't have time to answer it nor did I want to tell him what I was up to, just in case I was wrong. I didn't want to get him into any more trouble than I'd already gotten him into. I'd call him back once I was sure I could back up my theory with evidence. I raced past Charles, leaving the persistent phone on the counter.

As I turned to lock the door, I saw Pandora and Ranger looking at me curiously. Charles was standing there, smiling.

"Go get 'em!" I heard him yell as I locked the door and raced to my car.

CHAPTER TWENTY-FOUR

I was glad the entire police force of Mystic Notch was at the station processing Gladys, because I surely would have been pulled over for speeding if any of them had seen me race out of town.

I was going on gut instinct now, trying to prove my theory and, of course, I could still be wrong. Gladys *could* have done it and Charles might just be too loyal to see. Or maybe it was Claire ... or even Bruce.

But one thing still bugged me. The argument between Bruce and Les Price in the Mystic Cafe the night before Bruce died just didn't ring true. No reasonable person would get that upset over what Les was writing. Sure, most of the people put that down to Bruce having dementia, but just looking through his house, I could tell Bruce was as sharp as a tack—especially with the way he'd organized and arranged the clues on his dining room table.

What if Les Price knew about Bruce and Charles and was going to write about that in his book? Bruce had hidden the affair all these years and maybe he wanted it to remain a secret. But if that was the case, why didn't Les tell me about Bruce and Charles when I told him about my theory on Gladys? Instead, he'd played along. Maybe he didn't want to let on about the affair so it could be a shocking surprise in his book. But would he go so far as to try to incriminate an innocent person?

I sped past Van Dorn's, glancing over at the stream gauging station. The murder weapon had been found there ... on a clue I'd gotten from Les Price. Then, it hit me like a medicine ball to the gut as I stared at the sign SGS 17 06-82. That wasn't an identification number at the end—it was a date. The station was built in 1982—almost *thirty* years after Charles had died.

I remembered a conversation with Pepper about Ruth Walters complaining about the traffic on that road. Pepper had said 'she's been complaining since they put that in thirty years ago'. I could have kicked myself for not picking up on it at the time. Either Les Price had been lying, or he'd been lied *to*. He'd said his father had seen Gladys coming out of the gauging station, but that was impossible—it hadn't been built yet.

It was all coming into place. I just needed to check

one thing and then I could call Jimmy with more confidence in my theory. I pulled up in front of Bruce's cabin, my nerves suddenly on edge. I didn't think anyone had followed me, so why did I feel so uneasy? Probably because I was about to break into Bruce's cottage.

But I didn't have to break in. The door was still unlocked from my earlier visit with Jimmy. I remembered how I'd had to run back in to get Ranger's things after we'd left. Jimmy and I had already been almost to the car when I realized I'd never picked them up. Jimmy had given me the key and I'd run back in while Jimmy waited in the car. I was supposed to lock it, but must have forgotten in the excitement. I realized that twenty years ago, I never would have forgotten, but now my slipping memory was paying off. Maybe pushing fifty had its benefits.

The door creaked open and I stepped inside. It was eerily silent and I felt a little creeped out being there by myself. I hurried over to Bruce's evidence table.

Sliding out Charles' death scene picture, I squinted down at the note. It was definitely in fountain pen, but it didn't have the blotches and ink dots that Charles said he hated about using those pens. The penmanship was neat and tidy—someone had taken great care when writing the note ... and who would take such care when writing a note more than a professional writer?

I slid the ticket stubs out. Just as I suspected, they

were for the train, dated the night Charles died. One early, probably before Charles' time of death and one for the midnight train. Someone had bought two tickets and only used one. The first was merely to provide an alibi.

I picked up the bag with the cuttlebone, tapping the edges so the powder settled on the corner. White powder. Just like the powder found in Lily's hair. My memory conjured up the image of the vial I'd found under Lily's bed. I figured it had contained pounce—a powder used to make ink dry quicker. Centuries ago, people spread it on paper to make writing smoother and some people still did this today. Cuttlebone powder was absorbent—it would make a great powder for pounce.

And if the killer was someone who took pride in their writing, he or she might have carried that vial in their top pocket. The vial might have opened and the powder might have spilled out as they bent over Lily's dead body. And the vial might have slipped out and rolled under the bed.

My eyes went back to the picture of Charles. That orange fountain pen was such an unusual color. Then I noticed the cherry-red pen on Bruce's desk. I'd originally thought it was one of Bruce's pens, but now looking at the picture, I could see the pen matched the one in the picture of Charles. The pen in the picture only looked orange because of the yellow-tinted aging of the photo. I picked up the pen. It was a beauty ... a vintage Waterman.

My mind wandered back to the day I'd met Les Price in the cafe—his cherry red mechanical pencil was also a Waterman. My blood chilled as I realized it was probably from the same set as this very pen.

"Bruce wasn't arguing about what Les Price was writing, he was arguing about what he was writing *with*!" I said it aloud, to what I thought was an empty cabin.

"That's right ... that's my father's pen. Charles Van Dorn's suicide note was written by my father."

My heart seized and I spun around at the sound of Les' angry voice.

"Your father killed Charles Van Dorn?"

"That's right."

"And Lily, too?"

"Yep."

"But, why?" Les took a step toward me and I realized I was backed into a corner—he was between me and both the exit doors.

Les' face pinched. "My father was in love with Lily, or so he said. But she didn't return his affections. He killed her in a fit of passion."

"But why did he mark her forehead and why kill Charles?" I tried to keep him talking, hoping to distract him as I inched my way to the side, waiting for an opportunity to slip past him and out the door.

"He panicked after he killed her and knew he had to frame someone. Who better than Charles? He knew Lily had a thing for him and figured he could write it off as a lovers' quarrel. At first, he was just going to frame Charles, but then Charles wouldn't let go of trying to figure out who killed Lily, so he had to kill him, too."

"And you knew about it all these years?"

"Oh no, I didn't know a thing until he confessed to me on his deathbed this past winter."

"But he got away with it ... why come here now?"

"I wouldn't have, except I read about the house being inherited and the contents for sale. My father always felt that he got away with it because everyone lost interest after Charles died. The police stopped investigating ... it was a neat, tidy ending for them. But he always feared there might be something he left behind in the house that would lead back to him."

"So that's why you really came here? You're not writing a book?"

"No, I really am finishing the book, but I had to come and make sure his name wasn't tarnished."

"And you killed Bruce?"

"I had to." He gestured toward the table. "As you've deduced, he recognized the pen. I didn't understand at first why he would have even noticed it, but then once I realized the suicide note had been written with my father's favorite Waterman, I knew he'd been collecting clues."

I scrunched up my face, remembering how surprised Les had been when I'd told him about Bruce's death in the cafe. I could have sworn he had no idea. If only he'd acted the least bit suspicious, I might have figured all this out a lot sooner. "But you seemed so surprised when I told you Bruce had been killed that day in the cafe."

He laughed—not a mirthful laugh—a dark, evil one. "That's because I *was* surprised ... about the mark on his head. And a little freaked out. He didn't have that when I left him."

"Right, Steve did that." I slid my eyes to the right, judging the distance to the door.

He caught my look and stepped firmly in the path between freedom and me. "Yes, and that almost turned out to be my saving grace. When the police brought Steve in, I hoped the murder would be pinned on him and the house would get closed up again."

"So, you were the one who put the murder weapon out by the gauging station and made up the story about your father seeing Gladys out there fifty years ago?"

A malevolent smile cracked his lips. "Yep. Ingenious, don't you think? I'd actually hidden it there after the murder, then when you told me about your 'Gladys theory', I went back and planted the hair. It almost got screwed up, though. I had initially buried it so that the police wouldn't find it and when I went back to plant the clues, some animals had dug it up. I was just lucky they hadn't moved it and I could still find the thing."

Animals? My mind flashed on Pandora and Ranger. Had they been there before me?

"Anyway," Les continued, "you played right into that one."

It was true. I'd wanted my theory to be right so badly that all Les had to do was give me a gentle nudge in that direction.

"But, if that's true, how did Gladys' hair get on the murder weapon?"

"Another ingenious idea." He puffed out his chest. "I went to interview her on the pretext of writing the book, used her bathroom, got some hair from her brush and then planted it on the murder weapon. I was a little nervous that you might discover the weapon first, but you didn't and it all worked out in the end."

Under other circumstances, I might have found it amusing that he used the same technique to get Gladys' hair as Jimmy did, but not right now. Right now, I was busy trying to figure out how to get past him. I was running out of things to say and my leg was starting to burn.

"Not so ingenious, really."

"Oh, why is that?"

"Because the gauging station was put in thirty years

ago—*after* Charles' murder. Your father couldn't have told you he saw Gladys coming from there. I'm sure the police will figure that one out very soon and come looking for you."

He narrowed his eyes. "So, that's why you came back here? I wondered."

"But how did you know that I'd be coming here?"

"I've been following you. It was obvious you were getting close. I thought I'd framed that housekeeper, but when I saw you come here, I got nervous. You're just a loose end I need to tie up—just like all this evidence." He spread his hands to indicate the evidence table.

So it had been Les following me and not Claire and Felicity. Of course, now I wished Claire and Felicity *were* following me. I didn't know if they'd realize I was in danger and help me, but I would have felt a little better if *someone* knew I was out here—I didn't like the way Les had said he needed to 'tie up the loose ends'.

"The police have Gladys in custody right now, so, as soon as I get rid of this evidence and you, both my father and I will be scot-free."

Icy tendrils of fear squeezed my heart. My mind whirled to come up with an escape plan. An image of the bottle I found in Lily's room flashed through it. That pounce bottle was sitting in my purse right now.

"Not necessarily," I said. "Your father left a clue and I found it. It won't be long until they trace it, and with these clues from Bruce, both you and your father will be nailed."

Les let out a slow, unnerving chuckle. "Poor Willa, you are a little slow aren't you? The police aren't going to find these clues because I'm going to destroy them ... and you!"

Adrenalin shot through my veins as he lunged for me. I darted to the left, twisting my bad leg painfully. It gave out and I stumbled forward.

Les reached out, grabbing a fistful of my hair. Pain seared through my scalp as he jerked me to my feet. I flailed my arms wildly, trying to connect with any part of him, but he was amazingly wiry and strong for his size. He wound his fist tighter into my hair and started pushing me in front of him.

"Wait! You can't do this! The police are sure to find out!"

He laughed. "Don't be silly, Willa. I *can* do it. Thanks to your help, I've already gotten away with killing Bruce, and now I will get away with killing you!"

I tried to kick out at him, but I couldn't put any pressure on my bad leg so I was virtually helpless as he dragged me by my hair over to the door. I knew it led to the cellar because I'd opened it when I'd been there with Jimmy looking for birds. Apparently, he did, too.

He ripped the door open with one hand. "It's too bad

that your snoopiness is going to cause you to have an unfortunate accident."

He shoved me through the door, but I shot my arms out at the last second and grabbed the sides. I teetered on the top step as Les tried to shove me down. There were only five steps down to the crawl space. I knew the fall down wouldn't kill me, but I still had no intention of going down easy.

He shoved harder and I tried to maintain my hold, but my leg was throbbing with nauseating, white-hot searing pain. Stars floated across my line of sight and I hoped I wasn't going to pass out. Then he let go of my hair, and for a split second, I thought I was going to get free ... until the sole of his foot connected with my back and I toppled forward into the dark.

CHAPTER TWENTY-FIVE

*T*woke up with a mouthful of dirt and a throbbing leg. I opened my eyes to total darkness.

Where was I?

Then I remembered. I was in Bruce's basement, along with spiders, centipedes and lots of other creepy crawlies that I didn't want to think about. I bolted upright, hitting my head painfully on the ceiling. I had forgotten, Bruce's basement was a crawl space—not even tall enough for me to sit straight up in.

I rolled to my hands and knees, sharp pain tearing at my leg. Gritting my teeth, I inched forward, my hand in front of me feeling for the steps, my injured leg dragging behind me.

My hand connected with wood and I breathed a sigh of relief. The opening for the stairway was tall, so I tried to stand, crying out in pain when I put pressure on my leg.

"Damn!"

I knelt on the first step, and then used the railing to pull myself to a standing position. I hobbled up the steps and reached a tentative hand out toward the knob, not expecting it to be unlocked, but hoping it would be.

Was Les up there hatching his plan to do me in? I had no idea how long I'd been lying unconscious on the dirt floor. Hopefully, he'd left and I could bust my way out.

I tried the knob, but it didn't turn—it was locked. I pressed my ear to the door and held my breath. It was silent on the other side.

I pounded on the door.

"Hello! Anyone out there?" I knew no one would hear me. Bruce's house was too remote, but I yelled anyway because it seemed like the thing to do. I wasn't surprised when no one answered.

Taking a deep breath, I shoved my shoulder as hard as I could against the door. It didn't give an inch, but I kept at it. It was almost impossible for me to get leverage with my bad leg feeling like someone was running hot skewers through it every time I put any weight on it. I pushed and lurched, but my attempts got weaker and weaker, my stomach sinking further and further with each failed thrust.

I glanced back down into the dark basement. I couldn't budge the door, so finding an exit down there was my only hope. The house was too remote for anyone to happen by and hear me and I couldn't call for help, either, I realized, as I pictured my cell phone sitting on the counter in my shop where I'd left it.

Too bad no one knew where I was.

I leaned against the door as I contemplated my next move. I didn't relish the idea of crawling around in the pitch-dark crawl space. There was probably no way out anyway, but maybe I could find something that I could use to batter down the door.

And then I smelled it.

Smoke.

My heart froze in my chest—Les had lit the place on fire.

I rushed back down the steps, hitting my head and seeing stars again. I crawled forward, my hand out in front of me, my stomach tight with fear. I didn't know what I was more afraid of, the fire or my hand coming into contact with something creepy and crawly.

It was too dark to actually see more than a few inches in front of me and I had no idea where I was going. I closed my eyes, trying to picture Bruce's house from the outside. The basement wasn't tall enough for a door, but were there any windows? I seemed to recall it was set on concrete blocks and I figured they must have been cemented together pretty well since there were no cracks of light.

I swiveled my head around, looking for even the tiniest slice of light, but each direction was as black as the other. I had no idea which direction to go in.

The smell of smoke was getting stronger. How long before it engulfed the basement, or worse, the flaming structure collapsed on top of me? Tears pricked my eyes as I crouched frozen with indecision.

"Meow!"

A cat? Down here? No, not in the basement, the meow was too muffled. The cat was outside.

"Meow!"

Scratch, scratch, scratch.

The cat was digging. Maybe I could dig my way out? I crawled in the direction of the scratching, hope budding in my chest.

As I got closer, an oily smell permeated my senses. Oil! Bruce must have kept his oil tank down here. Then my heart seized—oil and fire didn't mix. If the fire got down here ...

I bumped into something metal. The tank, I assumed, but it was light. I remembered seeing a large propane canister tank out in the yard. Bruce had probably switched to propane and left the old oil tank in here, empty.

I pushed it aside and saw a miraculous thin circle

outline of light, the opening where they put the nozzle to fill the tank.

"Meow!" A piece of cement dropped out, making a dot of light in the circle—the rain must have been seeping in through this hole for years and probably weakened the cement.

Maybe I could scrape out enough cement to wiggle a couple of the concrete blocks loose and climb out.

With renewed vigor, I started digging at the cement, watching small points of light appear as chunks of the cement fell into the basement. The cat dug along with me on the other side and I wondered if it was Pandora. No, it couldn't be. I'd locked the cat door in the shop after her escapade at Van Dorn's and there was no way for her to get out.

"Meow." A pink nose poked its way through a small hole and I reached up and stroked the fur above the nose.

"I'm hurrying, Kitty."

It didn't take long before my fingers were raw and bleeding, but I ignored the pain and kept working. It was my only way out. Luckily, the cement crumbled easily and when I'd scratched out a good amount around an entire concrete block, I pried my fingers into one of the crevices I'd created and tugged.

The concrete block moved slightly.

I tugged again.

More movement.

I braced my feet against the wall and wedged my fingers in the crack. I tugged with all my might and the concrete block slid halfway out, revealing the sweet sight of daylight and the smell of fresh air.

"Willa! Are you in there?" Jimmy's voice rang from somewhere outside.

"Over here!"

I heard footsteps outside the wall. The cat stopped scratching and Jimmy yelled, "Get away from the wall and I'll see if I can kick the concrete block in."

I had to admit, I was a little peeved that he'd shown up when he did. A few minutes more and I'd have been able to get out on my own but, since there was a fire burning upstairs, I guess time was of the essence so I scurried out of the way.

"Okay, go!"

Jimmy kicked, and the cement block popped into the basement along with the one below it. I crawled back over and pushed my top half out of the hole. Jimmy grabbed my arms and pulled me the rest of the way out.

"Thanks!" I said after I was standing upright.

"Meow!"

I looked down to see the little black and white tuxedo cat from the cattery. "And thank you, too, but how did you get out here?"

Jimmy grabbed my arm. "There's no time for small talk. This house could blow at any minute."

My heart jerked as I looked up to see flames shooting out of the top of the other side of the cabin. They hadn't yet reached the side we were on but I could see it wasn't a good idea to hang around.

"Run!" I shouted as we headed for the woods. I wouldn't have thought I could do it, but an adrenalin spike caused by the fear of the fire must have blotted out the pain in my leg and I ran at full speed.

We were halfway to the woods when Jimmy suddenly turned and doubled back.

I skidded to a stop, turning toward him.

"What are you doing?" I yelled.

He gestured toward the woods. "Keep going!"

I did as he ordered. When I got to the safety of the woods, I turned just in time to see him scoop up the black and white cat that had remained beside the house, then turn and start back in my direction. He was about halfway to the woods when—

Kaboom!

JIMMY SOMERSAULTED into the woods and landed five feet away from me.

"Are you okay?" I asked as I watched burning pieces of wood fall to the ground some twenty feet away.

He nodded, then uncurled himself to reveal the little cat in his arms, unharmed.

"Mew." The cat looked up at Jimmy and placed its paw on his cheek.

"Aww. I guess you have a new friend," I said. "And thanks for helping me get out of there. How did you know I was there?"

"The fingerprint on the murder weapon didn't match Gladys' prints. We could tell the print was on top of the hair, and that seemed to indicate that Gladys was being framed. Then I realized Gladys had said Les was at her house before me and I figured he could have pulled the same trick with the hair and he might be the one framing her. I tried to call and warn you. When you didn't answer I got worried, so I drove up to Van Dorn's to see if you were there. I saw the smoke from the road and came here to check it out. When I saw your car in the drive-way, I ran around looking for you and that's when I saw Scooter digging." Jimmy frowned at me. "But why are *you* here?"

I told him how I had figured out Sal Price had killed Charles and Lily and I'd come to check a few of the clues Bruce had collected.

"Les was following me and knew I'd figure it out, so he decided to kill two birds with one stone and get rid of me *and* the clues in the fire." I looked at the house, my mouth set in a grim line. "He also confessed to killing

Bruce. Too bad all the evidence for Charles and Lily is now going up in flames and Les is getting away."

Jimmy rose to his feet. "He's not getting away. When I called in the fire, I told them my suspicions about Les. Hopefully, Augusta or Striker will be hot on his tail."

He extended his hand to help me up and I stood shakily, testing my leg. Some of the pain had returned, but it wasn't as bad as before. I waved off his offer of help and limped along beside him as we made our way to the front, the tuxedo cat still cradled in the nook of Jimmy's arm. The sirens got louder as we came around the side of the house and we'd just made it to the edge of the driveway when Striker pulled in.

"Chance! Are you okay?" Striker was out of the car before it even stopped. He scooped me into his arms, garnering a strange look from Jimmy who, I noticed, was still holding Scooter. The cat lounged contentedly against Jimmy's chest despite all the chaos, as if he trusted Jimmy wouldn't let any harm come to him. Emma was right; Scooter did have a good chance at getting adopted and I had a good idea by who.

"I'm fine." I wriggled to escape Striker's vise-like embrace. He held me at arm's length, checking me over.

"You look hurt. I'm calling an ambulance." He pulled a cell phone out of his top pocket.

I looked down at myself. I was covered in dirt, my shirt was ripped and I was sure my hair was sticking out like I'd been electrocuted. Not to mention my carefully applied mascara was probably running down my face, making me look like a demented mime. So much for the spiffing up I'd done earlier in the day for my date with Striker. He'd probably never want to go out with me again after seeing me like this.

I pushed Striker away. "We don't have time for that. The murderer is getting away!"

"You mean Les Price?"

"Yes!"

Striker put his hand on my shoulder, presumably to stop me from jumping up and down and scrunching my face up in pain.

"We've got that covered. After Jimmy called in the fire and told us his theory on how Les framed Gladys, Gus went out to the Moonlight Motel and brought Les in. If what Jimmy said is true, he'll soon be booked on murder charges. See, the police really do know what they are doing ... especially our rookie Jimmy here." Striker removed his hand from my shoulder and clapped Jimmy on the back. "Nice work!

Jimmy smiled proudly and my heart swelled for him.

"Well, I couldn't have done it without Willa's help."

"Oh, really?" Striker raised his left brow at me. "I thought Willa wasn't getting involved."

"Oh, I didn't ... not really. I just gave Jimmy a few

pointers. He did all the sleuthing on his own," I said, winking at Jimmy.

Striker slid his arm around my shoulder. "That's good because I don't think you need to get involved in any investigations. And judging by the way you look, I hope you've learned the lesson that it's much safer to leave the sleuthing to the cops."

I leaned into Striker. The weight of his arm on my shoulder felt warm and comfortable. He was right. It was much safer. Too bad I doubted that was going to stop me from investigating in the future.

The ambulance pulled in and Striker dragged me over.

"I'm fine, really," I insisted.

"Ohh, no ... I'm not going to listen to any of that. Your hands are all bloody and you look like you were buried alive." He picked up my hand and gently kissed the raw fingertips. "Besides, I don't want you using this as an excuse to stand me up for dinner tonight."

He still wanted to have dinner with me?

My heart warmed and I gave in, letting him lead me to the ambulance.

Gus called Striker while I submitted to the ministrations of the EMT. She'd brought Les in and the thumbprint had matched. She said he was confessing his heart out about Bruce's murder and about his father killing Lily and Charles Van Dorn.

Striker relayed the information, then his brows cut into a 'V'. "Les had some choice words about you, Willa. He said if it weren't for you poking your nose in, those murders would never have been uncovered."

I didn't know what to say, so I just shrugged.

"He said that's why you were here at Bruce's," Striker persisted.

I nodded. "Bruce had some evidence about the murders fifty years ago. I guess that's why Les had to kill him."

"Right. I get all that. But what I don't get is how you knew about those old murders and why you would poke your nose into them. Near as I can tell, you've been in the middle of this case the whole time and I can't help but wonder why, since it seems to have nothing to do with you."

I wasn't about to tell him it was because I was trying to make sure a ghost could move to the great beyond, so I plastered an innocent look on my face, shrugged my shoulders and said, "I don't know. I guess you could just say that I'm the inquisitive type."

EPILOGUE

The Van Dorn mansion had been spit-shined and polished. The boards had been removed from the windows, the sheets pulled off the furniture. The wood glowed, the chandeliers sparkled, and there wasn't a speck of dust to be seen.

I stood just inside the entry to the living room, the lemony smell of furniture polish tickling my nose as I stared into one of the many display cases that had been set up around the house. This one had a tasteful display of Charles Van Dorn's props that he used to work with, including the crystal orb, which looked amazingly similar to the paperweight that sat on my living room table. Steve had found it hidden in the fireplace in one of the guest bedrooms—the room Sal Price had stayed in the night before Charles died.

"So, what do you think?" Steve Van Dorn, decked out

in a new suit and tie with Ranger smiling at his side, spread his arms to indicate the room that had been turned into a museum.

"It cleaned up nice, and so did you." I bent to pet Ranger, stifling a smile at the pink blush that crept up Steve's neck. It turned out that Steve wasn't such a bad guy after all—just a little rough around the edges.

"Well, it certainly would fetch a lot of money on today's market," Ophelia said from the doorway, looking like she just came from a high-level meeting in her black pantsuit with beige piping. "But I am happy that if I can't make a big commission, at least the house is helping to preserve history."

I glanced around the room at the display cases, feeling a sense of pride. Sometime during this whole thing, Steve had stopped seeing his uncle and this house in the bad light his father had drilled into his head and started remembering the good times he'd had here. Instead of thinking of the items as a way to make money, he started to see the unique and interesting history of Charles Van Dorn's career.

He'd found that he couldn't bring himself to sell off the items, so he'd utilized the mystery of the Van Dorn curse in another way—he'd turned the house into a museum and tonight was the grand opening.

And the best part was, he was going to be able to

preserve his uncle's memory and treasures and make money for his cattery. He'd sold off enough items to cover the immediate need of his cattery and to do some of the much-needed repairs on the exterior of the house. Going forward, the proceeds from the museum would more than cover running both the museum and Steve's cattery back home.

I don't know if Charles knew that the home he'd loved and wanted to stay in was being preserved for history, but I felt like he would have been glad. I hadn't seen him since that last time at my shop, so I guessed he knew we'd found his killer and had gone off to wherever it is that ghosts go.

"I made you some tea to calm your opening night jitters." Pepper breezed into the room, a steaming mug in her hand. She glanced over at me, noticed my scowl and winked. I guessed since her herbal tea experiment with Jimmy seemed to have worked out, she was now going to try her teas out on Steve.

"This place looks great." Jimmy's voice boomed from the doorway and my brows shot up to see him dressed in a perfectly tailored dark gray suit. He stood tall, shoulders back, exuding an air of confidence.

When did that happen? His complexion seemed to have cleared up overnight, and I noticed for the first time that he had a rather attractive square jawline and boyish good looks.

He noticed us staring and spread his hands. "What? Am I overdressed?"

"No, you look amazing." Pepper beamed at him like a teacher watching her star pupil win the spelling bee.

He pulled at his tie. "Oh, good. I didn't have much time. I was getting ready for my new housemate."

"Housemate?" I asked.

"Do you mean Ranger?" Pepper looked from me to Jimmy. She knew I'd been considering Jimmy for Ranger's new master.

"No. Scooter, the tuxedo cat that helped save Willa." Jimmy's smile gave away his fondness for the little cat and I felt a tug at my heart—the little feral cat had saved my life and I was happy he was going to a forever home and couldn't think of anyone kinder than Jimmy to care for him. "I'm picking him up from Emma tomorrow."

"Ranger's staying with me," Steve said. Ranger looked up at him adoringly, and when Steve responded with the same look, I knew I'd made the right choice and Ranger had found the perfect master.

It was great that all these animals were getting good homes, but I didn't have time to bask in the warm and fuzzies about it because just then Gus appeared in the doorway, causing the room to fall silent. Her long blonde hair fell almost to her waist and she wore a slinky black dress that enhanced her hourglass figure. I couldn't remember the last time I'd seen her out of her sheriff's uniform, and apparently, no one else in the room could, either.

Gus ignored us as if she was used to being stared at in the slinky black dress, which made me wonder what, exactly, my sister did after hours. As far as I knew, she spent all her time crawling around crime scenes, but maybe I was wrong.

"Hi, everyone." Gus looked around the room. "Place looks good."

"Thanks." Steve shuffled his feet uncomfortably.

Gus simply glared at him for a second as if she still didn't trust him and then she turned to me.

"Willa, I wanted to thank you for helping us catch Bruce's killer." Gus scowled at me. "Jimmy tells me it was your tips that helped him break the case."

"Oh ... well ... I really didn't do anything," I stammered as Gus swooped me into an awkward hug.

"Just don't go poking around crime scenes anymore," she said. "You could have been killed and you're the only family I have."

My throat got tight and my eyes started to burn. I hoped I wasn't going to get all emotional.

Gus turned away, adopting an 'all business' attitude.

"Les Price caved in pretty quickly once we matched his fingerprints to those on the murder weapon. He made the mistake of pressing Gladys Primble's hair on top of the dried blood so it would stick, but the mere fact that the print was on the *dried* blood revealed that it was done long after the murder as a frame-up." Gus slid her amber eyes sideways at me. "He said Willa gave him the idea to frame Gladys ... apparently she had a motive for the murder of Charles Van Dorn and might have killed Bruce to cover it up."

"Yeah, well ... I did talk to him about that. You see, I was cataloguing the books here and got kind of involved in this whole Van Dorn curse." I shrugged.

Gus frowned at me. "And you felt that Charles' suicide was really a murder?"

"Yep."

She raised her brows. "Well, it turns out you were right. Les told us all about his father's deathbed confession and we found the other cuff link from Charles in Les' things. Then Steve gave us the vial you found under the bed. Turns out that was Sal Price's. He'd had to register his prints for a few of the journalistic assignments he'd had so we were able to match the prints on the vial to his. There was powder residue inside."

"The pounce that he used to dry the ink from his fountain pen," I said.

Gus nodded. "Right."

"So, Les Price will go away for murder and Charles' name will finally be cleared." I said as much for the benefit of any ghosts that might be lingering around, as for any of the humans.

"And Jimmy solved three murders, which I would say is a record for a new recruit." Gus beamed at Jimmy who shuffled his feet, his face turning pink.

"I hope that won't affect the museum badly," Ophelia said.

"Are you kidding?" Steve's lips quirked in a not-entirely unattractive—sideways smile. "The news of Charles' suicide now being proved to be murder is going to bring them in in droves. I plan to play it up big-time, too. I'm going to have a whole new display about it."

People had been steadily coming in as we'd been talking, and I decided to head down to the library. I was thrilled it was going to stay in the museum intact, but one thing still bugged me ... I'd never found the journals everyone had been looking for.

Bing, Cordelia, Hattie and Josiah were standing in the library and they turned as I entered.

"Willa, you look lovely," Hattie said, causing me to glance down at the silky, cinnamon-colored dress I'd bought especially for the occasion. I rarely wore dresses and a feeling of self-consciousness settled over me.

"Thanks," I answered, taking in the orange and yellow pantsuits the ladies wore—Hattie in orange and Cordelia in yellow with matching tops. "You guys look cheery."

Their eyes lit up.

"Thanks," they twittered.

"So, Willa." Bing raised his bushy, white brows at me. "Did you ever find those journals?"

"Did you say journals?" A voice interrupted from the doorway and we all turned to see Claire in a flowing silver dress.

Bing's eyes narrowed.

"Hello, Claire." His voice did not have friendly overtures.

Claire inclined her head at him. "Bingham. Long time, no see."

The two proceeded to turn their backs on one another and Claire fixed her gaze on me. "So, the journals went to Bing."

Bing spun around. "What? I don't have them ... you probably swooped in and charmed them out of Van Dorn."

"Charmed?" Claire's lips took on an amused tilt. "I didn't realize you thought I was charming."

Bing scowled at her. "*I* don't."

"Anyway, I don't have them." Claire crossed her arms over her chest.

"Well, *I* don't have them." Bing mimicked her crossing *his* arms over *his* chest.

They both turned to look at me.

I shrugged. "I don't have them."

"So, you mean they were never found in all this?" Claire waved her hand to indicate the room.

"Nope. But Steve's still going to continue looking for them." I smiled. "He said he might part with them if the price is right."

"Well, I certainly hope Steve isn't going to sell them to someone who keeps company with the likes of Idris Bates," Bing scoffed.

"Now, Bing, things are not always as they seem." Claire leaned toward him, her voice low. "As you well know."

Claire pulled me aside, out of earshot of the others. "Willa, I know you have a special gift and you must embrace it. You're one of the few that can help these poor souls."

And then she turned and floated out of the room, leaving a cloud of patchouli in her wake.

"What was *that* about?" Bing asked.

"Oh, nothing. She just wanted me to let her know if I found the journals."

"Well, I certainly hope you will tell me first."

"Of course, I will."

Cordelia and Hattie came over with a plate of miniature quiches and some napkins and we all took one and started to nibble and chat about Charles Van Dorn. I was into my second miniature quiche when I noticed Hattie and Cordelia had both stopped in mid-chew and were staring at something behind me.

Their cheeks turned pink and their eyes sparkled. What the heck was back there?

I spun around to see Striker, looking like he'd just stepped out of a magazine. Light gray suit, blue tie, fresh haircut and clean-shaven. The look on my face probably matched Hattie's and Cordelia's and I choked on my quiche.

Striker thumped my back. "Whoa, there. You don't have to gulp them down, there's plenty more."

I burned with embarrassment. "Thanks."

"You're welcome. And you look great." My eyes met his and I felt a trill of excitement. Striker always made me feel like a teenager on her first date and it was unnerving.

I picked up the plate of appetizers, partly to distract him and partly because I didn't know how to handle compliments. "Quiche?"

As he took one, my eyes drifted to a large mirror on the wall behind him. A big section was suddenly fogged up. I stared, as the words 'Thank You' appeared written in the fog. Then I saw the faces of Charles Van Dorn and Bruce Norton smiling at me in the mirror. They waved and winked, then turned and started walking away.

I gasped and spun around expecting to see them right behind me, but no one was there.

"Willa, are you okay?" Striker's face was a mask of concern.

I regained my composure, a smile quirking my lips. A feeling of self-satisfaction flowed through me as I realized that Charles knew we'd found his real killer and solved Lily's murder. And now, he and Bruce were spending the afterlife together. It felt good to know that I'd helped.

I turned to Striker. "Yeah, I'm fine, why do you ask?"

"Oh, for a minute there it looked like you'd seen a ghost."

PANDORA SAT *in the tall grass, watching the small house.*

"Are you sure about this?" Inkspot asked in a low growl.

"Absolutely," Euphoria purred. "I sensed the special energy as soon as my human came home with the journal."

"And you're sure this is the special journal and that she'll keep it safe?" Sasha asked.

"Yes." Euphoria's yellow eyes glowed in the moonlight. "A visitor came the other day and I sensed my human needed to fulfill her promise to Van Dorn for which he had paid her in kindness and money. She came back with the journal and the tingle in my whiskers tells me this is what we seek."

"A job well done." Otis purred beside Euphoria, and Pandora was amused to notice his eyes slitting to half-moons as he inched his way close to the curly-haired cat.

"But how do we know she will protect it?" Snowball asked.

"Just wait," Euphoria answered.

A few minutes later, the door of the small house cracked open, spilling a wedge of light into the backyard. Pandora and the others crouched down on their haunches, so the tips of their ears would be hidden by the grass, and watched as Gladys Primble hurried into the yard, a metal box in one hand and a notebook in the other.

"Is that the journal?" Scooter, the feral tuxedo cat, whispered.

Inkspot looked down at him fondly. "Yes, can you sense it?"

Pandora had introduced Scooter to Elspeth's clan after Scooter had performed a heroic deed on her behalf. Willa had locked Pandora in the bookstore when she went to Bruce's and when Pandora sensed Willa was in trouble, she couldn't get out to help her.

Pandora's caterwauling at the back door caught the attention of Scooter, who was rummaging in the dumpster, and the feral cat agreed to rush off to Bruce's and try to help the human. For this, Pandora would be forever grateful.

Inkspot had taken the little tuxedo cat under his wing and was teaching him the ways of the world.

"My whiskers are twitching. Is that what you mean?" Scooter asked.

"It's a start," Inkspot answered as they watched Gladys dig a small, but deep hole, then place the journal inside the metal box, put the box in the hole and cover it back up.

"The journal is now safe. No one will find it here and I will be on watch, protecting it," Euphoria said.

"Well, I guess we should call it a day, then." Tigger humped his rear end up, stretching his front legs out long in front of him.

"Wait. Are you sure it's safe there?" Sasha asked.

"Safe as it can be," Inkspot answered. "At least we know where it is and can keep an eye on it. No humans will think to look for it here."

"So neither the good side nor the evil side will have it," Snowball stated.

"And that's best for now." Inkspot groomed his shoulder blade, then stood. "It's time to go."

Pandora turned to Scooter. "I wanted to thank you again for looking out for my human for me."

Scooter puffed his fur out proudly. "No problem."

"Hey, what happened to that dog?" Sasha asked. "Is your human keeping him?"

"Thankfully, no. She found him a good home. He was okay, but I wouldn't want to live with one of those creatures for very long." Pandora ignored the hollow emptiness in her chest. Ranger had been an inconvenience if anything. Sure, he was warm and soft to lie beside, and sometimes he had been good company when *she was very, very bored, but she didn't want him in her home.*

She was glad he was gone, even if the strange feeling that squeezed her heart when she thought of him seemed to indicate otherwise. No, that feeling couldn't mean that she missed him. It is probably indigestion, Pandora thought, realizing it might not have been wise to eat that second field mouse—they never settled well with her.

"Now, Scooter," Inkspot was saying. "I hear you are getting a human and I wanted to give you some advice as to how to act. I know you have been in the wild and might be a bit overzealous toward your human at first, but it's important to maintain a cat-like demeanor and act disinterested in everything they do."

"Really?"

"Yes. And if they offer a tasty morsel, sniff it delicately and then turn your nose up before accepting it."

"Okay."

"And when they want to pet you, act aloof. Then, when they are reading or working on their computers, get right in between them and the book or screen and parade back and forth, interrupting their view and acting like you want to be petted."

"Got it."

Pandora chuckled at Inkspots' instructions. As they trotted off, she glanced behind her, noticing that Otis had lingered, probably putting the moves on Euphoria. She couldn't help but feel sorry for the Selkirk Rex, having to suffer the attentions of the loathsome Calico.

Better her than me, Pandora thought, as her gaze drifted past the two cats to the spot where Gladys had buried the journal. Her stomach tightened with apprehension. The journal was safe for now, but Gladys Primble was an old woman and Pandora had to wonder ... who would keep the journals safe after Gladys died?

THE END.

****

Sign up for my newsletter and get my latest releases at the lowest discount price, plus I'll send you a free copy of a book from one of my other series: https://mystic_notch.gr8.com/

WANT to see what happens next to Willa and the cats? Pick up the rest of the Mystic Notch series for your Kindle:

Ghostly Paws

A Spirited Tail
A Mew To A Kill
Paws and Effect
Probable Paws
Whisker of a Doubt
Wrong Side of the Claw

IF YOU WANT to receive a text message on your cell phone when I have a new release, text COZYMYS-TERY to 88202 (sorry, this only works for US cell phones!)

Join my readers group on Facebook - https://www.facebook.com/groups/ldobbsreaders

MORE BOOKS BY LEIGHANN DOBBS:

* * *

Dead Wrong
Dead & Buried
Dead Tide
Buried Secrets
Deadly Intentions
A Grave Mistake
Spell Found
Fatal Fortune
Hidden Secrets

Oyster Cove Guesthouse
Cat Cozy Mystery Series
***

A Twist in the Tail
A Whisker in the Dark
A Purrfect Alibi

Mystic Notch
Cat Cozy Mystery Series
* * *

Ghostly Paws
A Spirited Tail
A Mew To A Kill
Paws and Effect

Probable Paws
Whisker of a Doubt
Wrong Side of the Claw

Oyster Cove Guesthouse
Cat Cozy Mystery Series
***

A Twist in the Tail
A Whisker in the Dark

Kate Diamond Mystery Adventures
***

Hidden Agemda (Book 1)
Ancient Hiss Story (Book 2)
Heist Society (Book 3)

Mooseamuck Island
Cozy Mystery Series
* * *

A Zen For Murder
A Crabby Killer
A Treacherous Treasure

Lexy Baker
Cozy Mystery Series

* * *

Lexy Baker Cozy Mystery Series Boxed Set Vol 1 (Books 1-4)

Or buy the books separately:

Killer Cupcakes
Dying For Danish
Murder, Money and Marzipan
3 Bodies and a Biscotti
Brownies, Bodies & Bad Guys
Bake, Battle & Roll
Wedded Blintz
Scones, Skulls & Scams
Ice Cream Murder
Mummified Meringues
Brutal Brulee (Novella)
No Scone Unturned
Cream Puff Killer
Never Say Pie

Lady Katherine Regency Mysteries

***

An Invitation to Murder (Book 1)
The Baffling Burglaries of Bath (Book 2)

Murder at the Ice Ball (Book 3)
A Murderous Affair (Book 4)

Hazel Martin Historical Mystery Series
***

Murder at Lowry House (book 1)
Murder by Misunderstanding (book 2)

Sam Mason Mysteries
(As L. A. Dobbs)
***

Telling Lies (Book 1)
Keeping Secrets (Book 2)
Exposing Truths (Book 3)
Betraying Trust (Book 4)
Killing Dreams (Book 5)

Romantic Comedy
***
Corporate Chaos Series

In Over Her Head (book 1)
Can't Stand the Heat (book 2)

Regency Romance

* * *

Scandals and Spies Series:

Kissing The Enemy
Deceiving the Duke
Tempting the Rival
Charming the Spy
Pursuing the Traitor
Captivating the Captain

A NOTE FROM THE AUTHOR

A Note From The Author

Thanks so much for reading my cozy mystery, "*A Spirited Tail*". I hope you liked reading it as much as I loved writing it. If you did, and feel inclined to leave a review, I really would appreciate it.

This is book two of the Mystic Notch series. I plan to write many more books with Willa, Pandora and the rest of Mystic Notch. I have several other series that I write, too - you can find out more about them on my website http://www.leighanndobbs.com.

This book has been through many edits with several people and even some software programs, but since nothing is infallible (even the software programs), you might catch a spelling error or mistake and, if you do, I sure would appreciate it if you let me know - you can contact me at lee@leighanndobbs.com.

Oh, and I love to connect with my readers so please do visit me on facebook at http://www.facebook.com/leighanndobbsbooks

Sign up for my newsletter and get my latest releases at the lowest discount price:
https://mystic_notch.gr8.com/

ABOUT THE AUTHOR

Leighann Dobbs has had a passion for reading since she was old enough to hold a book, but she didn't put pen to paper until much later in life. After a twenty year career as a software engineer with a few side trips into selling antiques and making jewelry, she realized you can't make a living reading books, so she tried her hand at writing them and discovered she had a passion for that too! She lives in New Hampshire with her husband Bruce, their trusty Chihuahua mix Mojo and beautiful rescue cat, Kitty.

Find out about her latest books and how to get discounts on them by signing up at:

https://mystic_notch.gr8.com/

Connect with Leighann on Facebook:

http://facebook.com/leighanndobbsbooks